Dead Mule Swamp
Mistletoe

an Anastasia Raven mystery
Joan H. Young

Copyright © 2018 Joan H. Young
Published by Books Leaving Footprints

ISBN: 1-948910-06-3

ISBN-13: 978-1-948910-06-4

DEDICATION
To:

Those great writers who preceded me and created the tradition of English Country House Murders- Agatha Christie, Ngaio Marsh, P.D. James and all the rest.

1

The shadow separated itself from the black mold speckling the basement wall, creeping forward, a stealthy echo of shoulders, hips, and torso. Its head bulged with cancerous growths and serrations inflicted by the litter of bottles, pots, and a circular saw strewn haphazardly on rusting shelves. Slithering onward, the shape surrendered its bumps and notches with casual ease.

Quietly, quietly. Don't make a sound. It has to be here. Forgotten places. Mustn't forget. Mustn't forget.

2

Silver and blue glitter sprinkled across the black granite kitchen island. Jerry pushed the expensive creamy square of thick, hand-pressed paper toward me, the invitation sparkling with giant embossed snowflakes. "Come with us, Ana," he said.

"Do say yes," Cora agreed.

After all, what else could I say? Jerry and Cora were two of the best friends I'd made since moving to Forest County five years ago. I could hardly believe it had been that long since I'd kissed Roger goodbye. Not literally. I'd felt more like beating in his head with a crowbar when he decided to spend the rest of his life with a bedmate named Brian. I'd held my temper, and instead of a jail sentence ended up with a not-so-small fortune in alimony. Each and every month a sizable amount of cash was added to the assets of the local bank, via my account: in the name of Anastasia Raven. I was surprised to discover I didn't feel the slightest guilt at taking money I hadn't worked for.

I discovered other new things about myself too, here in the Northwoods, at the end of East South River Road where I bought an old farmhouse. The crowbar had been directed at ripping out walls, and the anger and frustration over the failed relationship served me well at that task. The house was now my sanctuary. I'd done as much of the work myself as I was able, honing a lifelong comfort with power tools and paintbrushes.

True, I'm no longer in my thirties, and my hips will never fit in Cora's size five slacks. On the other hand, a brisk daily walk will hopefully keep me from spreading quite as much as my other good friend, Adele. She owns Volger's Grocery, the only market in town. Jerry, that's Jerry Caulfield, publishes and edits the *Cherry Hill Herald*, and his wife Cora is the local historian. Small towns like Cherry Hill aren't quite the psychological mystery to me they once were, a transplant from the Chicago suburbs.

Somehow, right after I moved here, I got involved with sorting out the details of several suspicious deaths. Jerry eventually made me the local crime reporter. However, the most serious crime in more than a year was when the Morris boys set fire to their father's boat shed because he pulled up their not-quite-secret-enough marijuana crop. Oh, and Sarah Kellogg sliced her husband Prentice across his beer belly with a steak knife one evening when they'd both had a few too many. He laughed all the way to the hospital, didn't press charges, and rumor has it they're expecting another girl.

It's fine with me that no one seems bent on murdering a neighbor. I'll happily focus on DUIs and poaching in my regular column for the weekly paper.

Thus, unnatural death was the furthest thing from my mind that December. My only child, Chad, was coming to my house for Christmas, his last holiday as a student. In a few months he'd graduate from Michigan Tech, a newly-minted Master of Applied Ecology. Yes, Chad was coming.

"But what about Chad?" I blurted.

"Perfect!" Cora said. "He's welcome too. We've been told to bring two guests." She held up the coffee carafe and raised an eyebrow at me.

I slid my mug in her direction. "What exactly is this party?" I asked, suspecting the glitter might have temporarily dazzled my brain and muddled my thinking.

Jerry explained. "The event is at that big old mansion over at Janes Mill Fork, they call it Janes Mill Bed and Breakfast. You know the place. It's one of the few inholdings remaining within Thousand Lakes State Forest."

"That turret you can just see above the trees from the canoe rental place?" I asked.

Cora nodded, filling Jerry's cup as well. "That's it. Henry Janes cut a mill race in 1867 and built the shingle mill the next year. The big house came later, after he'd made a million. One of the richest men in the state."

"Anyway," Jerry said, cutting off what might possibly become a long exposition by Cora on the history of lumbering in the area, "Frank and Betty Farnsworth own it now. He used to be publisher of the *Emily City Ledger;* now he's the owner, but he likes to keep a hand in the day-to-day operations. Professionally, I feel somewhat obligated to show up. It would be much more pleasant if you'd come."

I turned over the frosty invitation. "Three days! The party lasts three whole days?"

"Why not?" Jerry tossed back. "They've turned the place into a posh bed and breakfast. At least, it's upper-crust by Forest County standards. I'd guess this is some sort of tax write-off."

"We've saved the best enticement for last," Cora said, a smug smile crossing her face.

"Which is?"

"You'll never guess who's catering the party."

Even Jerry was grinning now. They were right, I couldn't imagine what could make the food service arrangements have any bearing on my decision. Then it hit me... just as Cora said, "Jimmie Mosher."

Jimmie's obsession was to reestablish the Cherry Blossom Restaurant once owned by his deceased father. Details, such as the fact he was only sixteen, were minor annoyances to be overcome or waited out. "How is he able to do this?" I asked.

"His mother registered the business in her name," Jerry explained. "They're renting the old school kitchen at the museum because it's approved by the health department."

"I think we're getting special privileges to bring extra guests because we rescued their plans from disaster when we suggested Jimmie's new Cherry Blossom Cuisine," Jerry added.

"Disaster?" I asked. "That's a strong word."

Cora nodded knowingly, "They opened the B and B so recently they don't have a full staff for the winter yet, and couldn't get anyone to do food over Christmas. I think Betty Farnsworth doesn't like it when she can't get what she wants."

3

A stubby, rosy-cheeked apple dumpling of a woman opened the door and peered up at us. My strongest impression was of her floral perfume. "Come in! I'm Betty Farnsworth," the woman exclaimed, stepping back and admitting us to the wide entrance hall. A curved balustrade wound up the left side of the foyer, turning to the right at the top to form a balcony. It was wound with a swag of red bows and evergreen boughs— the real thing, judging by the piney scent. Oriental rugs muffled our footsteps as four of us tramped from the porch to the interior. We thumped our bags down to the side of the entrance. As Betty passed me to close the door, my left eye began to water from her strong fragrance. Unexpectedly, I detected the stale odor of cigarette smoke beneath the perfume.

Chad and I had ridden with the Caulfields. My son wasn't ecstatic about spending his holiday with a house full of strangers, but I had threatened to force him to play non-stop Scrabble for three days instead, and he acquiesced.

Frank appeared from beneath the far end of the elegant staircase carrying a stack of blankets. "Jerry, good to see you, you old rascal. Are you still trying to put my paper out of business?"

"There's plenty of room for two papers," Jerry replied cautiously. "Different counties, and all."

Frank barreled ahead, paying no attention to Jerry's response. "Good for you, good for you! Give the *Ledger* a run for its money. Put the screws to 'em." He balanced the blankets on one arm and playfully shook Jerry by the shoulder.

Jerry is six feet tall. He's my senior by quite a few years, but hale and fit, and physically shaking him is not a simple task. I noticed annoyance flicker across my friend's face, but it passed.

"Thanks for the invitation, Frank," he said.

Frank lifted the pile of blankets higher. "Just giving Sam a hand with these." He gave an apologetic laugh and started up the stairs.

"Who's Sam?" Chad asked.

Betty answered. "Samson Lyghtner. He's our handyman and general helper. But with so many guests coming all at one time he's a bit overwhelmed."

"Samson? Funny name," Chad said.

Betty giggled. "Parents were Biblical, I guess. He's strong as an ox. Keep your coats on. We want to give you an outside tour." She glanced upward. Frank was already descending, and she pulled their coats, scarves, and boots from a closet beneath the balcony.

"You're the first to arrive and we're so pleased to have you here. Frank and I have simply fallen in love with this house. Haven't we, Panda Bear? That's what I call my Frank; he's a dear old Panda Bear."

Frank nodded. If the nickname embarrassed him, he didn't let on. His bald head was noticeably square, and the angled planes of both his head and his black-framed glasses reflected the multiple lights of the chandelier. He was a tall man, ponderous, with the beginnings of an expanding gut. From the side, I noticed his chin was weak, and a stiff toothbrush mustache only exaggerated this unfortunate feature.

After Betty took our boxes containing presents for the gift exchange to the next room, we descended the six steps from the wraparound porch till we were standing on the lawn. There was a dusting of snow, but green was the predominant color.

"What do you think, Jerry? A white Christmas?" Frank asked.

Jerry shrugged.

"Now step back into the driveway so you can get a good view of this entire side," Betty said.

The Janes mansion certainly was impressive as it stretched northward toward the river. The Farnsworths had painted the clapboard siding an intriguing shade of blue-gray that seemed to shift in hue as the sun began to slide toward the treetops. It was trimmed in white, traditional but fitting, highlighting every angle and corner of the rambling Victorian house. The wrap-around porch and its sheltered windows were edged with white mini-lights which must have been on a timer because they began to twinkle as I watched. A long lightning rod, slightly bent, with a central white ceramic ball, rose from the point of the turret.

"Counting the top tower room, we have eleven guest bedrooms upstairs and ten additional rooms on the ground floor, plus the original servants' wing," Betty explained. "We use that section for storage as the rooms aren't repaired well enough for occupancy yet. I'm afraid staff will have to use the attic rooms this week. At least they won't be unbearably hot in December."

"How much extra help do you need?" Jerry asked.

"Samson will be staying over for this party, he and the food service people. Friends of yours, right? We really appreciated the tip."

"The Mosher family is pretty special to us," Cora said with quiet pride. Although there was no biological relationship, she thought of the boy as a grandson. "Jimmie's greatest desire is to reopen the Cherry Blossom."

"That wreck on the west side of Cherry Hill?" Frank blustered. "Oughta be torn down."

Frank probably had a point, but Jimmie held a special place in all our hearts and I wanted to change the direction the conversation was going. "So there are twenty-one guest bedrooms?"

"Not quite. We have a personal suite on the ground floor. But some are guest rooms. Had to be for accessibility codes, since there's no elevator yet." Betty explained.

As we chatted, we worked our way around toward the back of the huge home.

"Servants' quarters," Frank said, sweeping an arm out.

"Staff. Panda Bear, please refer to them as staff."

"Whatever," Frank growled.

We passed the rear of the house, closest to the river, and turned a corner. Chad had been quiet, but now he perked up. "Holy cow, this is weird! Looks like some sort of dragon."

A single-story extension of the staff portion of the house was dark with peeling paint, some of the windows were boarded up with plywood. A blue tarp was nailed diagonally over the roof, a point hanging between two bare windows. The impression it gave, as we now faced west squinting into the sunset, was of glowing red eyes beneath a scaly forehead.

Chad continued speaking, "See, the house makes the hunched dragon's back, and the tall turret is its pointed tail. It even has a stinger."

Betty laughed nervously. "This part isn't rebuilt yet. Frank and I can't quite decide what to do with it."

"Maybe this spring," Frank said.

Car tires crunched on gravel at the far side of the house.

"Someone else just arrived. Hurry, Frank, I have no idea where Samson is." Betty took her husband's arm and hustled him toward the front of the house.

"OK, imagining a dragon is just kid stuff," Chad said, "but this place could be a little creepy in the dark, don't you think, Ma?"

"Beautiful lines. Victorian architecture is unparalleled," Jerry said.

Cora sniffed. "They'll need more than one handyman to keep this place operating."

4

As we returned to the front of the house, I saw a black GMC Yukon with skis clipped in a roof rack parked beside Jerry's Chrysler Sebring. A couple hovered around the hatchback, removing bags. The man could have been a pro fullback— he was immense and possibly the blackest person I'd ever seen. He manhandled two large purple duffles in one huge fist. The woman was also tall but thin as a sapling. That mental picture was enhanced when she raised a twiggy arm, fingers spread, to the unruly mop of long curls that bounced in all directions around her head. She was draping tote bags, extra blankets and scarves over her companion's other arm.

The man noted our approach and lifted his shaved head, calling out, "Hello, there! Earl and Doreen Pyrtle here. Sorry, I'll greet you properly in a minute."

"Not a problem," Frank Farnsworth replied, "Good to see you."

"He looks familiar. Isn't that Earl Pratt? Writes for the *Ledger*?" Jerry asked.

"He writes under that name. Pyrtle sounds too fussy for a sports editor," Frank explained. "He's a vet— touch of PTSD makes him overreact sometimes— but an OK guy."

I wondered how someone could suffer from a "touch of PTSD." It seemed like something you dealt with or not, like being pregnant, no middle ground.

We all detoured toward the porch. Doreen was now loaded with tote bags and an armload of winter coats, including what looked like fuchsia ski bibs. As we converged, I got a closer look at her face. She was heavily made up with sparkly eye shadow graded from silver to purple, long curling lashes and purple lipstick.

She stuck out a caramel hand from beneath the bulging nylon

winter wear. Her nails were perfect, and matched the lipstick. "I'm Doreen, Doree's Cosmetology. On Center Street. Maybe you've heard of it?"

I knew she was referring to Emily City, but I wasn't aware of her shop. My total lack of interest in makeup and hair probably labeled me in her mind as a potential future victim. I did well when I kept my longish pageboy under control. And my jeans and navy L.L. Bean parka were pretty drab compared to her expensive clothing.

"Let us help you," Cora said, reaching out to take some of the slippery items Doreen was clutching.

"Thanks! I should have put all these ski outfits in another duffle."

Chad grabbed one of the large bags from Earl.

"Thanks, man," the sportswriter said.

Betty opened the oak door and gestured for us to enter. "Upstairs and to the left," she instructed.

I didn't know if Cora and Jerry had been inside before, but it was definitely my first tour of the Janes Mansion. A dim, high-ceilinged hallway stretched ahead of us as we turned left at the top of the stairs. Frank was in the lead, and he passed one door before opening the next on the left and swinging it inward. We all entered a large bedroom, and everyone immediately dumped their heavy or awkward loads.

"Semi-private bath. You'll be sharing with Paul and Mariah Thomas. Mariah is Paul's daughter," Frank said as he veered and opened another door. "Hope that's acceptable. We weren't able to create individual toilets for every bedroom."

"No big deal," Earl said. But Doreen pulled her mouth to the side in displeasure.

"Each bedroom has a theme," Betty explained. "I know Cora is going to be particularly interested in this topic. This is the Caribbean room. Each mahogany piece was carefully selected. The bed is a genuine antique of the George Washington era. The rest are repros. For now."

The bed was fussy but magnificent. Four tapered and grooved posts rose from the corners, and a canopy was swaged overhead.

Every bit of fabric, from quilt to shams to the padded headboard and covering was decorated with elongated pink and white diamonds.

A dark look passed across Earl's face, but he said nothing. I suspected pink was not his favorite color. Not to mention the spindly legs of the chairs and the intricate carved backs looked way too delicate for someone who was probably six-foot five and a solid two-hundred thirty pounds.

Doreen obviously had no misgivings. "This is splendid! What gorgeous decor." She was fingering an elegant pink wash basin and pitcher. The basin was recessed into a fragile ornate stand with attached mirror and towel racks, and the pitcher rested on a lower shelf.

Cora had wandered across the room to examine a framed cross-stitch sampler on the wall. "Susan Valentine, aged ten, July 4, 1789. Very nice work for a young girl. Where did you get it?" she asked Betty.

"Oh, I have a shopper who keeps an eye out for things I want," our hostess answered vaguely.

Frank headed back to the hallway and called over his shoulder, "Jerry, you and Cora will be over here."

Everyone shifted across the hall. We tried to peer into the next room to see and hear about its theme. I couldn't quite get to the doorway and only the Pyrtles were behind me.

"Do you think she did that on purpose?" Earl whispered. But his deep voice carried to my ears whether he wanted it to or not.

"Don't be ridiculous," Doreen responded quietly. "I don't think she's the brains of the family. She has no clue how you might feel. It's the largest bed in the house, that's all."

"I hope you're right," Earl said.

I didn't really see what the Caulfields' room was like. Frank pushed his way past me and stepped farther away from the stairway we'd mounted. He turned. "You and Chad will have these end rooms. They're also connected through a bath. Is that acceptable?"

Chad glanced at me and shrugged, "Sure," I said, following Frank.

"Good, these are singles, so we thought they would suit you."

The room we entered first had the appearance of a child's room. A Victorian rocking horse sat in front of the fireplace, one wild eye staring obliquely back at us. Ornate candlestands decorated with fresh greens and red ribbon flanked the fireplace. Large alphabet blocks were stacked to spell "BOY." But the bed was adult sized, covered with a woven blue-and-white cotton coverlet.

"Come through the bath," Betty said, leading the way. "I was so pleased to find that birds-eye bedspread and a similar one in the rose path pattern."

The bathroom was white tile, trimmed in green, with white fixtures. They were clearly of modern manufacture, but fit the Victorian period well. The adjoining room was a mirror image of the other. This bed had a red and white counterpane, there were several large dolls placed near the hearth, and the oversized blocks spelled "GIRL." The theme of the rooms may have been nursery, but there was a large dresser in each, writing desks in the nooks created by the addition of the bath, and several chairs. Comfortable spaces.

"It's pretty dark out already. I think I'll see about getting the rest of our luggage in," Chad said.

5

Cora, Jerry and I returned to the foyer and picked up the bags we'd originally brought in the house. We carried them upstairs, and were headed in the direction of our rooms when Jimmie Mosher, and his sisters Beth and Lindsey, approached us from the other direction.

"Nana!" Jimmie yelled, his voice squeaking at the end. He gave Cora a big hug and shook hands with Jerry, then hugged me, too. The girls clustered around, also giving and receiving hugs.

Jimmie was now sixteen and adolescent slender. Somehow, he'd dodged the acne buckshot and was becoming handsome with his fair skin and black hair. Beth and Lindsey looked similar to each other with round faces and light brown hair. The girls were technically Jimmie's half sisters, sharing the same mother. Beth was now twelve and Lindsey ten. They weren't chubby, but neither were they as thin as Jimmie. Cora had once told me the boy looked incredibly like his grandfather, also named Jimmie, who had been Cora's best friend when she was young. That Jimmie, his wife and their son had died in a car wreck when our Jimmie was a baby. He had also been in the car, the only survivor.

"You won't believe this house," Jimmie exclaimed.

"It's really creepy," Lindsey added, giving a little shiver, but grinning as if it were more exciting than fearful.

Chad was clomping down the hall behind us, bringing in the bags we hadn't been able to carry on the first trip.

"Let us show you where we're sleeping," Beth said.

"Is there time?" Cora asked. "Don't you have to help with dinner?"

"It's not even six yet, and we're eating late because some of the guests couldn't get here before seven. Mom sent us up here to take showers, so we'll be clean when we serve the food," Jimmie explained.

"Lindsey and I get to be waitresses," Beth said with a giggle. "We even have uniforms. I'm going to feel like I'm some sort of English maid."

"Yeah, but we have to be really careful not to dump the peas in someone's lap." Lindsey added.

"Peas aren't on the menu, silly," Beth reminded her sister.

Chad shoved the luggage into our rooms, and we followed our own private staff tour which began just outside our doors, at the north end of the hall. The hall was divided, with a closed door on the right and a narrow extension of the hallway to the left.

"If you walk through here, there are steps that go down to get to the kitchen and laundry room and stuff," Beth said, pointing into the shadows in the narrowed hallway. "That's what we're supposed to use instead of the big staircase. I don't like it much. The basement smells bad."

Jimmie pulled an old-fashioned key from his pocket, unlocked the door we were facing and flipped a switch. A bare bulb glowed weakly above us. There was no landing, and a steep set of narrow stairs rose immediately.

"That'll be awkward, coming down," Chad commented.

We climbed in single file and emerged at the north gable of the attic. I knew this because from the small uncurtained window at the top I looked down on the long wing used for storage and then the blue tarp covering the damaged roof we'd seen earlier. Beyond, the ice along the river edge shimmered in the light of a nearly full moon. There was no time to study the scene because our young guides practically dragged us down a dimly lit, but wide, hallway.

"This is Sam's room," Jimmie said, pointing to a door on the right, "and beyond that is Mom's room."

"We three each have our own because they're so dinky," Beth said.

Jimmie opened the first door on the left. "This is mine."

It was a typical attic room with sloping ceiling, except it had been cleaned, dry-walled, painted white, and modernized with basic amenities including electric baseboard heat. It was furnished with a dormitory-style bunk-over-desk unit, a dresser, a desk chair and one comfortable armchair with a side table. A small dormer window overlooked the east lawn, and the rising moon cast a gray path across the dark low-pile commercial carpeting. The hallway had been poorly lit, but the room was bright with an overhead light and lamps.

"Over here is a space we share, like a living room," Lindsey said. She ran partway down the hall and disappeared into an open area on the right. It was a lounge with sofa, beanbag chairs, a television, a dinette, and a small kitchen unit.

"Neat, huh?" Beth said. "My room and Lindsey's are just like Jimmie's, but Mom's is different."

She skipped down the hall and opened the second door on the right. Structurally, it wasn't all that much different except now I realized that the hallway wasn't exactly centered in the attic because the rooms on the right were larger. Not only were they deeper, but with only two rooms on this side, they were much longer as well. We entered Dee Mosher's room and found a pleasant sitting area with a loveseat, two upholstered chairs and a small table with two straight chairs. The room was divided by a screen, and on the other side were a double bed, dresser and writing desk. Each section had a dormer window.

Lindsey spoke up, "Mom says it's like having her own cozy apartment."

"We haven't seen Sam's room, but I think he lives here most of the time, so it's probably like a little apartment, too," Jimmie added.

"Where is the elusive Samson?" Chad asked pointedly. "Nobody's seen him since we came."

"Who knows?" Jimmie answered. "Maybe they sent him to town for extra supplies or something. He was here earlier, but we've been in the kitchen since forever."

I had to admit the Farnsworths had done a nice job of renovating a potentially useless space. The furniture looked like it came from Ikea, but assembly-on-site was a smart choice given how narrow the stairway was. However, the spaces were pleasant, and Cora was right that a bed and breakfast of this size was going to need more than one person to keep things running smoothly.

"Hadn't you better clean up? Your mother will be waiting." Cora pointed out.

Jimmie answered, "Yeah, we will. We do have to share one bathroom, but we'll be quick. It's between the girls' rooms. There's a shower, and sinks. Toilets, too, with doors." He blushed.

The kids turned to leave their mother's room, but I stepped to the window. This side of the house was above the driveway and entrance. In the pinkish light of a sodium vapor lamp that had turned on at dusk, I saw a bulky young man open the doors of a large shed. He disappeared inside and a moment later emerged driving a golf cart. It seemed like an odd vehicle to use in the winter, but since there was only light snow on the ground it probably worked just fine. He waited for a moment as a red Subaru Forester bristling with skis, and emblazoned with a logo I didn't recognize on the door, came into the parking circle where the road ended at the mansion. The glaring LED headlights of the electric cart swept across the scene, and then the man, whom I assumed was Sam, soundlessly steered around the hatchback and drove away, down the road.

6

As I watched from the attic window, another set of lights approached the house, passing the golf cart cautiously. I couldn't discern the exact color of the vehicle, but it was dark and small. It pulled in behind the Subaru. I wondered where all the other cars had been taken. Had Frank parked them somewhere, or maybe this was what had been keeping Samson occupied?

Car doors slammed, but I couldn't hear what people were saying. It looked to me as if the new arrivals didn't know each other because there was a fair amount of hand shaking and nodding of heads as they pulled luggage from the cars. Betty and Frank appeared beneath me, from the vicinity of the main door.

"I'm next," one of Jimmie's sisters shouted from the hall. I heard bare feet slapping in the hallway and a great deal of giggling. Pipes clanged and a shower door slammed, vibrating as the Plexiglas hit the aluminum frame. I hoped Beth and Lindsey were going to be able to act mature enough to serve a houseful of guests at meals. They seemed so very young to me.

Everyone except the kids had already returned to the second floor. Jimmie called to me, "I'm supposed to keep the attic door locked, Ana. Can you go down now, so I can take my shower too?"

"Sure," I answered, but I wondered why keep the attic locked. Wasn't that a fire hazard? As I left Dee's room I realized there was also a window at this end of the hall. I looked out and saw the tower that defined the mansion directly across a section of house that was not three stories high.

At least my concerns about safety were alleviated a bit. A metal ladder extended from the window down to the next roof, and then across it and presumably down the back side of the house.

Returning the way I'd come, I opened the door at the bottom

of the steps where there was no landing. Just as I'd suspected, it was awkward to reach the knob. You had to either lean down from about two steps too high, or angle your feet sideways on the bottom step while trying to keep the knob from jamming you in the ribs. Jimmie had followed me down, and I heard him turn the key in the lock after closing the door behind me.

Simultaneously, Chad poked his head out of his bedroom, while some of the new arrivals were spilling into the other end of the hallway.

"Ana, Chad, come meet the Crocketts," Betty said, but she pronounced my name Anna. This hallway was narrower than the attic one, and there was a lot of thumping of bags against walls and clattering of wheeled suitcases over the hardwood floor. It wasn't an ideal space to host introductions of large groups of people, but we managed.

Ray and Jessi Crockett were a very young couple, probably in their mid-twenties. Betty showed them into a room on the east, the same side as the suite Chad and I were sharing. This room was decorated for a sportsman. There were paintings, or maybe prints, of dogs pointing at pheasants, and men in red wool with shotguns. The wallpaper was a mossy plaid with a border of woven creels, ducks and speckled fish.

Chad perked up immediately at the sight of some guests closer to his age. "Hey, nice Fitbit," he said to Ray. "Isn't that the Charge?"

"It is. Not the top of the line, but it gives me the most value for the price," Ray answered.

The two guys drifted off talking fitness watches, and I sized up Jessi. She was slim and fit with a silver nose ring at the side of one nostril. She unzipped her puffy parka and tossed it on the bed. With one fluid motion she drew something from a pocket, smoothed back her long blonde hair and flipped it through a scrunchie into a pony tail.

Jessi raised her voice, teasingly. "You'll have to excuse Ray. We are an outfitter, and he's always on the lookout for someone who can discuss the latest toys. I'm more interested in the clothing side of the business. But we're both passionate about skiing." She flashed a toothy but warm smile in Ray's general direction.

"Crockett Outfitters?" Chad said, envy creeping into his voice. "I've been wishing they'd open a branch in the UP."

"You're a Yooper? Jessi asked. "I thought Betty said you came over from Cherry Hill."

"Not really either one. I'm just finishing grad school at Houghton. Don't know where I'm headed next. Spending the holidays with my mom." Chad jerked his head towards me.

"My name's Ana Raven. It pretty much rhymes with Donna," I said, correcting Betty's pronunciation.

Another round of clattering and thumping was heard in the hallway. Frank stuck his head in the door. "Drinks and appetizers downstairs in the main room whenever you're ready. Dress casual. Just heard the weather. Snow's coming tonight, so we should be able to groom the ski trails tomorrow."

His head popped back out, and a door opened across the hall.

"That's good news," Jessi said. "Having a chance to ski some new trails was the main reason I came. I hardly know the Farnsworths."

I shook my head. "Me neither."

"I think we were invited because the *Ledger* wants to keep our advertising dollars," Ray said.

We went into the hall.

"Paul Thomas, and his daughter Mariah," Frank said. They used to live in Cold Rapids, but I enticed Paul to come work for me. Ana, Chad, Ray, Jessi." He pointed to each of us in turn, and he got my name right.

Paul snorted and rolled his eyes. "More like you rescued me. I got laid off in the last round of electronics company failures," he explained to the rest of us.

"Well, their loss was our gain. You're a whiz at dealing with our new offset plate machine. We're upgrading the presses, too," he added, apparently for our benefit since Paul must have already known that fact. It was also curious that Frank was supposedly retired, and yet he spoke as if he was very much involved with the operations of the paper. But Jerry had implied as much.

Mariah didn't look anything like her father. Paul was blocky with a dark complexion and wavy black hair. I couldn't decide if his heritage was Mexican or Italian. She was petite, and fine-boned with shoulder-length brown hair and sideswept bangs. But their deep brown eyes were the same.

"Are you still in school?" I asked her.

"One semester to go at State, and I'll be looking for my first job."

Chad spoke up. "I'm almost done with my Masters. What's your major?"

"Special Ed. I'm really interested in autism. How about you?"

"Applied Ecology," he answered. "You want to go find the snacks?"

The four young people traipsed down the hall toward the main staircase, but Betty wanted to show off the decor in this room which seemed to be an Americana public education theme. There were twin spindle beds with red, white, and blue schoolhouse quilts. Instead of bedside tables there were antique school desks. A print of boys in knickers running through a schoolyard dominated the space above the headboard, and various slates with shabby-chic stencils of stars, pencils and books dotted the walls.

Paul looked around. "I'm not sure this is going to work."

"What's wrong?" Frank said, his eyes darting from bed to walls to doors.

"Mariah is hardly a child any longer. It would be better if we didn't have to share a room."

"I can see that," Betty said. "We'll make up the Beach Room across the hall. I'll have it ready before dinner is served."

"But..." Frank protested.

Betty pointed us in the direction of the food. My last glimpse of them before I started down the stairs was of Frank with one hand on Betty's shoulder and his head bent low, gesturing emphatically and whispering.

7

Getting some appetizers in my stomach was rapidly becoming a priority. Dinner at seven or later wasn't ideal for my body rhythms. I only hoped I wouldn't stuff myself with crackers and cheese and then be too full to eat a meal.

We all headed down to the ground floor. It was easy to tell by the blaring Christmas music and hum of voices that people had congregated in the room across from the main staircase. This turned out to be the dining room, at least I supposed that's what it was called. It was immense— large enough to be divided up into an efficiency apartment, and so large there were two pillars to help support the ceiling. Tables had been arranged the length of the front wall, set for the evening meal. The inner two-thirds of the room was dotted with the guests that had already arrived.

Along the inside wall was a large ornate fireplace, but it wasn't in use. I didn't know if it was no longer functional, or if the Farnsworth's didn't want the bother of a wood fire when Sam already had so much to do. The cold fireplace was flanked by two large Ficus in decorative pots strung with white mini lights, and fussy needlepoint stockings hung from the mantle. A pass-through with closed shutters, and just beyond that a swinging door, suggested the kitchen was on the far side of the wall. In front of that wall was a long table, set with trays of hors d'oeuvres, my immediate destination.

The selection of tidbits was worthy of a hotel banquet. If Dee Ward, Jimmie, and the girls had made all these, they had certainly been busy. There were tiny rolls wrapped in bacon; festive wedges of tomato topped with mozzarella and basil leaves; an already-ravaged Christmas tree created from rounds of hard sausage, cheese and grape tomatoes; deviled eggs sprinkled with paprika and parsley; and oval cucumber-slice boats filled with a dollop of something creamy, topped with red pepper. A serve-yourself punch bowl of green frothy liquid held down the far end of the table. Stars of golden ice floated on the surface.

I filled a small holiday paper plate, adding items until there was a sizeable mound. When I reached the punch, I realized a bar had been set up along the south wall with Jerry acting as bartender. I wandered over his way and asked for a glass of white wine. Beyond the bar was the sitting room, where a huge Christmas tree twinkled with colored lights, gold ornaments and bows.

"Who else is coming?" I asked Jerry. "There are already ten guests here. I hope I can keep them straight. I don't know anybody except you and Cora."

"Not my party. And this job keeps me out of the tedious self-introductory conversations," Jerry said with a smile, waving the wine bottle to take in the entirety of the room.

"Well, Cora can fill you in later," I smiled in return.

"That she will."

Earl Pyrtle/Pratt appeared on my right and asked for a Gibson and a scotch on the rocks. As Jerry fixed the drinks, Earl leaned in close and asked him, "How well do you know the Farnsworths?"

Jerry raised his head, looking mildly surprised. "I've known them professionally for decades, but we aren't close. Why?"

"This is a pretty odd group of people they've collected here, don't you think?"

Jerry scanned the room. "Two of you work for the *Ledger*, I own the *Cherry Hill Herald*. That leaves the Crocketts and the Thomases. I guess I'm not sure of their connection to Frank and Betty, but nothing strikes me as overly strange. Frank knows lots of people. Betty must, too. She's been involved in multi-level marketing for years."

"If you say so," Earl responded, "but I just don't see the couples here choosing to mingle with each other on an ordinary Saturday, if you catch my drift."

Jerry shrugged.

Earl picked up the drinks and walked away.

"Is he sensitive about his race?" I asked quietly, noticing that he and Doreen were the only black couple.

"Could be, but his writing style doesn't suggest it. And he wouldn't last long in a newsroom if he was too touchy," Jerry answered.

"Maybe Doreen feels awkward," I suggested.

"She's a businesswoman. Looks successful enough. Doesn't seem logical that she'd mind a diverse group."

Folding chairs had been arranged in small groupings throughout the room. Chad, Mariah and the Crocketts had formed a cozy circle near the empty fireplace. Doreen, Earl, and Paul had grouped near one of the pillars, sipping drinks. Cora was nowhere in sight. I suspected she'd gone to the kitchen; her connection with the "staff" was stronger than to the guests. Maybe Earl was onto something.

I felt a cold draft creep through the room, and raised my eyes to look into the foyer. The main door was open, and Betty Farnsworth was squeezing an overweight woman wearing a long gray blanket coat. A lumpy man in a cheap parka, past middle age, came into view behind her. The man pulled off a wool hat with ear flaps, and static electricity lifted long thin strands of light brown hair. He smoothed them across his skull with a hand from which a chunky gold ring gleamed. Frank collected their jackets and bags and started up the stairs, while Betty directed the newcomers toward the dining room.

"Everyone! Hello! May I have your attention?" Betty fluted.

The room quieted.

"This is my good friend, Belinda Kramer, and her husband Harry Hack. Harry will be sure to try to lure you to one of his rentals over on Lake Michigan this summer, so keep your guard up. Please introduce yourselves." She laughed and propelled Harry toward Earl, Doreen, and Paul. Belinda headed for the food table.

"I'd better be sociable," I told Jerry, and went to introduce myself to Belinda who looked like she might be the outlier in this room full of svelte professional people. She wore a flowing kaftan, which only made her look even larger, in deep shades of red and maroon. A gold belt, loopy necklaces, bracelets and hoop earrings sparkled, and an image of a vintage aluminum Christmas tree floated into my head.

Just as I reached her, with my hand extended, there was a crash from beyond the kitchen door. Heads turned in curiosity, but Belinda gasped and dropped the paper plate she was holding. A grape tomato rolled slowly in the direction of the bar.

8

"Sorry," Belinda said with a tentative smile. "I sometimes get nervous at parties."

She and I leaned over to pick up the fallen appetizers just as the kitchen door swung toward us. The burly young man I'd seen on the golf cart held it open, but he faced the kitchen.

"And as far as I'm concerned you little kids have no business being here. Just stay out of my way from now on. You got that?"

"Sam," Betty called, approaching him from across the room.

Sam pushed his way past me, nearly knocking me off balance, and stormed out the main door. Betty turned and followed, trotting in an effort to catch up.

I needed to dispose of the dropped food anyway, so I entered the kitchen. Warm fragrances— clam chowder and something tomato-y— enveloped me.

Lindsey was sitting on the floor, tears running down her cheeks. Boxes of food, and bags of marshmallows and chocolate bars littered the sand-colored squares around her. Two torn plastic shopping bags bulged like dying jellyfish on a vinyl beach.

Cora was, indeed, in the kitchen, and she was bent over, helping the girl up.

"I didn't do anything," Lindsey wailed.

"We know, honey," her mother said. Then Dee turned to me and added, "Sam just burst through the back door with his hands full of bags, and the door hit Lindsey. It wasn't her fault at all. If Sam is going to be like that all week, I don't know how we're going to be able to work with him."

"At least most of what he does keeps him out of the kitchen," Jimmie said, patting his sister on the back.

"Why was he coming in the kitchen now?" I asked.

Cora answered, "He took the truck to town to get a few extra supplies— mostly batteries and more liquor, but Betty decided to have an après-ski campfire, and she wanted the makings of s'mores, too.

"But the truck broke down," Jimmie cut in, "so he's mad anyway. It's over on the other side of that little bridge, and he had walk the rest of the way here and then go get the stuff."

"What little bridge?" I asked. But that explained why I'd seen Sam leaving on the golf cart.

"Didn't you see it when you came in? There's some big stream that feeds into the river. Mr. Farnsworth said they had to pay a fortune to get the bridge put in because it's beyond the end of the county road."

I shook my head. Apparently I hadn't been paying attention when we were in the car.

"Janes Creek, of course," Cora said dryly. "That family managed to name just about everything in the neighborhood after themselves."

Betty entered through the swinging door with Sam trailing behind her. His eyebrows were pushed together in a scowl.

"Sam," Betty said, raising her voice at the end of his name.

"Yeah, OK. I'm sorry. What's your name?" he said to the younger girl.

"Lindsey, Lindsey Ward," she sniffled.

"Sorry I'm grumpy. It's just that the truck is completely unusable. I think an axle broke. It's out of commission until we can get it towed. I can't fix that."

"And the girl I had hired as general housekeeper for this party backed out at the last minute," Betty added. "We're all a little stressed right now."

"Maybe I could help with some of those duties," I heard myself say. Where did that come from?

"Oh, no, I couldn't ask you to do that," Betty said.

I thought about it for a couple of seconds. "I'd be happy to. I don't know any of the guests except Cora and Jerry, and Chad has already started making friends. I'm clearly the odd person."

"Are you sure?" Betty asked again, but I could tell she was going to give in.

"What would I need to do?"

Sam answered. "Mostly just make sure each guest has clean towels every day, and clean up any accidental messes; vacuum the dining room after meals. Check the bathrooms. Maybe run some laundry. We aren't doing any major cleaning during this party."

"Sounds fine to me," I said.

Sam's face opened up a bit. "Sorry we crashed, Lindsey. Are you hurt?"

"No," she said, wiping her nose.

Sam turned to me. "Come with me, and I'll show you where the supplies and the linens are. Who are you?"

"I'm Ana Raven."

"Thank you, Sam," Betty said with a sigh.

Cora and Dee were placing the spilled groceries on a counter. "Maybe some of the crackers will be broken, but no real damage," Cora said.

"How soon until we serve dinner?" Dee asked. "Things are pretty much ready, and we're all dressed."

Indeed, Jimmie was wearing black pants and vest with a white shirt. Dee and the girls matched, but with black skirts instead of pants.

"Just one more couple to arrive," Betty said. "Let's wait a few more minutes."

Sam looked at me and pointed toward the rear of the kitchen. I followed him. It looked like I was going to get to see even more parts of the house.

9

We exited at the north end of the room and stepped into a large open area that served as a laundry and utility room.

It was my first chance to get a good look at the handyman. He was probably in his mid-twenties, about five-foot-ten, and his muscles bulged under a long-sleeved t-shirt. He had a thick wrestler's neck. I guessed he lifted weights in his spare time. His brown hair was shaved in a short brush cut that hugged his round head.

"Cleaning supplies over here, washer and dryer there, obviously," Sam said. "Oh, open this door to access the circuit breakers and stuff like that. Half bath in the corner."

I looked around and realized someone had done a good job of planning this space. I knew from personal experience that old houses were not noted for having the utilities and emergency panels organized.

"Here's where it gets a little weird," Sam continued. "When the house was first built, the kitchen was in the basement, so we have to go down to get to the servants' hallway. Mrs. F calls us 'staff,' but it was 'servants' when these spaces were built." He opened a door and flipped switches.

We descended open wooden steps into a large cool space. This was obviously the old kitchen, and appeared to be underneath the current laundry room and kitchen. There were two huge fireplaces that hadn't been used in years, discarded tables and chairs, crates and barrels and various shadowy piles of stored junk.

"Through there is an exercise room for guests." He pointed ahead toward a door that I guessed must lead to a space below the dining room. "Sometimes people do make a mess in there, so you need to know where it is. Water heaters, furnace, shut-off valves here. We go this way."

He turned right and entered a chilly stone hallway that disappeared into gloom ahead of us.

"The lights are all wired with switches at both ends of the hall, and at the tops and bottoms of stairways. Try to remember to turn 'em off after you've passed through." As he said this, he fiddled at the wall and the light behind us went out and a harsh glare that dazzled my eyes blazed on the stones ahead.

"Those must be LEDs," I said. "They're awfully bright."

"Yeah. We should probably put in some with lower wattage equivalents, but they sure save energy. Especially if someone leaves them on. Like those kids."

"Have they done that?" I asked.

"No, but they're kids. It'll happen," Sam predicted. We reached the end and climbed another set of stairs. Sam dutifully flipped all the light switches. "Motion sensors would be great for these spaces, but they're expensive."

We were at the end of a hallway I hadn't yet seen, but it had to be the north end of the ground floor guest room hallway. It was pretty much like the upstairs hall, but the wallpaper was patterned in gold, while the hallway where my room was located was a pale blue.

"Is anyone staying in these rooms?" I asked.

"Not this week. Just the Farnsworths are here, in their own apartment suite. You don't have to do anything about their linens or bathroom. Upstairs are the guest rooms you've seen."

Sam pointed again and we circled round to climb to the second floor.

"Now I know where I am," I said, as we emerged very near my own assigned room.

"Yup. There's a linen closet on each floor, right here by the stairs." He pulled open some shutter-style bifold doors to reveal sheets, towels and extra blankets stacked neatly on shelves. "At the other end of the hall, see the matching doors?"

I nodded.

"In that closet are cleaning supplies for the bathrooms and

stuff like toothpaste and shampoo that guests might have forgotten."

"Seems simple enough," I said.

"If you go up one more flight, the staff has quarters in the attic."

"I've seen it."

Sam's piggy features were all scrunched into the middle of his round face, and when he scowled he looked mean. "That's our private space. I suppose those kids took you up there."

"Look, Sam, 'those kids' are good friends of mine. Cora Caulfield even considers Jimmie her grandson. He's been helping to cook food for groups for several years already, and his mother took out the license for them to be caterers. I know the girls are younger, but why not give them a chance? It just makes them nervous when you act gruff."

"If you say so."

I tried to reason with him. "This party is obviously short-staffed, and we'll need to try to get along to make things go more smoothly. You don't think you could do it all by yourself, do you?"

"No, of course not. There should be even more people to help. No one wanted to work on Christmas. Dumb time to have a party if you ask me, but I'm not the boss, and it's no big deal to me to work."

"Don't you have family?" I asked.

"A cousin. He's a jerk," Sam clipped the answer and continued. "The guest rooms aren't full, but even so, there's an awful lot to do. I'm just worried, I guess. With the truck out of commission for who knows how long, I sure hope we don't have to move anything big. I better call for a tow service tomorrow. That golf cart will be no use at all if we get enough snow for skiing. Dang it all! I have to get wood out to the fire ring before noon. I'll have to hitch a sled to the back of the snowmobile because I sure don't have time now."

Maybe I had misjudged Sam. He was obviously overworked and concerned about making the Farnsworths' planned events come off smoothly.

"I'm sure my son Chad would be glad to give you a hand with

any of the heavy jobs," I offered. "It's not like we're still living in Victorian times when the servants and family were on different social rungs. We're just regular people."

"Yeah, yeah," he said. "But Mrs. F doesn't like guests to be reminded that this is a hotel instead of a home."

"All the more reason for everyone to pitch in," I countered.

"I mean... she kind of likes to keep up the distinction between them and us. Except now you're both. It's going to get complicated."

"I don't see how," I said.

"Look, since you aren't really staff, you don't have to use the passage I showed you unless you're carrying cleaning supplies or stuff that makes it look as if you're working. But try not to be obvious when you're helping out."

I sighed. There were clearly some conflicts in philosophies. "OK, I can do that."

"And, I've got no authority to keep you off the third floor, except out of my own room, but I don't have to like it."

10

We returned to the kitchen via the basement passage. At least I should get a good workout climbing so many stairs.

Jimmie and the girls were nowhere in sight, but the pass-through to the dining room was open. Dee flipped a hand in that direction, "The final guests came, and we started serving. You'd better get out there."

I pushed open the swinging door. Everyone except me was seated, but there was an empty chair between Chad and Earl Pyrtle, on the other side of the long table. Chad caught my eye, raised an arm and pointed at the vacant seat.

Scanning faces, I discovered the newcomers. One was a petite black woman with a long neck, sharp nose and a cap of very short hair runneled with streaks of gray, an aging Ethiopian queen. Seated next to her was a tall man of average weight with slightly lighter skin. They both seemed overdressed for what was essentially to be a ski holiday and Christmas party. He wore a gray suit with a navy shirt and light blue tie, while she had on a calf-length winter-white dress. An iridescent purple scarf was wound around her neck, and its long tails spilled over one shoulder and down her back. Her wrists and ears glittered with real, or possibly faux, diamonds

Betty stood, "Ana, there you are! Meet our recent arrivals, and our most distinguished guest. This is Her Honor, Viviette VondaVay Velvet and her husband Branson Owens. I'm sure you've seen the judge on television."

"Hello, sorry I'm late." I apologized, nodding to the judge and then various people.

"Call me Bran," Branson Owens said in a cultured voice. "I'm a Gemini, and it's a special pleasure to meet new people."

Doreen squealed. "I'm Aquarius, we might be best friends after we get acquainted."

"I'm Viviette, not Vi or Viv, it's Viviette, and I'm Scorpio. Watch your step," the judge said, giving Doreen an evil eye. Her familiar voice was scratchy but powerful, and it carried throughout the room.

I'm ignorant when it comes to astrology, and didn't completely follow that exchange. However, although I haven't owned a television since moving to Forest County, I did indeed know who the judge was by reputation. She was the prime force in one of those reality courtroom dramas. It had been on the air for years and her snarky attitude made the show a hit.

Fat mugs of white clam chowder had been placed in front of each person. The aroma rising from baskets of hot cheese sticks was divine, and we all got down to the business of eating. I was glad I didn't have a new acquaintance on both my left and right, or for that matter, someone as large as Earl. Cautiously, I scooted a little closer to Chad to give myself room to operate the soup spoon with my right arm.

Earl apparently saw the extra space as a vacuum which needed to be filled. He leaned in close to me. "I know you heard what I said to Doreen upstairs."

I was trying to recall the conversation, something that made me uncomfortable.

"You remember, when I wondered why the Farnsworths gave us that hideous room."

"Oh, yes," I said. "But it's a remarkable collection of period furniture, even if it's not all genuine. Why don't you like it?"

"Mahogany. All of it. Are you ignorant of the history of that wood?"

It seemed as if the question could have been phrased in a way that didn't make me feel stupid, but I just shrugged.

"Slaves were brought to the Caribbean islands by the thousands to harvest the mahogany. Forests were leveled to fill the mansions of the rich and white. My ancestors were among those who felled the timber."

Diatribes of this sort irritate me, and Earl's opening nettled even more. I countered but tried to keep my tone light. "The white pine were leveled to build mansions just like this one. It's history, not a personal attack. Should I be offended by this whole party if my great-grandfather was a lumberjack who worked for a pittance and lost his feet to frostbite?"

Earl turned and looked at me under lowered brows. "But insensitive, don't you think? I doubt your forebears were slaves."

I sighed. "Probably not. I don't even know about the lumberjack part. I made that up. Look, I'm not trying to start something, but I also heard Doreen suggest it was the largest bed in the house. You're a big guy. Betty doesn't seem like a real history buff beyond trying to coordinate the decor. Maybe you should just take things at face value."

Lindsey was suddenly at my left elbow, saying, "Excuse me, may I take your bowl?"

I made an opening for her, and she cleared the dirty dish and spoon, placing them on a rolling cart. Her actions were smooth and professional. She'd apparently recovered from the mishap in the kitchen, and other diners would never guess she hadn't done this before.

Right behind her came Jimmie with another cart. He put a crisp winter salad of arugula, pear, walnuts and cranberries in front of Chad, followed by a plate of roasted root vegetables with a pulled pork sandwich that instantly made my mouth water. As he served me, he whispered, "How do they like the food?"

"The chowder was perfect, and if these vegetables taste as good as they look, you'll have catering jobs lined up for months," I told him, stabbing a carrot.

"I've been watching people, and they do seem pretty happy. Were the cheese sticks still crisp? We had to hold them longer than we wanted."

"Mine were great. But you know I'm happy any time I don't have to cook the food myself."

Jimmie grinned and gave me a slight bow, then moved along to serve Earl.

Directly across the table from me was Mariah Thomas. Her father, Paul, was on her right, across from Chad. Earl reached for the basket of cheese sticks, but perhaps it was to give him an excuse to lean across the table toward Paul.

"Viviette VondaVay Velvet! What's she doing here?" Earl whispered.

"You know what they call her behind the scenes?" Paul asked Chad out of the corner of his mouth.

"No clue," Chad responded.

"The Velvet Hammer."

From beyond Chad I heard a snort. That had to be Jessi, the young co-owner of Crockett Outfitters. Her head appeared over Chad's shoulder. "Have you seen her show? It should be the Velvet Velociraptor. She's vicious. Hey, that's another V."

Earl leaned toward me again. "More like the Vain Vicious Velvet Vivisectionist. That's got enough Vs. She's a piece of work. On and off the set. I served in Desert Storm, and she's more deadly than an IED."

"You know her?" I asked.

"For way too long," Earl said, shaking his head. He straightened in his chair, picked up his sandwich and took a huge bite, finally giving me some breathing space.

11

After the main course, Frank rose and announced that dessert and coffee would be served casually, and we were free to socialize without structured activity for the evening. He said the weather forecast still promised several inches of snow, and Sam would be available any time after ten in the morning to help fit people who hadn't brought skis or snowshoes of their own. Earlier than ten, he'd be out grooming trails. Continental breakfast would begin at seven.

Jessi and Ray spoke up to say they were looking forward to giving beginning skiers tips and assistance.

There was a smattering of polite applause, which seemed to be an overly formal reaction, and then chairs scraped as people stood.

I ran upstairs to my room to retrieve a hostess gift I'd brought. I'd actually gotten organized enough to do something crafty, but then I'd forgotten and left it in my suitcase. When I returned to the main floor, the dining room was rearranged. The tables had been separated and taken over for games by the group of people Chad's age. I thought I recognized the board for Settlers of Catan, although I'd never played it. Plates of brownies and butterscotch bars, and coffee urns— "regular" and "decaf"— were arranged on the side table. Jerry wasn't manning the bar, but bottles and decanters were sitting out.

Frank was kneeling at the fireplace in the front room of the house, the room with the Christmas tree. As I entered, I saw flames begin to lick around the logs that had been laid in the grate. He rose and placed a decorative fire screen on the hearth.

The lights were dimmed in this room, and the glow of the firelight and the Christmas tree created a golden atmosphere that made me feel mellow the minute I walked in. A calming hum of soft conversations contrasted with the earlier tension. The music had been turned down to a soothing background level. The setting was perfect for a holiday party.

My preference was to deliver the hostess gift to Betty, but she was nowhere in sight, so I set the gift bag beneath the tree. Turning back to the dining room, I grabbed a cup of coffee and a brownie, then made my way toward an empty chair, the only one left in the inviting room with the Christmas tree. Unless I moved the furniture, this forced me into a grouping with Doreen Pyrtle and Belinda Kramer. *Might as well get acquainted*, I thought.

Balancing the plate of chocolate goodness, and calories, on one knee, I sipped the coffee and tuned in to what the women were saying.

Doreen was speaking. "Even so, I can't emphasize enough how Earl stuck with me through those difficult days. I was so lost, such a mess."

"Remarkable," Belinda replied.

"You name it, I tried it. Weed of course, but coke, alcohol, pharming."

"Farming?" Belinda asked. "You were living in some sort of commune?"

Doreen giggled, a rather annoying high-pitched haw-hawing. "Oh, no. P-H-A-R-M. It's a party where everyone dumps a bottle of pills in a bowl and then you mix 'em up and take a handful and wash them down with a drink. No one knows what might happen."

Belinda looked aghast. "People do that and live through it?" She stuffed half a butterscotch brownie in her mouth and wiped crumbs from her chin.

"Sure, but it is pretty risky. I suppose that's why it happened."

"What happened?"

"We lost our kids for a while." Doreen lowered her enhanced eyelashes and looked down at the rug.

"That's too bad," I said.

Both women started and looked my way as if they hadn't yet realized I was there.

"Hi," I said, "keep going with your story. I didn't mean to

derail you."

Simultaneously they turned their heads, shutting me out of the conversation. That was fine with me. I didn't need more personal interactions to feel good about the day. But I kept listening, and Doreen continued.

"Anyway, I don't like the judge. I don't know anyone who likes the Sixpack V— who has six Vs in their name?— except maybe the Farnsworths since they invited her to this party."

"Oh, but Harry and I have her to thank that we found each other," Belinda said.

"Seriously?" Doreen asked, "How did that happen?"

"Well, we were on the same show, but with different cases. We both lost that day, but we ultimately won, because that's how I met Harry."

"What was your case about?" Doreen asked.

"I owned some rentals back then. I was holding a tenant's things because he never paid me a security deposit, but he was demanding them back because they were supposedly worth more than what he owed me. The judge made me return his stupid junk. It wasn't such a big deal anyway. Both parties have to agree ahead of time to split the judgment. It's all about television drama, not law, you know. So I got half the security deposit."

"What about Harry?"

"Well, his was tougher. He had a dog that he was really fond of, but she bit a woman, and the Velvet Hammer ordered her put down."

I couldn't resist jumping in. "They can do that? It's not a real courtroom."

"No, it's not," Belinda agreed. "But both parties have to sign an agreement that the arbitration is binding, and unless the judge says something that isn't in the paperwork, it's all legal. So Harry thought he would just have to pay some money because he didn't read it carefully. He lost his dog. He sure loved his Sparky."

"That's rough. Excuse me," I said, setting my plate and mug beside the chair. Betty had just entered the room. I retrieved my gift bag from under the tree and took it to her. "Just a little something I made for your party."

Betty pulled the tissue paper away and drew out my creation. "A mistletoe ball!" she exclaimed loudly, which got the attention of everyone.

"Well, it isn't really," I protested. "I suppose you could call it Dead Mule Swamp mistletoe. It's made from leatherleaf and dogwood berries from along the river near my house, but I think it looks like the genuine article."

"Oh, it does." She paused. "Frank, where can we hang this? And the gold ribbon is perfect. It fits right in with our decorations. We'll have everyone kissing," she giggled.

"I'll put it up there in the morning," Frank said, pointing to the high point of the archway to the dining room.

"If it's fake mistletoe, that means the kisses don't count." Harry hooted. I turned and saw Paul Thomas staring hard at the judge, Ms. Sixpack V herself.

12

"Hey, have any of you looked outside?" Ray Crockett asked, sticking his head through the archway. "It's beautiful. We're all going out. Anyone else want to come?"

"I believe I will," Doreen said.

"Yes," said Frank, rising. He'd been chatting with Cora, Jerry, and Paul, near the fireplace.

There was a general rummaging in closets, clomping of feet on the stairs and opening and closing of doors as people scrambled for coats. But the warm, sleepy atmosphere still prevailed. As the first blast of cold air rushed in when the outside door was opened, the dreamy spell was broken.

Not all of us, but a sizeable group, stepped off the porch into the cold brittle air of a completely cloudless winter night. The stars seemed to be raining needles of ice, and a nearly full moon was so bright it cast tall jagged shadows behind the spruce trees lining the driveway.

"Gorgeous!" Cora sounded a little breathless. "Even in a small town like Cherry Hill we don't have the dark sky that makes this view possible."

"Temperature's really dropped," Jerry added unromantically.

"Sure doesn't look to me like snow's coming," Paul said, rubbing his ungloved hands together and then sticking them in his pockets.

"Not for a while anyway," Frank agreed. "Let's walk down by the river."

He turned to the right and led us past a detached garage and a couple of sheds. I learned where all our cars were parked— tightly wedged back here out of sight. We walked in silence for a few minutes. I looked behind us at the house. Lights glowed from the public rooms at the south end and I imagined I could see the flickering of firelight. The tower rose, dark, from the farthest corner.

"Does anyone use the tower rooms," I asked.

"Oh, sure," Frank answered. "We have a music room and activities up there. Sometimes we even rent out the top turret. Costs extra, though because we have to move stuff around. Families like it because it's big— keeps 'em all together. Hurry up. I don't want folks getting too far ahead. It can be dangerous by the river."

The younger crowd had quickly separated from the rest of us and we could barely hear their chatter any more.

"Hey, hold up!" Frank called.

They stopped and turned around, but it looked as if they'd reached the river anyway.

"Wonder what Frank is worried about," I said to Cora. She and Jerry were just ahead of me.

"The old mill was on the river. Maybe the ruins are still there," she responded.

That was exactly what was on Frank's mind. The rest of us caught up, and stopped abruptly at a sheer drop to the water. Voices in the darkness cautioned "watch out," and "that's all ice."

"Here's where the mill race began. You can just see the ruins of the outer wall there in the rapids." Frank pointed at the dark water as curls of foam gleamed in the moonlight where they lifted over hidden obstructions. "But it's begun to erode here along the edge of the remaining wall. One bad step, especially with the ice, and we could have a hard time getting you out of that trench. Or worse yet, you'd be in the river. Not good in these temperatures."

Mariah had been standing right at the edge, and she now took a step back, apparently realizing the wisdom of Frank's words. Suddenly she slipped and Chad reached out to steady her. I caught a flash of smile and lowered eyelids as she gratefully leaned into my son's side.

"Where was the mill?" Cora asked. No large building was visible.

Frank pointed downstream. "Just at that bend. You can see the bricks and bits of walls when its not so icy, but everything that wasn't built right into the riverbank has fallen down. It's mostly a big pile of rubble. And it keeps getting larger because debris catches on it at the curve."

"I'm going back. I'm freezing," Paul said.

In a straggling line we returned to the house. Ray, Jessi, Mariah, and Chad quickly outdistanced the rest of us. Mariah and Chad were still walking together. He slipped an arm around her waist and she didn't pull away.

Cora poked me and nodded at their backs. "Nice that those two seem to be hitting it off," she said.

My feelings were mixed. I knew Chad had dated. After all, he'd been on his own at college for six years, but I'd never met any of his girlfriends. I'd only really seen him interact with another girl his age when he and some friends came to reenact a local history event for Cherry Hill's very first Harvest Ball. But I was pretty sure he never dated either of the two girls who helped with that. Chad was hardly a child, and yet I'd never seriously thought about how it would feel to see him pay attention to a young woman.

It was nearly ten when we entered the house. "I'm heading upstairs," I said. I glanced into the empty front room first and realized that the guests who had not ventured outside must already have gone to their rooms.

"I'll just make a cup of tea to take up with me," Cora said.

She pushed open the kitchen door, and I followed. The kitchen was cold and dim. Dee, Jimmie and the girls were not there; they'd probably gone to bed. Covered trays sat on the counters. I peeked and saw delicious pastries arranged and waiting for breakfast. Tea bags and packets of hot chocolate mix had been left out. Cora filled a hot water pot and plugged it in.

"Are you having a good time, Ana?" Cora asked.

"So far, although I'm not sure what I'm doing here. Other people seem to at least know the judge and the Farnsworths. I don't know any guests except you two. Well, and Chad, of course."

"I suppose business parties like this are always a bit strained. It's one of the things about being married to Jerry that I find difficult to understand. Is there a point to spending time with people who are nearly strangers?"

"We won't be strangers when the party's over," I predicted.

The water pot heated quickly, and it began to make noise and then shut off. Cora and I steeped mugs of tea. She headed upstairs, and I quickly vacuumed the dining room then took my drink and went up as well.

Chad was sitting in a chair beside my bed when I entered my room, flipping through a magazine. "Ma, I have to tell you about Ray and Jessi," he said without any other greeting.

"What's so important?" I asked. I wanted to prod him gently about Mariah, but stopped myself. Maybe I should just wait till he brought up that subject. He looked so vulnerable sitting there in his pajamas, like the little boy he once had been, eyes bright, waiting for a bedtime story.

13

"You won't believe what the Crocketts told me. I know that sounds gossipy, but I can't figure out why these particular people were invited here. Don't you think it's a strange group of guests? Most of them don't even know each other."

I set my tea down on the bedside table, kicked off my shoes, and stretched out on the bed, stacking the pillows behind my head. "People keep asking me that, but I don't know anyone either. Why do you think so?"

"Everybody seems to be one step away from hating someone else."

"Everybody?"

"Well, I heard things, but I only really know the Crockett's story."

"OK, fill me in," I said, sitting up and sipping my drink, recalling other bits and pieces I'd heard that evening.

Chad turned to face me. "Ray and Jessi have this really neat store and business. I've actually shopped there. Remember last summer when my friends and I were driving back to school from North Carolina and stopped over to see friends in Cold Rapids?"

"Vaguely."

"Anyway, a bunch of us went there. I only bought some socks and a shirt, but they sell quality camping equipment. I looked at the tents and backpacks. This is their catalog," He tossed me the glossy booklet he'd been looking at. "They lead outings, too. Long hikes, rock climbing, kayaking expeditions, stuff like that."

I glanced at a couple pages in the book. The equipment was more expensive than I was used to. Not your discount store tents and sleeping bags. "So you feel as if you know them?"

"Well, I'm pretty sure I did meet Ray back then, but that doesn't matter. It's what they do that's important. And I know them now. Good people, Ma."

I wondered if it was possible to tell how good people were after less than a day together. "Tell me what happened."

"On one of the trips they led two years ago, someone got hurt. A girl slipped down a cliff, and she broke her leg. She's all right now, but there were a whole lot of medical expenses that insurance wouldn't cover. Her family sued the Crocketts."

I held up a hand. "Let me guess. They ended up in Judge Viviette's courtroom."

"They did."

"And they lost their shirts?"

I heard creaking and, from the hallway, the scraping of a key in a lock. Someone knocked at my door.

"I'll get it," Chad said. He opened the door, and Jimmie stood there.

He grinned. "Hi Ana, can I come in a minute?"

"Sure," I said. "You've met Chad, I think. Chad, Jimmie Mosher."

"Yeah, I remember when he was in that play a few years ago, when Jerry proposed to Nana," Jimmie said.

"That was a fun event. You're bigger now. Are you going to be able to go skiing tomorrow?" Chad asked him.

Jimmie laughed. "I don't know. I'm a working man. Maybe. But I'll probably let the girls go first if we can spare anyone."

"That's nice of you," I said. "What can we do for you?"

"Well, um... I just wanted to say I like it that you're here. And I thought you should know that Sam isn't as mean as we thought."

"Oh?" I asked.

"He was all stressed out about the truck. But a tow service is coming tomorrow, even though it's the day before Christmas. He thinks we have all the supplies we need, and he can use the snowmobile or the golf cart to haul things around the property."

"That's good to know," Chad put in.

"But what I really wanted to tell you is that he's being nice to Beth and Lindsey. They're upstairs watching TV. The dish gets a lot of channels, and they found some old, old stuff, one called the Honeymooners. It's funny even though it's really old. They're showing a lot of Christmas ones in a row, and everybody's up there laughing."

"I'm glad to hear this. Things were going to be tough if your family had to cook and serve the food under a lot of stress," I said.

"It's great," Jimmie said. He came across the room and gave me a hug. "I'm going to go tell Nana, too. She's been worried about us."

"Good thinking," I said.

"Don't work too hard," Chad advised, grinning and clapping Jimmie on the shoulder.

Jimmie grinned back at Chad and ducked out the door.

"Where were we?" I asked, finishing off my tea, before it got any colder.

"Ray and Jessi lost their court case on television."

"Right, and so they lost their shirts? But they're still in business."

"No, no, that's not how it works. They didn't lose that much money," Chad explained. "Those TV shows are really arbitration courts. So everyone had signed agreements ahead of time on how much damages could be awarded, and Ray and Jessi would have to pay a lot less money even if they lost."

I was confused. "So, what was the problem?"

"That judge. I've already heard a few really cutting names for her tonight."

"Me, too."

"Anyway, the accident wasn't Ray and Jessi's fault at all. The girl was wandering around outside the campsite after dark with no light. She claimed to be looking for a place to pee, even though everyone had been shown the latrine location in the trees when they set up."

"How can Ray and Jessi be responsible for that?"

"The girl's family claimed they were negligent in not showing the campers the steep bank on the one side."

"They hadn't signed some sort of release?"

"Sure they did, but those things don't hold up well, legally.

The rest of the campers on the trip said the Crocketts had showed them around when they set up and pointed out the dangers, but it didn't help because no one could prove this girl heard it all, and she said she didn't."

"So the judge held Ray and Jessi responsible."

"Yup. But even that wouldn't have mattered too much. It was what Judge Viviette said afterwards."

"Uh, oh. Overkill?"

"It sure was. She called Ray and Jessi unfit to lead trips and told them they were children who shouldn't be trying to organize dangerous activities. Their biggest competitor ran clips of that show wherever he thought he could get away with it."

"And really hurt their business."

"You got it. That was two years ago, and they're just beginning to recover from the bad publicity."

14

Knuckles tapping in the dark. Ears straining. Tock, tock, tock, thunk. *Again.* Tock, tock, tock, tock, thunk. *There it is. But how...?*

15

I thought I would sleep in but then remembered my promise to help with some housekeeping duties. Well, people wouldn't want their bathrooms cleaned while they were still trying to shower or shave. The desire for a solid rest won out, and when I came to in the morning, the most noticeable quality was the quiet. If I had calculated correctly, there were thirteen people with rooms off our hallway, not to mention the five overhead in the attic, and yet, I heard nothing. It was beyond eerie. Had something happened and everyone left the house, forgetting to count heads— mine in particular? Was I suddenly struck deaf? Had I missed breakfast?

A roaring whine beyond the window made me jerk, and my heart beat wildly. I jumped out of bed and ran to push back the curtain. In gray light, I saw Sam on the snowmobile skidding to a stop beside the unfinished portion of the house. Snowmobile! When we'd all gone to bed there was barely a dusting of snow. Now, there had to be eight or nine inches on the ground and it was still thickly coming down from a low sky.

Hitched behind the snowmobile was a large flat sled, unlike anything I'd seen before. My eyes wandered back along the route the machine had taken, and I realized Sam must have been out grooming the trails for skiing. A long compacted pathway with two grooves in it meandered across the wide open area and disappeared into a break in the tree line.

Sam unhooked the groomer, maneuvered it out of the way and connected a simple box sled to the snowmobile. He opened a door I hadn't really been aware of and ducked inside, emerging a moment later with a load of dry wood which he tossed in the box. Getting ready for the campfire lunch, I assumed.

Leaving Sam to do his chores without my supervision, I

staggered, still a bit groggy, to the bath Chad and I shared, where I found a note taped to the mirror.

"Ma- Didn't want to wake you. Breakfast buffet was great! Plenty left for you. Mariah and I are going to try some new kind of skis the Crockett's brought. Catch you later."

Mariah and I, eh? I thought, as I cleaned up and dressed in jeans and a turtleneck. I'd eat and get my housekeeping chores out of the way before going out to ski. Not that I knew much about how to do that, but maybe Jessi and Ray Crockett would give me a few pointers. I figured I couldn't embarrass myself more than the overweight Belinda Kramer. She probably wouldn't even try skiing. I wondered if Cora would. I had no idea if she'd ever been interested in winter sports.

The dining room wasn't quite empty. The long tables separated into squares and were now scattered around the room with four chairs at each. Belinda and Harry lingered over cups of coffee with our hostess, Betty.

"I *know* that coin collection was worth over a hundred grand, and I almost had it," I heard Belinda say. She looked up, startled to see someone, and quickly bit into a pastry.

Did I sense an undercurrent of alarm? Well, she'd told me she was a nervous person. It was probably nothing.

"Ana!" Betty rose and came forward. "Did you sleep well?" Strong cigarette odors clung to her sweater, along with that stifling perfume.

"Like the dead, apparently. I can't believe I just woke up."

"Almost everyone is out back getting fitted up with skis. Some brought their own, as I'm sure you noticed."

I laughed. "I'll head out as soon as I can. Let me grab some food first." I started to add something about cleaning bathrooms, but remembered that Sam had asked me to try not to advertize my dual role of guest and helper.

The breakfast buffet was set with an egg dish in a warming tray and plenty of tasty muffins, pastries and fruit. I grabbed some juice and a plate of food and wandered toward the sitting room. The Christmas tree was glossy-magazine lovely and I wanted to enjoy the atmosphere. Passing through the archway,

I noticed the mistletoe ball had not been hung overhead. Maybe my homemade gift wasn't quite nice enough to suit Betty. I shrugged involuntarily.

Setting my plate on an end table and taking in the beautiful tree with a sigh, I then wandered across the room, muffin in hand. A small vestibule had caught my attention. As I turned the corner into it, I saw a spiral staircase and a round room beyond it. The tower! The ground level housed a library— the walls were lined with books, and comfortable chairs had been randomly placed. Window seats were recessed into the three tall casings hung with velvet drapes.

I took a bite of the warm bread. Orange cranberry! It didn't take long to finish off the muffin.

Feeling conspiratorial, although we certainly would have been told if we weren't supposed to enter the tower, I climbed the stairs. The second floor was a music room. There was a baby grand piano, a drum set, hammered dulcimer and, oddly, a marimba of some sort. Too curious, I picked up a hammer and struck several of the bars, which produced the mellow, woody tones I'd expected. Shelves held an assortment of ukuleles, guitars, harmonicas and small rhythm instruments. How could the Farnsworths afford all these extra touches, in addition to completely renovating such an old house?

Sitting at the piano, I opened the music book that had been left on the rack. It contained simplified versions of hit tunes of the 70s, and I struggled through "Imagine." No one appeared to tell me to stop. I played it again, only slightly better. It had been years since I'd tried to read music. "Unrealistic," I commented to no one as I slid off the bench.

At the top floor, the door was locked, and I descended. But I couldn't understand why the foyer beside the stairs was so large. Taking a step into the darkened space I realized it was still under construction. An elevator was being installed, the blocked off shaft blank and chilly.

I retrieved my cooling cup of coffee and headed for the kitchen.

Beth and Lindsey were packing a plastic tub with hot dog buns and condiments.

Dee looked up. "Hi Ana. Have you been skiing?"

"Not yet. What time is it?"

Jimmie came through the back door, snow swirling around his thin shoulders. "Got another tub ready?" he asked.

Lindsey snapped the cover in place and pushed the container across the floor toward her brother.

"It's almost ten," Dee said, in answer to my question, taking the empty mug and plate from my hands.

"Wow! Gotta get busy or I won't get to play outside today."

16

The skeleton key for the guest rooms Sam had entrusted to me was shaped like an antique. I realized when I used it, however, that the locks were reproductions with more modern and secure internal mechanisms. Rushing as much as I could through unfamiliar spaces, I cleaned up the guest bathrooms and put out dry towels. The room directly across the hall from my own was not in use. Since I knew all the other assignments, it had to be the judge and her husband who were not staying on the same floor as the rest of us.

Gathering up the awkward bundle of damp towels—tomorrow I'd bring a basket up with me— I started down to the laundry room. Then I recalled that wasn't allowed. Not down the main stairs anyway. Just as I turned around to head for the back stairs, the judge's husband, Branson, entered through the main door. His shoulders and red stocking cap were covered with snow. He stamped his feet and the fresh smell of winter air drifted my way. I thought of calling to him and asking what room they were in, but then my "secret" role would be revealed. I watched to see if he would head down the first floor corridor.

Instead, he opened the closet beneath the staircase. From my position— he was almost beneath me— I couldn't see what he was doing, but a moment later he turned and headed back outside, carrying a pair of red ski poles. He never noticed me, for which I was oddly thankful.

I hurried back through the hallway, down the two flights of stairs, along the stone passage in the basement, and climbed back to the laundry room. What a bother! And I still needed to find where Viviette Velociraptor, or whatever her name was, and Bran were staying.

The kitchen was empty. I'd get no help from Jimmie's family.

So I returned to the dining room, also empty. However, there were voices coming from the sitting room. Betty, Belinda, and Harry had moved to more comfortable chairs but were still visiting, their heads together, conspiratorially. This suggestion was strengthened when Belinda gave a little scream and jerked in her chair when I said, "Excuse me." Apparently she was easily startled, but no food ended up on the floor this time.

Harry straightened and twisted his thick neck, as if to get out a kink.

"Yes?" Betty responded.

"I need to know... " I began, but then realized Harry and Belinda were guests. "May I see you for a minute?"

"I'll be right back," Betty said to her friends.

She came into the dining room. "What's the problem?" she asked quietly.

"Nothing major, it's just that I don't know what room the judge is staying in, and I need to change the towels."

"Of course, my apologies. They asked if they could have more privacy, and I moved them to our most luxurious guest room. I'm sure you don't even know where it is. Top floor of the tower. You'll have to use the circular stairs across the living room. We're putting in an elevator, but the shaft isn't finished yet."

I didn't want to admit I'd already become somewhat familiar with the tower so I only said, "Then I'll need to bring the laundry down that way. Your guests will see me." I nodded toward the front room.

"Belinda? Don't worry about her. She's truly an old friend, and I've told her and Harry how kind you were to offer to help. The same key opens the tower. Sam did give you the key?"

"Yes, the other rooms are already done. Thanks."

Betty returned to her friends, and I crossed past them and climbed the spiral stair again. Splendid and spacious appropriately described the third floor of the tower. The furniture was Chippendale, or perhaps a quality reproduction. Baby blue accents were brocaded with fine gold thread. The room had been decorated with its own small Christmas tree, making me think it was no last-minute decision to offer this room to Viviette and

Branson, or to someone, anyway. Next to the bathroom door hung a long curtain. Since it didn't match the windows, I peeked. It was apparently temporary, to hide the unfinished elevator shaft, which was heavily barricaded with plywood and warning signs.

With windows all around the room, the views were sweeping and enlightening. Sam's disabled truck was visible just beyond the bridge, the one I hadn't noticed when we drove in. The large black vehicle almost blocked the narrow road— its right rear corner angled awkwardly toward the ground. Obviously, the tow truck hadn't arrived yet. With the lawn and surrounding clearing white with snow, I could see the dark ribbon of Janes Creek cutting through the bright landscape and flowing toward the river. I suddenly realized the mansion was marooned on a point with the bridge the only overland access. To the east the dark line of trees was nearly solid between the river and the creek. A light at the top of a distant cell tower blinked through the scrim of falling snow. It was the only sign of human influence I could see beyond the mansion property, and I remembered Cora explaining this was an isolated inholding surrounded by state forest.

Brightly outfitted skiers were emerging from the woods and causing small eddies in the thickly falling snowflakes. I couldn't hear anything, but they seemed to be laughing and having a grand time. Maybe someone would want to go around the trail again if I could just finish the chores and get into appropriate clothes.

17

Doreen Pyrtle in her fuchsia bibs waved to me as I stepped off the porch. She and several other people were coming from the rear of the house, no longer on skis.

"Whew," Doreen said. "They need an easier way to get to a bathroom than coming to the main door."

"You can go in the utility room on the other side. Right by the kitchen door," I said. "There's a half bath in there." I was glad to have useful knowledge.

"I'll remember that. Are you going to ski?"

"I want to, but I'll need help getting fitted." My black ski pants were secondhand, and I wore my regular navy jacket. I felt underdressed and small next to Doreen. Maybe skiing was more about looking good than athletics.

Jessi Crockett said, "Sam's around back with all the equipment. Go see him, and we'll be right out. I'll ski with you if you want."

"That would be great. Except for a couple of basic lessons two years ago, I haven't done this since college."

Jessi patted my shoulder. "You'll do fine."

The farthest end of the unfinished section of the house must have been a stable or tack room of some sort. Maybe an early garage when cars were smaller. It had wide double doors that swung outward which were now latched open. The room was unheated and unfurnished except for benches along the walls. But it was perfect as a ski shelter and sports equipment storage.

"Ana," Cora said, looking up and smiling as she removed a tiny ski boot, "where have you been?"

"I slept in, and it felt great," I answered, pulling off my stocking cap and pushing my hair behind my ears before replacing the hat. "But I hope there's time to ski a little before lunch. Jessi said she'd go with me. I'm supposed to find Sam."

"Right here," Sam said, leaning back and revealing himself. He'd been partially hidden by Earl and Bran, the two largest men, who were stacking their skis and poles near the door. "Have a seat. What size shoe do you wear?"

Jessi, Ray, Chad, Doreen, Paul, Mariah, and I were soon making our way toward the tree line. Already, I was having trouble keeping up, even though the others had at least an hour of exercise behind them.

"It's not how hard you work," Jessi said. She had positioned herself behind me, and the others were ahead. "Let the skis glide, and push all the way back with the poles. Let me show you how to wrap your hand in the loops."

We stopped and she arranged the pole straps so my wrists leveraged against them. We started again.

"Now you're getting it."

I hoped she was right, and it did feel better. I'd been sort of shuffling, but now I was definitely moving faster.

"I guess the older folks aren't big on fitness," Doreen said. She was a couple people ahead of me and I missed some of the words, but I couldn't let this pass.

"Jerry and Cora skied, didn't they?" I asked, pretty sure of the answer.

"You're right about that," Paul said. "But they don't seem old. I haven't seen that overweight couple, though. What are their names?"

"Harry and Belinda," I supplied. "I think they don't have the same last name."

"Judge Viviette and her husband went snowshoeing," Jessi added.

"Good," Paul said. He was directly ahead of me, and I could hear him without any trouble. His tone suggested his pleasure had nothing to do with their fitness regimen.

"You seem happy about that," I laughed.

"You've got that right. That way they're nowhere near me. I

can't believe the Farnsworths invited the judge to this party. She's making too many people uncomfortable."

"What do you mean?"

Paul growled, but didn't explain himself. Just then we headed around a curve and my ski tip caught on a small branch— not much more than a twig. However, it was more than I could deal with at the speed we were going, and I went down in a heap.

I wasn't hurt and started laughing almost immediately, but it was a struggle to get up again. Jessi coached me, but by the time I got to my feet the others were out of sight among the trees.

After I righted myself, Jessi took hold of my jacket sleeve so I couldn't fall, or maybe so I couldn't leave for a minute. "Chad told me you are good at solving mysteries," she said.

Where was this going? "Not in any special way. I've just had some success at asking the right questions."

"I know you know about our situation— the business. Why don't you try to find out what Betty and Frank are up to? Betty is way passive aggressive, and I haven't heard anyone say they're glad the judge is here. "

"Harry and Belinda credit her with introducing them. I heard her say so last night," I said.

"Well, that's something, I guess."

"And I don't know that Jerry and Cora have any particular feelings about her." I felt defensive for my friends.

"Ask them. I know I'm young and maybe don't know everything, but I just have a bad feeling about this whole party. There's something *off*, if you know what I mean. Toxic."

I feigned a thoughtful attitude, as if this was new information. "I have heard several people make comments to that effect," I admitted. But Betty and Frank couldn't be responsible for how guests felt about each other. Suddenly, the mental image of the Farnsworths secretively tête-à-tête with Harry and Belinda popped into my mind. However, I wasn't about to commit myself to something that was probably nothing at all, at an event where I was determined to relax and enjoy myself. I brushed snowflakes away that had collected on my eyelashes and nodded down the trail. "Let's try to catch up."

"OK," Jessi said. She shivered and looked around as if the gorgeous winter woods were ominous. "But I think something bad is going to happen. I can feel things."

18

The campfire circle was near the river, east of the house. Most everyone must have taken their gear back to the equipment room before walking out that way, but there were a few pairs of skis leaning against a board nailed between frame uprights. People were standing or sitting near the fire. Some held plates or cups.

"Want to go directly there?" Jessi asked, pointing toward the warm orange flames leaping skyward. We never had caught up to the others.

"Sounds good," I said, and we veered along an ungroomed but previously used track to join the lunch crowd.

Rough benches surrounded the fire, and a number of nylon fabric lawn chairs were also occupied. There were two picnic tables laden with food and draped with plastic sheeting since there was no pavilion. That was when I realized just how hard it was snowing. As soon as anyone lifted an edge of the plastic to reach underneath for a bun or plate, a thick line of hard dry snow gathered in the fold. This wasn't the ordinary wet snow of early winter; this was the real thing. At least the day was calm. If the wind picked up, it would be too miserable to stay outside. I unclipped my bindings, and stacked the skis with the others.

Jimmie and Dee stood near the fire holding flat wire cages filled with hot dogs over the blaze. Beth and Lindsey were at the tables helping people work around the awkward plastic to fix their frankfurters and fill plates with chips and the makings for s'mores. The girls had bundled up in snow pants and cheerful Christmas hats— no uniforms out here. I headed their way.

"What's to drink?" I asked.

"Hot chocolate, and there's pop and beer in the coolers," Beth said. "But you have to get your own if you want the beer. We're too young to hand it out."

"I'll have the cocoa, " I said.

Beth filled a cup from an air pot and handed it to me. "Fix your bun now. More hot dogs will be ready in just a minute."

Chad and Mariah stood by the fire chatting. Chad and Mariah again! Jessi joined them, and I watched to see how they would react. They didn't seem put out that someone had broken into their conversation, but I decided to let the younger folks have a good time without me. I took Beth's advice and filled a plate, making sure I had graham crackers, a chocolate bar and two marshmallows.

Jimmie approached with a rack of sizzling wieners. "Just for you," he said, grinning. I took two of them, as well.

Earl was seated in a blue nylon chair, scowling and talking with Harry. "Give me a good football game any day instead of pansy sports like skiing." He was emphasizing the point by jabbing a can of beer toward the sky.

Harry sipped quietly from a foam cup and nodded. He didn't seem interested in the conversation. His face was blotchy red; and he looked cold in a thin parka. He probably hadn't brought many clothes for outdoor recreation.

Ray Crockett stepped toward Earl. "Why do you insist on belittling sports that don't interest you? Just because you'd rather watch people get closed head injuries and chase a ball..."

Earl slipped the beer can into the cup holder in the arm of the chair, with some difficulty, I noticed. He stood up, towering over Ray. "Are you trying to start something, little man?"

"You're drunk, and lunch isn't even over yet." Ray shook his head and turned around.

"Too scared to hold up one end of a discussion?"

Ray walked away, and Doreen ran to Earl's side. "Calm down, honey," she soothed. "Let's get some food in your stomach. That will help."

Earl seemed unexpectedly belligerent to me, even if he was drunk. Surely he skied regularly. He and Doreen had brought their own equipment. Did he just enjoy challenging people and starting arguments? Maybe he had something against Ray in particular.

Cora and Jerry sat on a bench at the other side of the fire, and I decided to put as much space between myself and Earl as possible.

"Ana, I haven't seen you since yesterday," Cora said with a smile as I approached.

Jerry slid over and indicated I should sit between them.

"I know! It seems like there are a lot of people here, but then somehow we all spread out and don't find each other."

"Are you enjoying yourself?" she asked.

"I'm not sure. Somehow this party is a little crazy. Whenever people start to have a good time, something boils over, and then it seems like everyone hates someone else."

"I've noticed that," Jerry said. "I saw Earl and Ray going at it just now. And no one seems happy Judge Viviette is here."

That reminded me. "So, do you know her? Everyone seems to, and not just from watching TV."

Jerry sighed. "We went to college together. She wasn't anybody special then, but I was editor of the literary magazine— just student stuff— no budding classics, but not shabby. She matriculated when I was a senior and she was jealous of my position. Didn't matter to her that she was a lowly freshman. Went out of her way to spread rumors. Stuff that was patently false."

"Not a person who won friends even then," I grinned.

"She was not," Jerry said, and took a large bite of hot dog. He wiped a spot of mustard from his mustache. "But she got the editorial position the next year. I didn't care; I was gone. She just liked power. Still does."

"How about you?" I asked Cora. It was beginning to look like a lot of the guests did have some outside connection to the judge.

"Never met her till yesterday," Cora said. "But I don't think we'll be making friends anytime soon. Oops, here she comes."

Viviette and her husband Bran were approaching on snowshoes. She wore a long, deep purple down coat. Bran's red ski poles matched his jacket but clashed violently with his wife's purple outfit.

"Jerry, how nice to see you. I didn't get to say hello last night," the judge said, holding out a hand that was obviously long and slender even inside her gloves.

"Viviette. How are you?" Jerry said with some reserve, standing and shaking the extended hand. Cautiously, I thought.

We went through all the polite introductions. Branson and Viviette removed their snowshoes and sat on the bench.

"We've been down along the river," Bran said, leaning forward in order to more or less look at us.

"Oh, where the mill used to stand?" Cora asked.

"In fact, yes," he answered. "It's fascinating."

Viviette snorted.

"It is to some of us," Bran continued. "You can't see any of it from here, through that band of trees, but there are a lot of partial walls still standing. You can tell where various rooms were— mostly full of water and debris now. I wonder if there's a copy of the original blueprints anywhere."

"I'm sure Cora would know, with that little hobby of hers," Viviette put in.

I could practically see Cora swell and bristle. "What *little* hobby would that be?" she asked.

"All that fooling around you do with local history. It must be nice for you that Jerry can support your pastime."

To her credit, Cora held her temper. "We do have several pictures of the mill at the museum, but to my knowledge no drawings of the interior layout have survived. I'd love to locate a set."

Wow. Couldn't anyone hold a civil conversation? If Cora hadn't known Viviette before, she certainly did now. I looked toward the back door, wishing I had never agreed to come to this party, or whatever it was supposed to be. Someone was coming from the house, blurry through the falling snow.

Belinda charged toward us, waving her arms. "I can't find Betty anywhere. Is she out here with you?"

19

"Oh, for Pete's sake," growled Frank, straightening his back. He'd been leaning over to tend the campfire where several people were toasting marshmallows. "She's probably just gone for a smoke. We don't allow it in the house. That woman is nuts." He pointed a piece of firewood in Belinda's general direction, then threw it on the fire in exasperation, and began walking toward her.

The mood changed following Frank's callous accusation.

"Well, nice to meet you," Viviette said with a smile that was clearly camera practiced. She stood and turned to Bran. "Let's have lunch before they pack everything up. Then how about a little nap?"

Bran nodded, gathered the snowshoes and poles together, and somehow he still managed to help the judge to her feet. They headed for the food table.

Jerry rose too. "Give me your plates and trash. Here comes Chad. At least he'll be civil, I expect."

Cora and I laughed half-heartedly. I stuffed a raw marshmallow in my mouth and slipped the chocolate bar in a pocket.

Mariah was still with Chad. Were they becoming inseparable?

"Hey, Ma. Do you want to try snowshoeing this afternoon? It's lots easier than skiing. Oh, your still wearing ski boots."

"It takes a different kind?" I asked.

"Just regular ones. These will be too stiff."

"Aren't your feet cold?" Mariah asked.

Now that I thought about it, they were. I looked at my son and this girl who was full of life. Her cheeks were pink from the cold, and her smile was natural and infectious, unlike Viviette's. Chad's eyes were sparkling. I hadn't seen him this happy for a while. Not that he was a sullen or negative person, but something about this girl was really holding his attention. "I think I've had enough exercise for a few hours. You two go have fun."

Mariah wanted to be sure I meant that, and she invited me again, but I told her I'd catch them later and get better acquainted then.

Almost everyone except Dee and the kids had begun to wander toward the house. "I think I'll go help pack up the food," I said.

Chad and Mariah ran off awkwardly— the snow was getting deeper— toward the equipment room, laughing. I realized my normal boots were still there, so I retrieved my skis, and after Dee assured me they didn't need help I followed the young couple. Entering the gloomy interior of the former garage, I headed for the bench where my ordinary boots were waiting. My eyes were still dazzled from the bright snow, but movement in the corner caught my attention.

"Ma!" Chad sounded annoyed. He and Mariah backed hurriedly away from each other.

"Sorry," I said. I grabbed my boots, held them up, and tried to hide a smile. "I'll change in the house."

I exited and turned toward the campfire area, but there was no one there. Instead, I shuffled through unshoveled snow along the back edge of the closed-up section of the house and entered the utility room. My feet and legs were wet, and I quickly changed into my own boots. Clunky but dry. The cheerful voices of Jimmie and his sisters, bantering in the kitchen, beckoned me. I was sick and tired of all the animosity among the adults. Maybe Jessi was right.

Beth and Lindsey were giggling and snapping damp towels at each other, and their mother was making no effort to curtail their glee. Jimmie unloaded tubs and occasionally swatted a sister on the behind if one ventured close to him. Snowpants and coats were piled in a corner.

Dee rolled her eyes and offered me a cup of coffee, which I gladly accepted, along with a cookie from the box on the counter.

"They need a chance to be children for a few minutes," she explained.

"No problem with me," I replied. "I'm mighty glad to see people having fun. I'm not sure everyone at this party is so happy."

"I've noticed that, too," Dee said. "It's that judge. She's made too many enemies."

"You've overhead things?" I asked.

"Not so much here. But all those years I was too fat to leave the house, like when you met me... I watched a lot of TV. I've seen some of these people before."

"Really? Got time to tell me about it?"

"Sure. I need a little break," she said, turning and clapping her hands. The towel chase stopped. "You three need to be back in the kitchen by four o'clock, but for now, get outside and build a snowman or something. Work off some of that energy."

"OK, Mom," Jimmie said. "I'll just put the rest of this stuff away. Linds, Beth, get your snow gear back on and I'll pull you on the toboggan. Then you can pull me."

Much squealing and swishing of wet nylon and the whine of zippers ensued, and soon Dee and I were alone in the kitchen.

"What's the scoop?" I asked.

Dee let herself down on a kitchen stool and sipped her coffee. "They weren't all on the TV show, but some were. That nice young couple with the outdoor store? That was some episode, I can tell you."

"Chad told me the story Ray and Jessi told him."

"That they almost lost their business because of *her*?"

"Yes. Was there more to it?" I asked.

"Not really, I guess. They won the lawsuit but Judge Viviette was so nasty to them. If it had been me, I'd feel like murdering her."

"Don't say things like that."

"Well, I wouldn't really do it, but that's how I'd feel. And Harry lost in her courtroom. He had to have his dog put down. That can be like losing a child for some people."

"I heard Belinda was on the same show and that's how they met. So they didn't care that they'd lost."

"Now that's a strange one. There was something going on besides her renter wanting his stuff back." Dee stretched her back and pulled down the hem of her shirt.

"Like what?"

"You couldn't really tell on the show. But I've seen it several times on re-runs, and I read about the cases in magazines. Well, I used to. I have a life now." Dee reached over and touched my arm.

We shared a moment of unspoken sadness over how she'd lived when Bert was alive.

She continued. "I've always thought Belinda wanted to keep the tenant's things a lot more than she wanted the deposit money. There was something involved that wasn't just cash."

An overheard comment came to mind. "Something about a coin collection?" I asked.

"That's an idea," Dee said. "What if there was something really valuable in his stuff that she wanted to keep?"

"Why wouldn't he have just said so? If his property was worth way more than what he owed, he could have gotten it back without a fake court case."

"Maybe he wasn't supposed to have it. Stolen? It belonged to a family member who didn't realize it was missing?"

I raised my eyebrows and took another bite of cookie.

Dee looked down at her hands and then up at me with pain in her eyes. "I actually know a lot more about the judge than just from television." The coffee cup on her lap vibrated as her legs began to shake.

"Dee, what's wrong?" I reached out and took the cup from her as a tear spilled from the corner of her eye.

"Did you know she was a real judge in family court before she got a TV show?"

I shook my head.

"It was before I met that horrible man you saved me from. The four of us, the kids and I, were doing all right; we just didn't have a very good place to live at the time." Dee wiped her cheeks with trembling fingers. "She's the one who took the girls away from me."

20

I placed her cup on the counter, grabbed a paper napkin and handed it to Dee. She blew her nose. "There's more," she said.

"About you and the judge?" I felt numb.

"No, about Paul Thomas. I'm shocked he was invited. It's really in very bad taste."

"How's that?"

Dee glanced around. We were alone in the kitchen. There wasn't even a buzz of voices coming from the next room, but she seemed extremely concerned that no one overhear.

"You have to understand that for a while I became somewhat obsessed with following Judge Viviette. Not only did I read the tabloids, but I searched their ads and sent for books and other papers that supposedly gave the deep inside 'dirt' on people. What I'm going to tell you isn't common knowledge at all."

"Are you sure it's even true?" I was uncomfortable with this level of gossipy information, but if I were to learn what was really going on, I'd have to hear it all.

"Who can be certain about any of that stuff?" Dee shrugged. "I don't read that garbage any more, but I was at a certain place in life... and I hated the Velvet Hammer. I kept wishing for hurtful things to happen to her."

"And you found something? Something about her and Paul?"

"I did."

"I don't know her age, but he looks a lot younger."

"Yes, she's old enough to be his mother, but she's not," Dee said. Her voice did not drop as it would if the thought were completed.

"But there's some connection," I prompted.

"He's the son of her first husband. They nearly broke up after Paul was born. When you look at him it's not obvious. He claims to be Italian, with his wavy hair and dark good looks. That helps him pretend he's not half black."

"Who cares about that stuff any more?" I asked.

"Not me, but he cares. He cares very much, and spending three days with his father's wife is just going to keep that fact right in the center of his thoughts."

"Where's Paul's father?" I asked.

"He died, so there's no one to let the secret out except Paul and the judge."

"Does his daughter know?"

"I have no idea. She seems like such a nice girl."

"Chad certainly thinks so," I agreed, laughing to lighten the conversation. "You've given me a lot to think about. Is there more?"

"No, no," Dee said, looking at me in consternation. "Isn't that enough?"

"It certainly is." I placed my coffee cup on the counter. "I think I'll find a cozy spot to hide from everyone till dinner. Too much drama."

"Good luck," Dee said, laughing with me as she tried to forget her past life.

My room would have provided privacy, but I was drawn instead to the library. I had to admit, Betty Farnsworth had a true talent for beautiful decorating. The window seats were cushioned with maroon velvet trimmed in gold braid and strewn with puffy pillows for reclining. Dark wood bookcases stretched floor to ceiling, and there was a ladder that rolled smoothly on a bar so one could access any shelf.

I studied the collection of books which interested me considerably— I'd taught literature in my former life. There was an entire section on Victorian architecture, restoration, and decor. That made sense. Soon, I discovered that a number of the volumes appeared to have been chosen based on when they were written, as opposed to their literary value. Shelf after shelf was filled with titles such as *The Courage of Captain Plum, Joyce of the Northwoods, and Girl of the Limberlost.* I actually knew some of them, but a quick glance assured me most of them were romantic drivel, lurid at the time they were written. However, the bindings looked perfect in the century-plus old library.

There was also a large selection of modern literary fiction and best-seller paperbacks. These were near the door so their out-of-character bindings weren't immediately seen if one glanced into the room, but they were near at hand for a reader.

Interspersed with the books were knick-knacks of decent quality: a marble miniature of The Thinker, a bronze boy riding a tricycle, and a rusted tangle of gears with doubtful artistic value.

I pulled a dark green book from the shelf of older novels, and settled into one of the leather chairs with *Lydia of the Pines.* Surprisingly, the story turned out to be compelling, but my thoughts distracted me in spite of the plucky Lydia.

Would it make any difference to Chad if he knew that the poisonous judge was the grandmother of the girl he liked? Well, Viviette wasn't her grandmother, really. Not truly any relation at all. That was confusing.

I was having trouble keeping track of who disliked whom. Doreen used to be on drugs, Belinda was obsessed with gold coins or something. Earl seemed mad at everybody. I wondered if Frank had located Betty.

"Hello, Ana. Would you care for some company? What a wonderful space!"

I looked up to find Cora peering in the library door.

"I think the younger folks have gone snowshoeing, and most of the men went back out to huddle around the remains of the fire. Not my kind of conversation," she said.

"Did Betty turn up?"

"Oh yes. She was smoking in one of the storage rooms. She really blistered Belinda's ear for making such a fuss."

I had tucked my legs underneath me in the large chair, but now I unfolded and sat straighter. "I thought they were friends?"

"They are, but Betty's got a mouth on her. I've heard it once or twice before." Cora tried to look prim, but the effect came across as saucy.

I laughed out loud and leaned forward. "What do you make of this group of people she and Frank have collected here?"

"It does appear eclectic." She sighed. "Betty is an interesting person. She's actually related to the Janes."

"The family that built this place?"

"Yes. A distant cousin. I'd have to look at the records to get it exactly right. Anyway, she also has a ton of money."

"She's not just an aging housewife socialite?"

"Oh, no. Frank isn't exactly poor, of course. I'm sure his pension from the Emily City *Ledger* is quite generous, not to mention investments, but Betty got in on the early days of multi-level marketing with cosmetics. I don't know what she's worth, but I've heard rumors of seven figures."

"Well, that explains this house," I said.

Cora pulled her sweater tighter around her shoulders. "Partially. She wanted to be upper crust, but I'm afraid small town newspaper editors don't rise to that level."

"I've lived in the city. There's nothing wonderful about rarified social circles."

Cora shrugged. "Now that she's got the house mostly ready for the public, she wants to show it off. But..."

"But, she doesn't have the social skills to match her gift for decor?" I waved a hand to take in the room, implying the entire house.

"I think that's a fair assessment."

"And yet, that doesn't seem to quite explain how she managed to put together a group with so many grudges, does it? I think she wants to prove she's in control."

Cora's eyebrows lifted.

21

As darkness began to settle in at four-thirty, people made their way to the dining room and the bar. I left the protective atmosphere of the library and mingled, mostly to see what would happen next. The answer was— nothing as exciting as some of the previous outbursts. Maybe everyone was mellowing, which I thought was a good thing. It was almost Christmas, after all, and so far holiday spirit had seemed lacking. The Canadian Brass was playing "Silent Night" softly behind the hum of voices.

Doreen was now telling Ray and Jessi about her previous life on drugs. It was a curious subject to continually bring up, since it seemed to have been many years ago. At least long enough in the past to have established a successful business after her recovery.

I watched Belinda and Harry enter the room, hand in hand. They had to turn sideways to do it. However, Belinda looked less imperial tonight, in dark slacks and a red stretchy top. Harry was casual in clean jeans and a Hawaiian shirt. His extra fat kept him warm.

Paul and Mariah were chatting, wine glasses in hand. Mariah wore red and green patterned yoga pants with a long black sweater that curved seductively over her behind. I noticed this just about the same time as Chad did. He entered and looked around the room. He wasn't searching for me, and I caught his eyes following Mariah's hips before he focused on her face and crossed to her side. I knew his expression, only it used to come over him when receiving a new Lego set. This was the face of a boy in love.

The evening meal was cozy and, thankfully, free of tense exchanges. The tables had been left as individual squares rather than strung together in a long banquet format. This was a good plan, given the fractured relationships of those on the guest list. Of course the foursome of young people, Jessi and Ray with Chad and Mariah, took one table. Earl and Doreen paired up with Frank and Betty. I supposed this was due to the professional ties between Earl and Frank, and Betty and Doreen were both in the cosmetic business, although technically competitors.

I arrived in the dining room just in time to grab a seat with Jerry and Cora, by far the most comfortable grouping for me. Paul was the other single— since Mariah had attached herself to Chad— and when he asked if our fourth chair was free, we gladly welcomed him. This left Judge Viviette and Bran with Harry and Belinda, but I thought this was probably the safest combination for the unpopular judge, since they seemed unperturbed by her presence.

The menu was comfort food designed to fill people up after a day of exercise. We forked in Cobb salad and nibbled at tiny garlic rolls until the girls placed an individual pot pie in front of each guest. I chose beef, and it was delicious, obviously homemade, with a flaky crust. Jimmie was establishing himself as a seriously good cook.

With Chad and Mariah becoming something of an item, at least for the duration of this party, I was pleased to have a chance to get to know Paul better. I attempted to engage him in conversation about his background, but he dodged every question with some lighthearted response that missed the mark. Eventually, he managed to get Jerry discussing the evolution of printing processes. Cora tuned in, ever interested in the history of anything, but I half listened and decided Paul's evasive personal revelations tended to verify what Dee had told me.

The girls were bringing colorful bowls filled with small fruits- grapes, strawberries, chocolate-covered banana chunks— and cheese to each table as Betty stood and tapped a knife against her water glass.

"Good evening, everyone. I hope you've had a delightful day of visiting and enjoying the snow which we were pleased to be able to provide."

This claim was accepted with light laughter. I appreciated

that it sounded genuine rather than strained. Maybe we'd gotten past the rough patches.

"As you are well aware, each of you was asked to bring a generic gift for our group exchange on this gorgeous Christmas Eve. Thanks to another person who wishes to remain anonymous, there will be two gifts under the tree for each of us. Well," she qualified, "some are labeled to go to a couple rather than an individual."

There was a general nodding of heads and murmurs of anticipation.

"In about twenty minutes, let's all gather around the Christmas tree. Hot drinks and a luscious dessert will be served later by our caterers, Cherry Blossom Cuisine. Will someone bring them out, please."

Cora rose from her chair and pushed open the kitchen door. Dee and the three children bashfully entered the dining room, and a round of enthusiastic applause followed. There was no question but that the food was excellent, and this would establish a reputation for the renewed Cherry Blossom brand.

Betty tapped her glass again. "Twenty minutes. You won't want to be late."

I popped a chocolate banana chunk in my mouth and followed up with a strawberry.

22

Jessi passed the large red box to Ray, "You open it," she directed.

In addition to the couches, several huge lounge pillows were scattered around the room. I had made myself comfortable resting against one, with my legs tucked under me. Chad and Mariah were also curled into pillows on the floor. At Betty's command, Frank and Earl had carried in the leather chairs from the library, so everyone had a comfy seat. Logs glowed in the fireplace, and the scents of warm pine sap and wood smoke permeated the room.

Someone had re-wrapped all the gifts people had brought, because every single gift under the tree was now covered in matching red paper with a pattern of gold ornaments and bows. A bit OCD, I thought, but I was learning that Betty was often "over the top."

Ray eased a can of flavored popcorn from the paper. "Nice. Pass it around." He popped the lid, pulled open the plastic liner and took a handful. "Umm," he mumbled, rotating the can that he'd handed to Chad to read the label. "Dark chocolate drizzle."

Cora opened a multi-pack of colored gel pens. Belinda smiled and gushed her thanks, nodding to everyone, for a pair of gloves that allowed her to use a smart phone without baring her fingers. She pulled them on immediately and tried them. "I just sent my daughter in California a picture of our party," she announced as another red and gold package was being directed to Earl and Doreen.

Doreen eagerly ripped the paper away from a flat box and lifted the lid, but then she sucked in her breath with a sound of distress. The messy collection of paper, box, top, and gift slid to the floor. Earl reached down and retrieved the contents. He held up a picture frame designed to display a collage of pictures. The rustic frame was shaped like a house where the rooms were the photos, and the words "Our Family Memories" were wood-burned along the roof gable edge. Earl put a calming hand on Doreen's shoulder.

"It's very nice," he said. Although he looked less in shock than his wife, he didn't seem particularly pleased. What was that about?

Next Jerry opened a slim package. He pulled out a book that looked something like a school annual, except it had a soft cover. He held it up. "Well, this is a surprise at a gift exchange. It's quite personal. A copy of the student literary magazine from my college days. This was the final edition for which I served as editor." He smiled in appreciation, but I noticed him send a brief sharp glance toward Judge Viviette. Maybe she was the mysterious gift donor, but she didn't appear to be paying much attention.

A tall rectangular parcel was handed to Chad. He stripped off the paper and waved a wine bottle in the air. "Always a good choice at a party," he said. "I'll add it to the bar." He scrambled to his feet and headed for the dining room. I knew Chad rarely drank, but he wouldn't begrudge sharing with others.

My attention wavered from the gift exchange as I watched him. I was really proud of the man my boy was becoming. As he returned, Harry Hack was holding up a dog collar studded with spikes. His expression was a cross between anger and amazement. "Sparky," he said, his voice cracking. "It's engraved 'Sparky.' That was my favorite dog." His was no swift glance at the judge. He glared at her. "Did you bring this gift?"

"Of course not," Viviette snapped. "Why would I care enough to remember your dog's name?"

The judge herself was handed the next package. She balanced it on her palm. "Heavy," she commented before removing the paper. She arranged her face into the professional smile and held up a chunk of black marble engraved with the scales of justice tipped to one side and her name beneath. "A paperweight? Looks more like a tombstone," she said. "What's going on here?"

We all shook our heads. There was a lot of shifting of bodies— a result of the discomfort that was spreading through the room.

"Well," said Betty. "I think Frank and I will open one next." She carefully peeled the tape from the sides of a squarish box, and she smoothed and folded the paper deliberately. Eventually, she held up the imitation mistletoe ball I'd brought as a hostess gift. "How lovely! Frank and I would like to tell you a story, wouldn't we, Panda Bear?"

"Aw, you tell it, dear," Frank said, looking sheepish. Light reflected from his glasses giving him a blank expression.

Betty must have kept the ball and re-wrapped it in order to be able to stage this scene.

"All right, then. Tomorrow is our wedding anniversary. It will be forty years."

We all clapped politely, and several people murmured "Happy Anniversary."

"I suspect a lot of you are not aware that we were childhood sweethearts. We've known each other for as long as I can remember. Mine is the true 'boy-next-door' romance. Frank is a few years older than I am, and my earliest memories are of him coming over to play. But we have a story that includes the judge and mistletoe."

Frank took the ball and held it high. He leaned over and gave Betty a kiss. It wasn't a romantic kiss, but I guessed that after forty years of being called Panda Bear, it was something.

"Actually, I don't remember when this happened. I wasn't even born yet, but it's a family legend. Are you sure you won't tell it Frank?"

"You go ahead," he insisted in his gravelly voice.

"We've also known Viviette all our lives. She grew up in the same neighborhood."

The judge was still not paying much attention. Her fingers moved idly across the surface of the black marble slab in her lap. Maybe she had heard the story so often it was a complete bore.

Betty continued. "When Frank and Viviette were about five years old his parents threw a huge Christmas cocktail party. Apparently she climbed to the top of a decorated step ladder used to display house plants and held up a mistletoe ball, much like this." Betty stood and went to the archway into the dining room. She reached around the corner and retrieved a stepstool she must have placed there for just this purpose. "Help me, Panda Bear," she said.

Frank steadied the stool as she climbed the steps and suspended the ball from a hook at the center of the arch. She kissed Frank on the top of his bald head, and a purple flush rose above his collar.

"Anyway, little Viviette insisted that everyone come and exchange kisses beneath the mistletoe that year. It was apparently the hit of the party. Most of the guests had already had a little too much to drink, and there was a lot of kissing between non-spouses— very inappropriate back then."

"And much remorse the next day," Frank added with a hoarse chuckle.

23

Mariah received a mug with stick figures hugging which was imprinted with the saying "Brothers and Sisters Stick Together." She held it up and laughed. "That's the trouble with gift exchanges. Someone always gets a ringer. I'm an only." She set the mug back under the tree.

I opened a nice blue plaid scarf. It was soft— not at all scratchy. "This is a perfect gift for me. Sometimes you do get nice things," I said. "Thanks to whomever."

Betty cut me off before anyone had a chance to react. She waggled a finger and said, "Now, now, we're not going to have any guessing or intimations about who brought which gifts. That's strictly forbidden."

Branson Owens got a pair of Christmas socks with penguins wearing red and green scarves. He laughed and held them up for everyone to see. "Mariah and I should trade. I do have a sister, and these are too small for me."

"Oh, yummy," Belinda cried, yanking a net bag full of chocolates wrapped like gold and silver coins from her gift box. She peeled one oversize coin and popped it in her mouth. "Not the cheap ones, either." Unwilling to graciously share, she tucked the treasure away in the tote bag beside her chair. Then she turned and whispered something to Harry. I watched his eyes flick from the judge to our host and hostess as his wife continued to murmur. Belinda had sounded pleased with the gift, but her mouth was drawn into a scowl.

Betty and Frank got a travel mug that could heat water through a car's twelve-volt outlet.

Cora slid a rolled paper from its red tube. She opened out the poster and tried to display it so everyone could see. Jerry helped hold the corners. There were photographs of twelve outhouses, and across the top was printed "Great Moments in Forest County History."

Earl guffawed. "Are those actual historic shit-houses?"

Cora looked shocked, and her face colored. I wasn't sure if she was reacting to his crass choice of words. It was just as likely she was embarrassed because she might be unsure whether they were, indeed, local privies.

"That's very funny. I like it." Chad said. He reached over and gently knuckled Cora on the knee, which apparently broke her temporary spell.

She chuckled and recovered nicely. "Well, now I have a new category of items to explore and catalog," she quipped.

"Hey, when will it be my turn?" Paul blurted out. "I haven't had a gift at all, yet. Shall we place bets on whether it will be something fun, or in slightly bad taste?"

The pile of packages beneath the tree was diminished, and Mariah leaned forward and found one with her father's name on it.

Paul grinned at the chunky box. "Another mug?" he suggested. It was a mug, and Paul's face became stony. He set the gift down beside his chair.

"Come on, you have to show us," Doreen said, poking him in the upper arm. "We've all lived through it." She reached for the mug. "DNA doesn't lie," she read. "What's so bad about that?"

"Ha! It's the other side that has him in a dither. 'Ninety-eight percent chimp,'" Earl read from the mug. "Someone's having a freaking good time at our expense. Good thing I didn't get that one, or someone could plan on a broken jaw. As soon as we figure out who the prankster is." He rummaged through the remaining gifts. "Here's his other one. This should be OK."

Paul quickly unwrapped a small box about the size of a desk calendar. He held it up. Written on the top was "Insult Generator." Puzzled, he opened the lid, riffled his thumb across an edge and laughed out loud. "Yes, I think I can use this," he said, turning the box around again so the rest of us could see. There were two sets of cards that could be flipped to create random insults. The one that was showing was "Crap Wad."

Ray and Jessi received a decorative wall plaque of two short crossed canoe paddles. "Crocket Outfitters" was carved into the blades. Ray ran his finger over the first word and a funny look appeared on his face. "Very nice," he said in a flat tone. That's when I realized the name was misspelled.

A few more packages were opened with no awkward moments. I received a coloring book titled *I Hate My Ex-Husband*, but animosity toward Roger was no longer much of a problem for me, so I just laughed it off. Someone discovered there were boxes pushed toward the back with Dee's, Jimmie's and his sisters' names on them.

"It's time for pie and coffee," Betty announced. "I'll tell the staff, and they can open presents after dessert. Surely, their gifts will be in good taste." Her eyes paused for just a brief moment on Harry, and then Belinda, before she left for the kitchen.

Most everyone stood up to stretch or visit a bathroom. Cora pulled me into the library. "Someone has deliberately planned this." She looked more furious than I'd ever seen her.

"Sure, but why? That's the question."

"I'm thinking of telling Jerry we should leave. I'm not that much of a ski enthusiast, and parties where each person is purposely insulted are way beyond my interest."

I knew that parties of any kind with so many guests were pretty much beyond Cora's interest. "Don't go while it's dark. It's probably still snowing." I pulled one of the heavy drapes aside, and in the glow of the Christmas lights saw white curtains of snow being whipped by the wind. Although the moon had been bright the previous night, no hint of it was visible through the low clouds. "Wow, it's really coming down now."

"After breakfast then," Cora agreed. "You and Chad can stay. Jerry will come back for you later."

We returned to the living room. Beth and Lindsey were carrying trays loaded with plates of pie and a container of topping. "Cranberry-apple or pumpkin," Beth was asking people in turn.

Jimmie followed them, helping to scoop the topping for people who wanted some, and passing out forks. "Decaf coffee and hot cider on the table over there," he repeated every few steps.

"Sit down and join us. You have presents to unwrap," Betty invited after the food was distributed.

She handed Jimmie a package. He shook it, but nothing rattled. He shucked the red paper away from a long board with charred edges. "Oh boy, this is great!" he said and held up a sign with the words "Cherry Blossom Resta" on it.

"But it's burned. Ruined," Paul pointed out, his face reflecting the vague sense of horror that was overtaking all of us at the realization that the person behind these gifts would include children on his or her list of people to hurt.

"I don't care. It's the real thing. My history," Jimmie said without so much as a flicker of doubt. He whirled around. "Who do I thank?"

There was a communal shaking of heads. "No one knows who provided most of the gifts," Cora said stiffly.

As I scanned faces for any hints, it occurred to me that the only person not in the room was Sam. Could he have done this?

Dee's present was an apron made of various calico print fabrics. I had no idea what was wrong with it, but her face went white. "Thank you," she managed to respond weakly.

Beth and Lindsey opened their gifts last. They also received aprons with the same patterns of material as their mother. Lindsey ran to Dee and pushed the fabric into her hands. "Mom, didn't I used to have a dress that looked like this?" she asked.

"Me too," Beth said. She looked thoughtful.

Dee groaned and slumped to the floor in a faint.

White light flared through the windows accompanied by a deafening crash. The century-old window panes rattled, and thunder rumbled from one end of the sky to the other like a stereo speaker demonstration. Complete darkness and silence followed.

24

The smothering blackness became a heavy blanket, hindering even my breathing. I groped for Dee in the dark. Was she all right? Then, Frank's rough voice, usually so emotionless, spoke hope. "Don't panic. The backup generator will kick on in a few seconds."

"Better be quick. I can't take this for long," Earl rasped. He sounded genuinely panicked.

The generator did its thing, the lights flickered, then held steady, and restored us. There was a collective sigh of relief.

Earl was curled up with his arms wrapped protectively over his head.

Dee sat up, "What happened?"

"You fainted, and then the lights went out," Jimmie said. His matter-of-fact answer was somehow comforting in its simplicity. He helped his mother to her feet.

I heard her quietly assuring the girls that she was fine.

Doreen whispered something to Earl and he also stood. They moved to the side of the room. I noticed the usually abrasive veteran was trembling. His wife hugged and soothed him.

Frank rummaged behind the Christmas tree. He pulled the plug and the tree ceased to provide its golden cheer. Stepping to a window, he looked out and shook his head. "I'm going out to kill the light strings. The generator is adequate for basic needs, but keep electric use to a minimum. No watching TV in your rooms. We can check the weather on the one in the library. This is turning into one heck of a storm. Where in the blazes is Sam?"

"I'm going to finish my pie and go to bed," Jessi confided in a small voice. She sounded demoralized.

"Good idea," Belinda agreed.

Murmurs of general consent followed, but Harry and Viviette headed for the coffee urn.

Bed sounded nice to me too, but then I remembered I'd hadn't put away the clean towels. I probably needed to check the public bathrooms as well.

A bit later I was standing in front of the dryer, setting it to run briefly to warm the towels before I folded them. Dee came through the utility room, headed for bed herself.

"I already sent the kids upstairs," she said. "Betty tells me the generator is powerful enough to make coffee and everything we need for breakfast. And there are two underground propane tanks that fuel it. They aren't likely to run out. Do you think the utility company will actually work on the problem on Christmas day?"

"No idea. I suspect some guests will go home early, which should lighten the load. The party's supposed to end after lunch anyway, right?"

"Yup. We're serving soup and sandwiches. On the buffet," she added, turning to leave.

I put a hand on her arm. "Dee, what happened tonight? What was wrong with those aprons?"

She leaned against the dryer and wrapped her arms tight around her body. "Those prints? The designs of the fabric... they matched dresses the girls were wearing the day Judge Viviette took them away. I made those dresses. How could anyone remember that?"

"Wow. It almost had to be someone who was there. Unless there were pictures, I suppose."

"I don't know, Ana. I just don't know." Dee shook her head sadly. "I heard others got bad gifts too, not just us."

"Yes, although some people just took them in stride. Like Jimmie..."

"Isn't that boy something! He hardly sees any situation as negative."

I nodded in agreement and put a hand on her shoulder. "That day in court was painful for you, but it's all in the past now. Your girls are back where they belong, and you can just chuck those stupid aprons. Someone is trying to play with our heads. Don't give in to it."

"Thanks. I'll try," Dee said, hugging me fiercely. "Don't stay up too late."

The dryer buzzed, and I waved as Dee started down the stairway, closing the door to the cold basement behind her. Folding warm towels felt safe and homey, and I refused to think about needing to take that dank stone passageway myself in a few minutes.

Cora was waiting in the hall as I rounded the corner from the stairs. "We need to talk," she said.

"I agree." Deciding the towels could spend the night in my room instead of the linen closet, I balanced the pile in one arm and keyed open the door.

Cora's braids were hanging loose and she had already changed into pajamas, robe and slippers. She turned the desk chair around and pulled it close to the bed where I landed, putting my feet up and leaning into the pillows. Her robe fell open as she sat. I'd seldom pictured Cora as frail, but tonight she looked older than I knew her to be, small and maybe a little frightened.

"Who do you think planted all those horrible 'gifts?' she asked, Her mouth twisted in sarcasm.

"Not sure. I think Sam was the only one who didn't get one, but he wasn't even in the room."

"It doesn't make sense for it to be Sam. The person who did this wanted to watch our reactions. Did you see Paul's face when Mariah showed off that mug?"

"I didn't notice," I admitted.

"He was as upset about hers as he was his own," Cora said. "And that doesn't make sense."

I thought for a minute. "Did you notice anyone in particular watching faces? Or maybe someone who seemed to know what was going to happen before packages were opened?"

Cora rubbed her forehead as if that might stimulate her brain cells. "No, but it has to be someone who was there with us."

I agreed, and told her Dee's story about the fabric.

"That's just cruel. I think it must be the Vicious Viviette."

"That's too obvious," I said. "I still think the key has to be why, although I certainly don't have any good answers to that one. There were some gifts I didn't understand."

"Whose?"

"Like...why was Doreen so upset about a family picture frame?"

"That's easy enough. She's been telling everyone who will listen about how she used to be on drugs, but finally got her life together," Cora said.

"Yeah, I've heard some of that..."

Cora explained. "When things were really bad, Doreen's and Earl's children were placed in foster care. They got them back after she successfully went through rehab, but she missed the greater portion of their childhood."

"Don't tell me..."

"Of course. It was Viviette who took the kids away. But I think she was also responsible for giving them back. After all, she was the family court judge for years before getting into entertaining people in a fake courtroom."

"Still," I said, "I can't see why she would do this— it would just make people hate her more. And she got one too— that mini grave marker thing."

"So? Maybe she gave one to herself to avoid suspicion." Cora dismissed that argument.

"But not all the gifts seem connected to her."

"An awful lot were. She apparently despises my interest in local history. She was jealous of Jerry's position in college. She ruled in family court on both the Wards and the Pyrtles. She ruled in TV court against Harry, Belinda, and the Crocketts."

"Who didn't get one?" I asked.

"Hmmm. Branson. That's interesting. If she did it, she might not have wanted to embarrass her husband."

We fell silent. I was running through the evening in my head. "Chad didn't."

"I don't think we can set much importance by that. These gifts took a lot of planning, and he was added to the guest list at almost the last minute."

"So was I," I pointed out.

"True enough. But, your gift was more like a joke— an adult coloring book that probably isn't hard to find. Some of the gifts were personalized. The judge's paperweight, Ray and Jessi's canoe paddles."

"Your poster. It didn't have your name, but it had to be custom ordered. That takes time."

"And those aprons." Cora paused. "There must be video or pictures from that court date."

"I think so too."

We sat in silence for another minute.

"Does someone want to inflame everyone against the judge?" Cora asked.

"I think she's pretty unpopular already. That motive doesn't need help."

"Maybe someone, or a couple, wants this party to be so bad that it will ruin Frank and Betty."

"An intricate and expensive way to go about it," I said. "And why would anyone blame them? Too tough a puzzle for my brain tonight. Are you still leaving in the morning?"

Cora stood and wrapped her robe around her. "Yes. Jerry agreed to it. This is just not fun. I might skip breakfast. Call us when you're ready to come home."

"OK, I'll probably stay and help Cherry Blossom Cuisine unless Chad is in a big hurry," I said.

"Good night. Lock your door, Ana. I don't like the atmosphere in this house."

I couldn't disagree with that.

25

As I lay in bed listening to the wind shriek, I wondered who, besides Frank and Betty, had seen the guest list in advance. Maybe Belinda; she and Betty seemed to be thick as thieves. And Belinda would have told anyone. Earl's occasional nasty outbursts suggested he could be mean enough to sabotage a party. All I felt certain of was that my close friends and I were in the clear. Although, I had to admit to myself that Dee had the same reason to harbor hard feelings toward Judge Viviette as Doreen and Earl, and she probably had seen the guest list. But I had come to know Dee as a friend. I couldn't believe she'd faked the fainting.

Recurring dreams of ghostly snowmen streaming long comet tails of snow and ice, committing suicide by hurling themselves against my window, kept me restless for hours.

A laser beam drove between the edges of the curtains and snapped me awake. I glanced at the clock. Seven-thirty two. Sun! Throwing back the covers, I crossed to the window and was astonished at the white wasteland below. Every track from the day before was obliterated. The snow stretched unbroken from the house to the forest, appearing unvisited by humans with the exception of a blue nylon chair that had blown east and now quivered in the exhausted breeze against a tree trunk. I couldn't see the fire circle at all. Squinting in the dazzling light I found one dark triangle, the corner of a picnic table. The ski rack protruded from the snow but appeared to be a low fence instead of a high crossbar. Directly below the window, Sam was shoveling a path alongside the house.

Rushing through the connecting bath, I knocked on Chad's door. The response was a sleepy grunt. "Are you awake? Look outside. We must have over two feet of snow."

"Ma! Why'd you wake me, then? Go back to bed."

I cleaned up and dressed. As I entered the hall, Jimmie was coming down from the third floor. His dark eyes were shining.

"Did you see the snow? Gosh, it's so deep! Sam says we're really and truly snowed in. He's going to get new ski tracks laid down right away."

"You sound like being snowed in is a good thing," I said.

"Why not? It's a ski party. There's heat and electricity and food. We're having an adventure," he said, grabbing the door frame and propelling himself around the corner like a pole dancer. His feet pounded on the steps as he descended.

I went down the front stairs. Earl stood in the foyer with his hand on the doorknob, while Bran rummaged in the closet. "Going to clear the porch," Earl explained.

Branson Owens straightened, slapping a pair of heavy gloves together, and Earl pulled the door open. A wall of snow, almost to my eye level and imprinted with the pattern of the exterior door panels, blocked egress.

Earl stared at it stupidly. "Uh, now what?"

"Don't pull that snow into the house." Bran closed the door as stinging sparkles of ice blew against my cheek. "Betty will have a hernia."

I had the solution. "Go through the kitchen and out the back. Sam's opened that way already. There's probably an extra shovel in the utility room, too."

The men said "thanks" and followed me into the dining room, thumping toward the kitchen in their heavy boots.

Beth and Lindsey each grabbed one of my hands. "Merry Christmas, Ana. We're making waffles. It doesn't matter that they take a long time because no one can get out yet anyway. How many do you want. We'll tell Mom."

"Merry Christmas to you, too. Mmm, waffles," I said, approaching the buffet table where scents of warm butter and real maple syrup arose. "How about two?"

"Yippie! The snow is so much fun." Beth ran to Dee, who was stationed at the end of the buffet, opening the smoking waffle iron. "Mom, Ana wants two."

Dee looked up and smiled at me.

"Merry Christmas," I said.

Someone touched my arm. It was Cora. "I guess we're staying," she said, looking chagrined.

Jerry explained. "Sam can't plow without the truck and it will take forever to dig out by hand. Anyway, the county plow doesn't even come as far as the bridge. We'd have to shovel at least a half mile of road." He accepted a plate of two golden waffles and headed for the butter.

"Who wants to leave?" Mariah was at the table with Jessi. "As soon as Sam gets the trails groomed, the skiing will be awesome. Hope those lazy boys get down here soon." Mariah laughed and pointed toward the door where Chad appeared looking dazed. He'd forgotten to comb his hair.

"Just lead me to the coffee," he groaned in mock agony.

Harry stood beneath the mistletoe in the archway to the front room, but no one jumped up to kiss him. "We've got the fire going, for those who just want to stay inside and be cozy. I'm too old a dog to ski," he joked.

Frank appeared beside him. "I cleared the snow out of the TV dish. Weather forecast is for sun this morning, then more snow later. The county declared a state of emergency. No surprise there. Has anyone tried to use their cell phone this morning?

Jessi pulled hers from a pocket and poked at it. "No signal," she said. I have AT&T. "Who's got Verizon?"

"I do." Jerry tried his phone. "Nothing. What's up, Frank?"

"TV reported the wind taking out the main tower over east of here."

"How about the land line?" Doreen asked.

"None. We pulled that months ago. The wires were forever getting knocked down anyway," Frank said.

"Who cares?" Chad countered, from behind a steaming cup of coffee. "We want to play and have fun, not make phone calls. Don't anybody break an arm or leg. Make a note of that." He laughed. "There's no doctor among us, and my first aid skills are rusty."

Judge Viviette, in a killer white and lavender Nordic sweater that must have cost more than half my wardrobe, rose from the small table where she had been visiting with Belinda. Belinda, however, was not wearing a killer outfit. Her tacky Christmas sweater and cheap stretch jeans had probably come straight from Wal-Mart.

The roar of the snowmobile temporarily drowned out our voices, but the sound faded as Sam, presumably, headed toward the woods.

"Good. I'm going skiing," Viviette announced. Who's coming with me?

There was not an immediate positive response, but Mariah finally replied, "Four of us will be out soon. Ray still has to eat."

"Too cold for me. I'm finding a book in the library," Belinda said, heaving herself upright and see-sawing her hips as she tugged at the back of her pants.

Lindsey hung on my arm. "As soon as we're done in the kitchen, will you help me build a snowman?"

"Sure thing," I promised, forking the last of a delicious waffle in my mouth.

It was a fresh new day, and the beautiful snow and sunshine seemed to have lifted the gloomy atmosphere of Christmas Eve.

26

Stone. Black, cold sweat leaking from every pore. Rock is the enemy. *Owwwww.*

My first task was to check the bathrooms again. I did remember to take an empty laundry basket with me . Making my way along the upstairs hallway, from room to room, I almost finished undetected by guests. But with only one room to go, Belinda appeared. I flinched, then remembered Betty had said she already knew about my double role.

"I'll only be a minute. Just let me change your towels."

"No problem." Belinda held up a paperback. "There's too much noise downstairs. I decided it would be quieter to read up here."

Quickly, I wiped the sink and toilet and hung clean towels on the racks. "There you go. Enjoy your morning," I said.

Belinda closed her door, and I heard the bed springs creak. Footsteps sounded on the main stairs at the other end of the hall, so I popped into my own room with the basket of wet towels to stay out of sight. This was ridiculous. A door opened and closed, but I paid no attention to which one. Then I realized it would have been easier to simply hurry down the "staff" stairs to get out of sight, but since I was here, with a moment to breathe, I peeked out the window.

Fresh ski tracks, punctuated by periods and colons of pole marks, snaked along the groomed trail leading away from the house, but the return path was still pristine. The skiers were in the woods. Sam must have retrieved the blue chair. It was no longer caught against a tree, and "post-hole" boot tracks were visible from the snowmobile groomer's route to its former location and back.

The heavy-laden trees were beginning to shed their burdens of snow in the sunshine, and as I watched, a sparkling cascade slipped to the ground. Tendrils of snow whirled away in the light breeze that remained after last night's blow. Feeling slightly resentful that I'd agreed to household tasks that cut into my time to enjoy such beauty, I let the curtain drop into place, picked up the laundry basket and hurried down the back stairs.

As I rounded the first floor corner, my nose began to twitch from the unmistakable odor of a freshly lit cigarette. I wondered if Betty allowed herself to smoke in her own bedroom, since she and Frank were the only ones with a room on the first floor. Like most smokers, she probably didn't realize how easily non-smokers could pick up the scent, even long after the cigarette was finished.

Descending again, I flicked on the harsh LED light so I could see to navigate the basement hallway. A small motion caught the corner of my eye, making me turn to my right, and I realized there was a stony alcove I hadn't noticed before. A man hunkered there, holding something behind his back. Blue wisps curled around his thigh. I'd found the smoker.

"Hi, Sam," I said.

He looked sheepish. "You won't tell on me, will you?" he implored. "I usually don't do this, but I thought I could catch a quick puff or two without putting on my boots again." He dropped the cigarette and ground it out with an orange canvas-covered toe. The classic, but thin, high-tops wouldn't have been warm enough outside. His jeans had a fresh rip across the thigh.

"I'm no snitch, but the smell is going right up the stairwell. This probably isn't a great place to try to sneak a smoke." It seemed like a good idea to change the subject. "Has anyone used the exercise room? Should I clean it?"

"Naw. Outside stuff is making everyone good and tired," he said.

"Thanks, Sam. See you later."

I threw the towels in the washer, but before starting the cycle, I remembered the tower room. On the way there, I quickly ran the vacuum in the dining room and picked up a few stray plates and napkins still scattered around.

Betty and Doreen had a tall stack of publications spread on a table in the library. They were standing over them, backs toward the door, pointing at various things and sorting the magazines into piles. Since I was trying not to call attention to myself, I passed by them and climbed to the judge's room. Thankfully for me, it was empty.

I completed my household tasks without seeing anyone else. No one was in the kitchen, and I wasn't sure if Lindsey still had building a snowman on her mind. Not wanting to encounter Sam if he'd gone to the attic, I decided not to go up and look for the girls.

By ten o'clock, I was standing in the cold equipment shed contemplating whether to ski or snowshoe. Most likely, everyone that was going out was already on a trail, so I guessed I'd be going alone.

Jimmie came through the door into the dim light of the former garage. He saw me and said, "Hey, are you going out? I have a little time before we start lunch. I wanted to try snowshoes, 'cause I've never done it."

"Snowshoes it is. then. That is, if you want company."

"Sure, that would be great. Where do you want to go? Sam said to stay off the ski trails, though."

"Yes, it's bad manners to mess up the groomed tracks. That much I know," I chuckled.

We fumbled with the bindings of the traditional wooden snowshoes, since neither of us really knew what we were doing, but before long we were headed toward the river following fresh webbed and alternating ovals.

"How's your mom feeling this morning?" I asked.

"She's OK. Those gifts really shook her up, but we're a family now, and all that old stuff isn't going to bother us."

"I'm glad to hear it."

"Ana, can I ask you something?" Jimmie said.

"Of course."

"I've heard people talking. This party isn't very much fun for a lot of the grown-ups, is it?"

"Well, you weren't in the room for most of the gift exchange last night, and to be honest, that got pretty tense. It certainly seems as if someone is trying to offend almost everyone. On purpose," I added. "And some of the guests don't like each other."

"But the food is good? I mean, this is like our first big event. If the party is a flop, maybe no one will ever hire Cherry Blossom Cuisine." Jimmie stopped and turned around to face me. He looked forlorn.

I couldn't help but laugh. "I don't think you need to worry about that. As they say, any publicity is good publicity. People will say things like, 'Remember that awful Christmas party? The only good thing was the food.'"

"Do you really think so?"

"I do." Over Jimmie's shoulder I could see two people approaching. "Look, here come Cora and Jerry," I said.

28

The four of us awkwardly tramped around in the snow a while longer until Jimmie looked at his watch and decided he needed to get back to the kitchen.

"Uh, oh, I'm late," he said as we entered the back door and were enveloped with the delicious aroma of hot minestrone.

"You're fine; I started early," Dee assured him. "But go get into the right clothes. Be quick!. And hurry those girls along."

Jimmie ran toward the back stairs, and Cora, Jerry and I entered the dining room.

Belinda, Harry, Earl, and Doreen sat at a square table, playing euchre. "Two tricks for us," Belinda said, palming a stack of cards and laying them crosswise over another pile. One of her garish nails had broken. I didn't recall it being that way when I'd met her carrying the book.

"The hand isn't over yet," Earl countered, much more darkly than seemed warranted for a simple card game. The man just didn't like to be crossed.

Harry groaned and straightened his left leg. "Are you all right?" Belinda asked him.

"Just my bum knee. It'll be fine, but it's stiff," Harry said.

A background of piano, marimba, laughter, and tambourine filtered in from the front of the house. I guessed the younger crew had taken over the music room.

"Any change in our connections with the outside world," Jerry asked.

"None," Frank answered. "The snow is messing up dish reception again, but I was able to catch most of the noon weather. More snow on the way with the wind picking up. Some of us have been shoveling, trying to free up the Crockett's Subaru. At least it's got four-wheel drive."

"That's not going to help in three feet of snow," Earl said, laying down the nine of spades. "Trump. Our trick."

The main door opened and Bran stamped the snow off his feet. "Sam and I got one car free, and we're working on the driveway, but the wind is picking up again," he called out to anyone who cared to listen. Pulling off a pair of expensive sunglasses, and crossing through the room, he then announced, "I'm going to get into dry clothes before lunch. Too much physical labor to suit me."

"There's no use in those men doing all that work," Harry said, his own lack of participation obvious. "We're not getting out of here until the snowplow comes."

Sam had entered behind Earl. "That's true enough. But we're responsible to clear north of the county turnaround, and maybe you didn't know, but our truck had to be towed to the shop. We've got no plow."

"You can take the snowmobile out," Doreen suggested.

"Yeah, maybe I can go find someone else to clear our section, but it almost needs a front-end loader now. I don't think a regular truck can blast through this."

Dee pushed open the pass-through and stuck her head out. "Lunch is nearly ready."

"I'll get the music makers," I said and started for the tower stairs.

Doreen's head swiveled. "Where's Betty? She seems to disappear a lot."

"She's addicted to her nicotine," Belinda said. I thought that sounded catty, coming from someone who was supposed to be her good friend, but it seemed to be true.

"We haven't seen Paul or the judge since breakfast either," Doreen said.

That was the last remark I heard before heading upstairs. Bran pushed past me on the stairs just as I stepped into the music room. He wasn't exactly rude, but I had to sidestep to avoid being bumped, and he seemed preoccupied.

Paul, along with his daughter, the Crocketts, and Chad were arranged around the piano, singing "Jingle Bells." Mariah sat at the keyboard, playing rather well. She ended the chorus with a long rippling chord.

"I've been sent to collect you for lunch," I said. "But I think I should have come up sooner. Looks like you've found the holiday spirit."

"Is it lacking downstairs?" Paul asked with a dry smile.

"A bit," I admitted. "I think some people are realizing we may be stuck here longer than they had in mind."

"I'm cool with that, until we run out of food," Ray joked. He started down the stairs.

Lunch was already in progress as we entered the dining room. People were building multi-layer sandwiches and carrying mugs of hot soup to various tables. I noted that Betty had showed up. She was standing in the swinging door to the kitchen, presumably giving directions to the staff, and rubbing a fresh scratch on her forearm.

The soup and sandwiches hit the spot. The wind was, indeed, beginning to howl around the corners, and even a renovated house of that age couldn't stop all the drafts. I was glad I'd kept a sweater on. Jimmie and the girls began clearing the dishes.

Chad was rummaging in a cupboard beside the fireplace. "I've found the extension pack for Settlers," he announced. "We can have more players now. Paul, why don't you and Mom join us?"

I was about to say "yes," when Betty clapped her hands. "Has anyone see Viviette? She's going to miss lunch."

"The judge and her husband were heading out on the longer ski loop when we turned the corner to come back to the house," Jessi said.

All eyes turned to Bran, who answered, "Yes, we took the outer loop. It was pristine. You should have joined us."

"Did the judge come back with you?" Betty asked.

"She did. I left her taking off her skis when I went to find Sam and ended up helping with the shoveling."

"What time?"

Bran shrugged. "I didn't pay any attention. Maybe around eleven. She wasn't in our room when I took my sunglasses upstairs."

"Has anyone seen her in the house?" Frank asked. A faint edge of concern sharpened his voice.

"I'll go check the equipment room," Chad offered.

There was a tense shifting of bodies in squeaking chairs, and small breaths that weren't quite gasps punctuated an uneasy silence.

Ray brought us back to an emotional center. "She's an adult. There's certainly no need to worry about her yet. What I want to know is the food situation. We were all planning to leave this afternoon. Now, we'll be here at least until tomorrow." He turned toward Betty.

"Don't worry. We have a deep pantry, although the quality of meals is sure to change. It's mostly canned and packaged goods, you know. But, there's meat in the freezer. Let me talk to the staff." Having delivered that good news, Betty pushed open the kitchen door and left the room.

"I'm going up to look for Viviette again," Bran said. "Maybe she was in the bathroom and I didn't realize it." He headed toward the stairs.

"It won't hurt my feelings if that judge stays away from us as much as possible," Doreen said, not quite softly enough. Bran hesitated just a moment, then continued on his mission without looking back.

29

Paul and I joined the Settlers of Catan game. I had to learn the rules, but after a while I decided it wasn't going to be one of my favorites— or maybe I just had bad luck at getting the resource cards I needed. I was seriously losing. Nevertheless, it was fun to spend time with Chad and his new friends.

Bran had not come back downstairs, so I assumed he'd found his wife and perhaps they were taking a nap.

The euchre game broke up, and that foursome wandered away toward the library. Frank and Jerry came in through the front.

"We've got a wider path across the porch cleared," Jerry said with a deep sigh. His face was red. "I'm glad the stronger guys did most of the work, though. The snow was packed hard where it blew against the house."

With a whistling sound, a gust of wind blew open the main door. It banged hard against the wall and the instantly chilly air made me shiver. Chad ran to shut it.

"I'd like to get everyone together," Frank said to me. That sounded ominous. "Can you take a break from your game to go find the others?"

Everyone except the judge gathered in the dining room. Her absence, although somewhat welcome, was faintly troubling.

Ignoring that, Frank announced, "Listen, here's where we stand. As you can tell, the wind has strengthened, and a lot of what we shoveled has filled back in. We're going to need outside help to be able to leave, and I'm not sure the county is even aware there's a group of people stranded out here."

Mariah spoke up. "I've been trying to send a text message to 9-1-1. Sometimes those can get through when a call can't."

"Good idea," Frank admitted, "but if the tower actually came down, nothing is going to..."

"Has anyone see my wife?" Bran interrupted. "She isn't in our room. I wasn't worried before, but now..." his gaze shifted toward a window where a draft moved the curtain in uneven breaths.

Frank cleared his throat. "Yes. That's our next item of concern. I don't think Viviette would still be outside with the wind chill so low."

"Maybe she went back out on the trail and took a bad fall. Jessi and I can take a quick run around the loops," Ray offered.

The Cherry Blossom Cuisine crew huddled between the door and the bar. Cora stood with them, and she said, "We need to find her fast, if she's outdoors,"

Betty took charge of the indoor search. "Belinda, will you and Harry check all the public spaces."

"She'd be here if she heard Frank yelling to get us all together," Harry protested.

"Get off your fat behind," Belinda said. "Maybe she's fainted or knocked unconscious."

Harry groaned and stood up. "I wonder who'd be interested in helping with that," he mumbled.

Ray jumped up. "Come on, Jessi, we'll be fastest to check the ski trails. Chad, you and Mariah can follow any snowshoe tracks out there. Let's get going before it gets any worse out."

Earl growled, "I'm not hunting for that witch. It's my guess she's avoiding us on purpose."

At this point, I think we need to be certain of where she is," Frank pointed out, taking the sting out of Earl's words.

Turning to me, Betty said quietly, "You have the master key. Check all the bedrooms on the second floor."

"If they're locked, how would she get in one?" I asked.

"I don't know. Just look, please," Betty said, her eyes dark with worry. "I'll look down our wing. I'll get Sam to check the basement and outbuildings. Dee, could you look in the attic? Jimmie, please get some water heating and refresh the beverage service."

By three o'clock the mostly cheerful mood of the day had

shifted, We were again assembled in the dining room, but no one had found the judge. Jimmie and the girls were distributing cups of hot cocoa, tea, or coffee, which was helping people stay somewhat calm.

Ray took charge of speaking for those who had searched out-of-doors. "We checked all the ski and snowshoe trails. There were enough tracks still visible to be sure we followed every path. We didn't see where anyone had gone off trail. But the wind is filling everything in quickly."

Bran looked as stormy as the early gloom gathering beyond the windows where the sky was again dark solid gray. "She has to be somewhere. Maybe you kids didn't look very hard."

An angry look crossed Jessi's face, but Ray put a hand on her shoulder and answered, "We looked very thoroughly, Mr. Owens. We've been trained in search and rescue. And, if the judge has been outside with no shelter since before lunch, there's probably nothing we can do for her now, anyway."

"All right, all right," Betty fussed. I'm sure she's not lost in the woods. And she wouldn't have tried to ski to town without telling someone."

"Did someone check for tracks on the road?" Bran fired at Ray. He was becoming increasingly agitated.

"Yes, we looked," Jessi said.

Betty nodded her head vigorously, as if coming to some conclusion. "She must be in the house. Let's all look again."

"Sure thing," Earl said. "But let's just admit what we're doing. She's not anywhere one would find someone reading or napping." He paused. "Or even alive. Check cupboards, under beds. Everywhere."

"I'm afraid you're right," Frank admitted, his eyes flitting nervously from one face to another. "Let's meet here again in half an hour."

Betty herded Jimmie, Beth, and Lindsey into the kitchen, and I followed. "Did you hear all that?" she asked Dee. Without waiting for an answer, she continued. "If the worst has happened, this could be traumatic for the children. They shouldn't be part of the search team. Concentrate on keeping everyone full of warm drinks and as comfortable as possible."

"We can do that. We have plenty of leftovers for tonight. And I'm thawing bacon and more bread for breakfast. There are four dozen eggs," Dee assured Betty.

"What's the worst?" Jimmie wanted to know. "Do you think the judge is really dead?"

"She must be, dopey, or everyone wouldn't be so jumpy," Beth said, not sounding upset at all. But I knew the reality of a dead body hadn't registered with her. So far, it was all just an adventure to the children.

"Perhaps she's hurt and banged her head on something," Betty suggested.

Dee put a hand to her mouth. "Someone hurt her on purpose?"

Just then a woman's piercing scream split the air. "Help, oh help, I've found her!"

30

Whirling around and pushing through the swinging door, Betty hurried into the dining room.

Dee extended her arms in a sheltering way toward the children. "We'll stay here," she said.

I shot Dee a meaningful look and followed Betty. The screaming had lessened in volume but hadn't ceased. It was easy to follow the sound. Not to mention that everyone was now running toward the source. I turned left into the front room and joined a cluster of people gathered in the alcove beyond the circular stair.

Belinda was the screamer, and Harry pushed through the group to reach her side. He pulled her to him, turning her head to muffle the sound against his shoulder.

"Where's Frank?" Harry asked, his hands busy with Belinda, but his eyes were fiery and dark, searching each face.

The space was too small for more than a few people, but by now every person in the house had arrived to gawk and demand information, pushing to try to see what had set off Belinda's shrieks.

"Where is she? Is she all right?" Bran demanded to know.

Belinda took in a deep breath that ended in a moist sucking sound. "Down there. I don't know, but it looks bad."

"Down where?" Earl shouted from behind me.

Betty's voice commanded us to move out of her way. "She must be down the elevator shaft. I told Frank this floor needed a better barrier, but he said no one could fall in."

"Elevator? What elevator?" Doreen asked.

"It's being installed, I think," Paul said. "There's a sheet of plywood screwed to the wall in the music room. I wondered why. It must cover the opening on that floor."

In fact, I knew from my explorations that it would have been difficult, if not impossible, for someone to accidentally stumble into the hole from this level. You could see into the shaft, down to the basement and upwards into the tower if you craned your neck, but there was a solid piece of plywood four feet square fastened across the lower half of the doorway here and reinforced with a two-by-four at top and bottom. Nothing like being johnny-on-the-spot as the crime reporter.

"But why is this open at all?" I asked.

Betty answered. "It wasn't, but after the contractors finished for the season, somehow a raccoon got in and we had a devil of a time getting it out. This seemed a safe enough barrier."

Those in front let Betty pass, and Harry guided Belinda away from the group, which freed up quite a bit of space. I followed in Betty's wake and got a look at what had set Belinda to screaming. At the bottom of the square hole, a lump of something in an expensive white and lavender sweater shone through the gloom of the unlit shaft.

Frank and Jerry were hovering behind me. Jerry took charge.

"We've got no way to summon any help. So, let's be sure we deal with this in an orderly way." He tapped me on the shoulder. "Ana, have you got your camera?"

"In my room," I said.

"Send Chad for it. Don't leave the scene. We want to be able to state for a certainty that nothing was tampered with after she was found. Frank, how do we get to her?"

Chad was dispatched for the camera, and I heard him running up the front stairs.

Frank replied, "There's a basement entrance. I'll go open it up. Maybe she's alive. I'll need to check."

"That's acceptable, but move her as little as possible. After all, maybe her neck is broken but she's still breathing," Jerry told Frank.

Frank elbowed his way through the press of people who were hoping for a look, and was immediately replaced by Branson, the judge's husband.

Bran was unsteady on his feet and grabbed the edge of the

plywood barrier as he looked down on Judge Viviette. "Can't someone do anything? How can we get her out of there? This isn't right at all."

Cora spoke. I hadn't realized she was right beside me.

"If she's hurt that badly, we aren't going to know what to do to keep from causing more damage."

"Don't Ray and Jessi have search and rescue skills?" I asked.

"I'm here," Ray called. "Yes, we're wilderness first aid certified. That should be helpful."

Doreen spoke up. "Earl was a medic in Desert Storm."

I heard Frank say, "Good. Earl, Ray, Jessi, you three come with me, then."

Chad handed me my camera, and I began taking pictures of the elevator shaft and the still form of the judge.

"Get as many angles as you can," Jerry said quietly. "These are going to be the official crime photos."

I looked at him and raised an eyebrow.

"This was no accident." He reiterated my thoughts.

Thumping and banging, and the grating squeal of nails being pulled began to rise from below, and in a moment Ray's head was thrust into the square shaft. Then his whole body appeared, and he reached out to search for a pulse in the judge's neck. He looked up. We made eye contact and he shook his head.

"Don't move her," Jerry commanded. "We'll come down and take more pictures."

"Follow me. I know how to get to the basement," I said.

Jerry took my elbow and propelled me out of the alcove. "Everyone have a seat right here. Nobody else leave this room or the dining room. Ana, you go get those photos. Cora and I will stay here with the others."

I was pretty sure Jerry wanted to be certain that no one tried any monkey business. However, Viviette had been missing for hours. If someone had wanted to tamper with evidence in some way, there had been plenty of time before now.

Even though I didn't know exactly where the elevator emptied into the basement, I knew approximately where the opening for the eventual access had to be. And as soon as I got down the steps, I spotted the four people who'd previously gone down. Several crates and an old desk had been pulled out of the way to make a path.

"Over here," Ray said. "We had to move all that stuff, so she must have fallen from above. None of these things had been touched in a long time."

The judge was curled into a distorted semblance of a fetal position, lying more on her face than her side. There was no blood visible. I snapped pictures from every angle possible without disturbing the body.

"All right," I said.

Ray and Earl stepped in beside me. "Let's turn her over."

"Should we touch anything?" I asked rhetorically. Of course we shouldn't.

Earl was firm. "We can't leave her like this. Your pictures will have to do. She'll start to decompose long before any authorities can get out here. The body has to be put somewhere cold."

"Not so fast," Ray said.

But it was too late. Earl easily turned the petite judge face up. Rigor mortis had set in and she now lay curled and rocking on her back like a flipped turtle with clawed fingers grasping at the air. A splintered red rod protruded from her chest.

31

Branson was still staring down from the first floor as the scene featuring his dead wife unfolded. "That's my ski pole," he gasped.

It would have been tactful if someone had taken him aside and broken the facts to him more gently. However, once Belinda discovered the body, it all happened so quickly that Bran was left to deal with the situation in the same way as the rest of us.

At just the same moment as Bran spoke, Frank asked, "Why isn't there any blood?"

"It happens that way sometimes," Earl said. "I've seen it all too often. A puncture wound doesn't bleed until the foreign object is removed.

Frank reached for the jagged red pole.

No. Don't pull it out," Ray cautioned.

"Fingerprints, evidence," Jessi added.

"Oh, right," Frank said, looking abashed.

Above us, Paul was pulling Bran away from the elevator shaft. "Come sit down," I heard him say.

"Look, we've got to protect the evidence, and keep the body cold," Ray instructed. "We'll need to wrap her in something."

Frank stood, and his knees cracked. "I'll get a drop cloth. We've got plenty of those plastic ones. We bought a case of them for the renovations, but I need to find them. Sam will know where they are."

"Make sure it's big enough," Jessi said. "When the rigor lets go, she'll flatten out again."

Frank's undercut jaw pushed forward and his mouth set in a hard frown. "This is all too distasteful," he said. But he hurried away to find the plastic.

Jerry leaned through the opening above us. "What's going on down there?"

I answered him. "Frank is getting a plastic sheet to protect the body so we can move it somewhere cold. I've taken lots of pictures."

"Good. Have Ray or Jessi stay with the... down there... to watch things. Everyone else needs to come back upstairs. We've got to decide what to do," Jerry said.

Jessi agreed to the distasteful duty of body-sitting, claiming it didn't really bother her, and the rest of us returned to the dining room. Cora, Belinda and Doreen were seated together at one table. Belinda nervously plucked at pills on her cheap sweater. Chad and Mariah, with Paul, stood near a window, looking out at the blowing snow.

Betty was just entering the room from the foyer, and Bran sat alone with his head in his hands.

As Earl, Ray, and I came in from the kitchen, Earl turned belligerently toward Jerry, who was standing behind the makeshift bar. "Look, I don't know who appointed you to be in charge, but you've got just as much reason to want the judge dead as some of the rest of us. We need a neutral party to take over."

"After last night, I don't think there is such a thing as a neutral party," Cora retorted.

Jerry stroked his mustache. "Hmm. I don't think a little college spat, fifty years ago, about who was going to be editor of a magazine is much of a motive for murder. And someone needs to be in charge."

"He's right," Paul put in, turning away from the window. "Earl, according to your wife, you two should have much stronger feelings about the judge than Jerry."

"Is there anyone here who never met the judge before this week? How about the staff" Doreen asked.

"As far as I know, Sam didn't know her, but Dee's family certainly did," Betty answered without explaining how she knew about the Ward's connection to the judge. Maybe Dee had told her, too.

Earlier, I had been all too happy to say I hadn't known Judge Viviette VondaVay Velvet, but now that fact was placing me in the spotlight. "Neither Chad or I had met her before," I admitted.

"Then let's put that smart young college man in charge. That one over there." Earl pointed at Chad.

"Why not the other young fellow?" Paul asked.

Doreen pulled her sweater tighter around her shoulders as a cold draft blew through the room. "The handyman? Because he's got to get on the snowmobile and go get help. It's the only way out of here."

There was a general nodding of heads at this suggestion. Frank, Jessi, and Samson entered from the foyer.

"We've put the body in one of the empty storage rooms that has a lock on the door," Frank said. "It's better if only a few of us know which one."

"And so, we all begin to distrust each other," Harry chuckled, with ice in his voice. "But, yes, we need to get the police here as soon as possible. Someone with real authority."

Apparently Sam had heard the comment about the snowmobile. "I'll go gas up and ride into town. It's going to be a bad ride in the dark with the blowing snow, but I can make it." He pulled his gloves on and left through the main door causing another frigid breath to sweep through the house.

"Let's all go into the front room," Frank urged. "It's cozier. I'll get a fire going— we don't know how many days we might have to run the generator on the propane— and if that runs out we'll really be in a bind. Then we can discuss the situation calmly."

"Maybe it would be better not to discuss it at all," Chad said.

I wasn't sure if he was stepping into the role of person-in-charge as had been suggested for him, of if he just thought that was a good idea.

"I mean, if the police are coming, they'll want to hear our stories first," he added.

"The Sheriff's Department will be the responding unit," Jerry pointed out. "Not technically the police."

"OK, so noted," Chad said evenly. I was glad he didn't take offence at being corrected, but it wasn't clear to me that he was willing to be the one in charge. He still seemed very young to me, although certainly he was a man— no longer a child.

Frank headed for the front room and knelt in front of the

fireplace. He began placing logs. Slowly people started to rise and follow him into that potentially warmer refuge. The mistletoe and golden bows seemed garish and out of place in a house where someone had just been murdered. The unlit Christmas tree did nothing to cheer my spirits. As the shock of finding Viviette drained away, the mood was becoming dismal.

"I'll just see what's happening with dinner," Betty fussed, returning to the kitchen.

"Line up some of those bottles," Earl said to Jerry. "I need a drink."

"I agree," Belinda said. "Make mine a double Scotch."

Glass clinked and several other people requested beverages. It was probably good that Sam had bought extra liquor at the last minute.

Just then the foyer door banged open again, and Sam plowed into our midst without knocking the snow off his clothes or removing hat and gloves.

"What the hell!" He yelled. "Someone has dumped all the gas cans and punched holes in every gas tank. There's a puddle under every car. I can't go anywhere."

32

Chad stepped to the middle of the room. "You've all suggested I take charge because I don't... didn't know the judge, and I will try to. This has suddenly become more serious."

"The word you want is 'sinister,'" Bran's voice shook.

"Yes, I agree," Chad said. "First of all, no one should go anywhere alone. Both for safety and to have a witness to what they are doing. Someone in this group is up to no good."

"No couples going off together either," Mariah put in. Nobody that came together. Not Chad and Ana, not my dad and me."

Earl snickered. "Not you and Chad, either."

Mariah turned bright red. "All right. I can agree to that."

The wind was coming from a different direction from the night before and wailed like a crying child through a loose window casing.

"Can't someone stop that infernal noise?" Bran whined.

"Yes, that would help. It's very disturbing," Cora agreed.

Frank stepped to the pile of newspapers he'd used for kindling. He began to tear off a page which he folded into a long strip. He stuffed this into the gap beside the window, and the unwelcome noise ceased. Cora was right; it did help.

While Frank was busy with this task, Harry ponderously got to his feet and cleared his throat. "I did a little checking myself, before we made this rule about being alone. The first and best suspect is always the husband." He glared at Bran who had taken a seat near the fire that was just now beginning to lap up the larger logs.

We all looked at Bran. He was practically trembling, and had gone pale under his dark skin. This did not look like a guilty man unless his mien was fear rather than grief.

"And?" Paul prompted.

"It's his ski pole stuck through Viviette. He's the only one with those bright red ones. He went upstairs twice when the judge was missing. We have only his word that she wasn't there."

"These things don't prove much," Paul said.

Harry jabbed a finger in Paul's direction. "How about this? I went up and checked the tower room. There's a curtain over it for sure, but that plywood covering the elevator shaft up there... it's loose. Not fastened tight at all."

Bran leaped to his feet. "How did you get in my room? You... you..."

Harry shrugged, "It was unlocked."

"OK, OK." Chad placed himself between Harry and Branson. "This isn't productive, and it's why we can't go anywhere alone. You might just as well say that Sam dumped all the gasoline himself, just because no one saw him checking the jugs."

Belinda perked up. "That's an interesting idea. I mean, why would he think to check the vehicles to see if fuel had been siphoned. That seems a little fishy to me."

Sam slapped his gloves against his leg and tossed his head. "I'm the handyman. I think of things like other ways to get gas if the primary source is gone. Give me nuts and bolts and gasoline and engines, not this psycho stuff."

He turned to exit the room, but Earl grabbed his arm. "No you don't. You aren't leaving alone either."

Sam sighed and peeled off his heavy coat. "Is the dining room allowed? I'm not quite clean enough for this room," he sneered.

"I think it's time we stopped second-guessing each other. We'd better all tell our true relationships with the judge. Not everyone who disliked her has a significant reason to want her dead," Cora said. "I certainly wouldn't have killed her over a poster that is actually rather humorous. But I'd never met her before Wednesday."

There were several minutes of silence in which everyone looked around the room at the faces of the other guests. Paul actually looked frightened. I wondered what that was about. Maybe Mariah didn't know Viviette was technically her step-grandmother. I thought I had that relationship figured out.

Belinda had recovered to some extent from the trauma of finding the judge. She asked, "Is there any chance this was a bizarre accident? Maybe we're jumping the gun at calling it murder."

Earl laughed out loud. "It would be some crazy-ass accident. Climbing over a four-foot barrier, or removing a piece of plywood, to fall down an elevator shaft with a ski pole in your hand. One that was already broken, at that. The rest of the pole wasn't at the bottom."

"Oh," Belinda said. It came out like a gasp.

Harry added, "She didn't throw herself from the tower room. There were only a couple of screws holding the plywood, but she couldn't have put the board back after she fell. That's where the husband comes in."

"Could two people be involved?" Jessi asked.

"Of course. And, she might have been killed somewhere else and then thrown down the elevator shaft," Ray pointed out.

Chad spoke up. "How do we even know the ski pole killed her? Maybe she was strangled first. Then she wouldn't bleed when she was stabbed, I don't think. Nobody here is a medical examiner. That's the problem. We don't really know much at all."

"We know she's dead, and at least one of us had something to do with it," Harry said forcefully. A little spray of spit gleamed in the flickering firelight.

"Let's concentrate on what we can really determine," Chad said. "Jerry, will you and Ray go up and verify what Harry says about the plywood in the tower, and also check the panel in the music room?"

"I'll go too," I offered. "I have a key." Harry had said the room was unlocked, but it shouldn't have been, and I didn't want to be left out.

This admission earned me a piercing look from Branson. "So, there are people besides me who can get in my room."

My secret would have to come out, although it seemed rather silly to withhold it at this point. "Yes, I agreed to help with housekeeping. I've been changing the towels and cleaning the bathrooms. I have a master key, but so does Sam, and the

Farnsworths, of course." I did wonder how Harry had gotten in the tower room. Maybe I'd forgotten to lock it behind me? No that couldn't be right. Bran had been up there after I was.

We three climbed to the tower. It was nearly dark by now, and with so many of the lights turned off, the upper landing was dim and gloomy. I inserted the key into the lock and twisted it. The doorknob wouldn't turn. I fiddled with the key again, and opened the door. The room must have been unlocked, as Harry had said. The men went immediately to the curtain.

"Should we be wearing gloves?" Ray asked.

"I think we can check the security of the plywood panel without touching much," Jerry said, pushing the covering away with the backs of his fingers.

It was just as Harry had reported. There were only two screws holding the plywood in place, and it was very loose. However, it didn't appear to have been moved recently. There were no scratch marks on the walls and no tell-tale pile of dust or splinters on the floor.

"Pictures, Ana," Jerry commanded, and I complied.

We then checked the music room, but that plywood, also covered with a temporary curtain, was screwed tight to the wall. Again, there were no signs anyone had removed it recently. I took pictures of that access as well, just to be thorough.

As we returned to the first floor, Jessi was saying, "...not that easy to kill someone. I mean, we're just regular people. I saw someone I didn't know die in an avalanche once, in Colorado, and helped recover the body, but to actually murder? Has anyone here ever killed someone? By accident, I mean."

"I was in Iraq, remember?" Earl said. "Killing people was our job."

"Oh, but war is.... different, somehow," Jessi said.

"But he's done it before," Harry said. "That makes it easier to do again."

Doreen glared at Harry. "Watch out who you're pointing fingers at."

Chad tried to smile. "Our search party is back. What did you find?"

"It doesn't look as if anyone's removed the panels covering the shaft on either floor," Jerry reported. "Yes, the plywood is loose in the tower, but there's no indication that it was taken off since the room was last cleaned."

"That would have been on Monday or Tuesday. Before the party." Betty explained. She must have left the kitchen and joined the group while we were upstairs.

Jerry turned to her. "Are these the only potential access points to the elevator shaft? I just don't see how anyone could have carried a body through the house on this floor, to throw it down, without being seen."

Frank coughed loudly, and all eyes focused on our host. "There is the ballroom," he said.

33

Frank pointed at the ceiling at the same time as his wife stepped to the south wall and pulled aside one of the long drapes. This revealed an exterior door with a large oval glass panel. "There's the front door," she said. "We tried to disguise it by making these, she shook the fabric in her hand, match all the window curtains and letting them reach the floor. I wanted to discourage foot traffic from coming directly into this room. But it's functional, and easily seen from outside if you are on this side of the house."

"I still think it would have been very difficult to carry someone through here without being noticed," Jerry insisted.

"Were these rooms both empty at any time this morning?" Chad asked.

"Don't forget the library," Cora added. "There's a clear sight line from anywhere in there."

I shared what I knew. "No one was here when I came through a little before eleven, except Doreen in the library. But she wasn't looking this way."

"Still, that would have been an awful risk for someone to take, to count on not being heard," Jerry pointed out.

Mariah wanted to know what the door sounded like when it was opened.

Betty held back the heavy drapes and turned the doorknob. "We keep it unlocked during the day in case of an emergency."

The original-to-the-house oak door was swollen from the damp, and a lower corner stuck as our hostess tugged at the knob. The corner broke free with a wrenching snap, and the seldom-used hinges moaned loudly as she opened the door. With the upper edge restricted by the long drapes, after being opened about a foot, the door wouldn't move any farther. As Betty tried to close it again, the cloth buckled behind the door. Cold air swept through the room and a menacing shower of sparks flew up the chimney or popped as they died against the mesh fire screen.

"Close it," Earl demanded. "No one snuck in that way."

"Yes, there's no doubt I would have heard that racket," Doreen agreed.

Jerry and Earl were tall enough to free the corners of the door from the draping fabric, and working together with Betty, the swollen door was forced closed.

"Much too difficult for anyone to come in that way," Cora said.

"That leaves the ballroom," Paul said. "Where is it anyway?"

"Tell them, Panda Bear," Betty said, needlessly.

Frank pointed upwards again. "Right over our heads. It's above this room and the dining room. Not finished for public use at all yet."

"How do you get there?" Mariah asked.

"I'm confused. If the elevator isn't working, can anyone go up there at all?" Belinda said.

Ray shook his head. "Why are ballrooms on the second floor, anyway?"

"That's a good question," Cora, ever the historian, said. "But, I don't know the answer. I can only tell you that in many private houses of this age, they are."

I recalled the narrow gallery opposite and above the main door and realized I had a pretty good idea of how to get to the ballroom. It wasn't all that difficult to discern. Anyone, even Mariah or Belinda, could have figured it out. Or accidentally discovered it.

"The entrance hall is off the foyer balcony," Betty confirmed.

Chad asserted himself again. "Frank, why don't you and my mother go up and check that out. She can take pictures of whatever you find."

"Not so fast," Earl said. "Let's all go."

Doreen nodded. "I agree. It's the only access we haven't checked, right? And I'd like to watch faces when we find out what condition it's in."

"Sure, OK, " Frank said. "It's safe enough to be up there.

That's why those support pillars are in the dining room. It's just not clean or decorated."

"Do you keep it locked?" Bran asked.

Frank hesitated. "I... I'm not sure. I don't know when anyone was last in there." He turned expectantly to Sam, who had come closer during the experiment with the front door.

Sam shrugged. "Beats me. I haven't been in it for months. Since you had me pull out the stage steps, I think."

"Betty?"

But his wife wasn't sure either. She explained they had decided months ago not to attempt to refurbish that room in time for the Christmas party, and there had been no reason to use the space. Without a functional elevator the room was essentially a large dead end. Using it for storage was counter-productive, since it would need to be cleared as soon as renovations resumed.

"Let's go. Frank, you lead the way," Chad directed.

As all of us climbed to the balcony, I did wonder about the structural integrity of that narrow elevated space. There were so many whispered conversations occurring and so much general commotion that we wouldn't have heard the joists groaning as the balcony gave way. But the floor held firm.

"Ma, get up there in front with your camera," Chad yelled.

Frank waited for me at the door to the ballroom, which was a double-wide opening. Although the panels had been devised to look like two doors, it was actually a single pocket door. As we all watched, he noiselessly slid the heavy wood panel into the east wall. It had not been locked. He then reached around the corner and flipped on the lights. Crystal chandeliers dazzled brilliantly, the glass pendalogues throwing patterned shadows and highlights on bare walls and hardwood floor.

There was a collective intake of breath. I snapped pictures as Frank whirled around and extended his arms to prevent people from entering the room. A moment later, I realized I should have taken photos of people's reactions instead of the empty room. That might have been far more useful.

A wide track where something had been dragged through the dust led from our feet to the open elevator shaft on the opposite wall. The only barrier was two sawhorses placed in front of the yawning black space. Red and jagged, the lower end of a ski pole lay in the center of the dustless pathway that had traced Judge Viviette's last dance.

34

"Nobody goes inside," I yelled. "There could be footprints to preserve."

"Back up so we can see too," Belinda shouted back. "Some of us are short, and you don't get special privileges just because you're supposed to be some kind of reporter."

"Actually, she does," Jerry insisted, "But it's reasonable to let others have a look. Frank, just keep people from stepping inside."

I had decided I'd at least record what reactions I could. Although no one looked happy with me, I photographed each person who stepped up to the human gate and peered into the ballroom.

Chad and Mariah were directing those who had looked through the ballroom door back toward the front of the house. Before long, only Frank, Jerry and I were left on the balcony.

"You'd better lock that door now," Jerry said.

"Yes, of course you're right," Frank responded. Sweat glistened on his forehead. "It takes a different key, though. I keep it in my office, not on me."

"You can't go get it by yourself. House rules," I said.

"And one of us can't stay here alone," Jerry added. "Mariah! Come back up here a minute."

Mariah nodded and jogged up the stairs.

The girl was holding up well, I thought. She was pretty young to be involved in something this sordid. And what were Dee and her children doing, I wondered. If they were alone together in the kitchen, they were violating the house rules— a family unit with no one else present. I certainly couldn't picture Dee as a murderess, although her reason to dislike the judge was pretty intense. Still, she had the girls living with her again. Would she jeopardize the current family status for pure revenge? I hated myself for even considering the possibility, but obviously someone had expressed their feelings about Viviette to the ultimate extent. Separating children from their parents was highly emotional. Earl and Doreen had also been affected in that same way by the judge. And Earl could be a powder keg with his PTSD. Maybe Earl had snapped and accidentally killed her in a confrontation that went south and then tried to cover it up. The Velvet Hammer would never have backed down, even to someone as tall and strong as Earl. She carried herself like the Ethiopian queen she wasn't, but she certainly had thought of herself as royalty.

"What do you want me for?" Mariah asked breathlessly, as she skidded to a stop.

"You can stay here and babysit me, to be sure I don't contaminate the scene," Jerry chuckled. "Frank and Ana are off to find the key to lock this door."

Frank gave Jerry a sideways glance, and his thick glasses distorted his eyes enough to impart a portentous gleam. "We'll be right back," he said and headed for the stairs without a word to me.

Apparently I was supposed to keep up.

Turning the corner under the stairs into the first floor hallway, Frank finally spoke to me. "The office is next to our suite."

I followed him about halfway down the gold-papered corridor where he stopped at a door and unlocked it with a key he pulled from his pocket. We stepped into a room that was exactly what one would expect of an office. A large roll-top desk was littered with papers and pens, an empty mug, and half a waffle covered in gelatinous syrup on a plate— so someone had been in here this morning— probably Frank himself, since he didn't seem surprised to see the cold food. Framed photos covered the walls. File cabinets were jammed between the windows, and partially emptied boxes of supplies— paper towels, toilet cleaner, and a whole case of castors— spilled their contents onto the floor.

Frank sat down in the wooden desk chair which rocked and squealed under his weight. He rummaged in the top drawer. "It should be here. Aha." He held up another key with an antique shape, but I could tell it was significantly different from my master key.

I tried to study the photographs on the walls, but I didn't recognize anyone other than Frank and Betty in the short time Frank had been at his desk.

We returned to the ballroom door, closed it, and Frank turned the key in the lock.

Jerry then tested the door, but it was held firmly shut. "Good enough. You all saw that it's secure now. Let's join the others, shall we?"

I won't say that Mariah didn't trust Jerry, but she also tried to open the sliding panel. "OK, I agree," she said.

When we returned to the dining room, people were divided between the buffet and the smaller tables. Soup and sandwiches were on the menu again, along with Christmas cookies.

The pass-through was open, and Dee was handing plates of pie across to Jimmie. I could see the girls beyond their mother. I wanted to know if they'd been in the kitchen all afternoon. Not that I thought they had been involved with the judge's death, but perhaps they'd seen or heard something earlier that might put them in danger. They needed to be protected, not watched.

"I think we should each make an account of how we spent the morning," Earl said loudly.

"Oh, give it a rest," Belinda shot back. "Let us eat in peace. You don't seriously think someone is going to admit, 'I stabbed her and threw the body into the basement,' do you?"

35

The mood was not exactly that of a holly jolly Christmas, despite the voice of Burl Ives booming from the CD player, insisting we have one.

"Can someone turn that horrible man down? It's enough to give me a nervous breakdown," Doreen whined.

No one rose to adjust the volume, and I thought it was a good thing to have enough noise to cover stray comments, so I didn't take any initiative. Each little grouping of people seemed wrapped in a cocoon of its own thoughts and feelings, as if the music were irrelevant to any of them, and yet it provided a blanket of security, holding whatever evil lurked among us at bay.

Earl calmed down, and an intermittent conversational hum burred beneath the songs. After Belinda's likely truthful prediction, some visiting was far better than the awkward silence that might have been expected.

I built a sandwich and pulled a chair into the corner of the square table occupied by the four twenty-somethings who seemed to be forging a real friendship.

"Here, we'll make room," Ray said. He stood and moved his dishes to an empty table then dragged it over to mate up with the one where Jessi, Chad, and Mariah still sat. I took an unoccupied side, and Paul also joined us.

Chad jumped right in with the question on all our minds, "Do we have any good ideas about who might have done in the judge? Assuming it's not one of us."

"Yes, let's assume that," Paul said, his mouth pulled into a grimace.

Mariah leaned forward and flipped her long bangs away from large liquid brown eyes. She reminded me of a doe I'd caught in my headlights once this autumn. "You know every table is having this same conversation, but someone here has to be the one. It's too creepy"

Chad reached out and put his hand over Mariah's. She had been gripping the edge of the table with white knuckles. "I think the judge was the specific target. There's no danger to any of the rest of us."

"Right. Unless someone figures it out, and the guilty person sees them as a threat," Jessi said. Her eyes flicked from table to table.

I noticed that Chad and Mariah's hands moved out of sight, and she relaxed, even tried to smile at Chad.

"I think it's Earl. He makes too much commotion about the whole thing," Paul said. "The man doth protest too much, you know," he mis-quoted.

"But Doreen keeps saying they got their kids back, so why would he, or they, do it?" Jessi asked.

"Revenge, lost memories, spite. He's a loose cannon, too—maybe he just went nuts," Paul theorized.

Jessi shook her head. "It's too obvious. Look at Harry instead. I don't trust him. He tries to keep a low profile, but he's not as harmless as he looks."

"Belinda's the same way, except her sharp tongue gets the best of her occasionally," Ray said.

I hated conversations like this. We'd all be at each other's throats by morning. "Look, Chad," I said. "Earl may be obnoxious, but he has a point. I think after dinner you need to get people together and see if we can re-construct the morning, determine when Viviette died."

"I agree," Paul said.

All the heads around the table nodded in agreement.

We finished our sandwiches and soup in silence.

Chad stood and called for attention. "After you've finished eating, let's move into the front room. It's warmer there anyway. We can try to figure out when the judge was seen last. I know it's difficult to keep from speculation, but let's see if we can pin down some facts."

Sam built up the fire once more, and extra chairs were carried in from the library so that everyone had a seat. I went into the kitchen and invited Dee and the kids to join us. I didn't want the girls traumatized, but they insisted it was much worse to be isolated than to know what was happening. "It's mostly like a TV show," Beth said. "She was just an old lady we didn't really know."

"That's not polite," Jimmie said.

Beth stuck out her tongue at him. "An *elderly* lady, then."

"Ho, ho. Don't let Nana catch you calling someone younger than she is, 'elderly.'"

"We'll just listen and not get in the way," Lindsey promised.

When the arranging of chairs had ended, and everyone was settled with hot drinks, and with napkins filled with cookies balanced on knees or side tables, Chad began.

"Since I've been more or less appointed leader, I'll be the first to tell what I know. I came down late to breakfast... most of you saw me... and the judge was in the dining room. Then the four of us that have been hanging out together went skiing. We saw— no, let's just tell what we personally know— I saw the judge and her husband skiing ahead of us."

"Yes, but are you sure it was them?" Harry said.

"I suppose I can't be positive, but Mr. Owens is tall and has that bright red jacket, and the judge is petite. She had on the same fancy sweater she wore at breakfast. And they are very good skiers. We... I couldn't catch up to them. They went on straight at a junction to take the long ski loop, but our group turned left on the shorter route. I never saw her again."

"I'll go next," Mariah said. "My story is exactly the same as Chad's. That makes it easy."

"But where were you for the rest of the morning?" Doreen asked. "We can't just say 'we didn't see the judge;' we have to account for our time."

Mariah turned red and looked at Chad.

"We were together," Chad said. "We switched to snowshoes

and went to explore the ruins of the mill. Even though the wheel is gone, some of the walls are still there and we tried to figure out the old floor plan. But it's a real puzzle."

"And got better acquainted, I suppose," Earl said sarcastically.

Doreen made a clucking noise. "Hush, dear. They're young, and they like each other. What do you expect?"

"It is a portentous month for starting relationships," Bran added, as if he couldn't stop himself from spouting horoscopes.

My son sounded calm, but I could tell he was working hard to keep his voice even. "If you're suggesting we were acting inappropriately, I take issue with that. We exchanged a few kisses. It was certainly too cold out there to do anything more... um... "

"We understand," Betty soothed as she glared at Earl. "No one is finding fault. So you two can vouch for each other until lunch?"

"Yes, absolutely," Mariah said, sounding glad to have something definite to say that wasn't defensive. "And we passed the Caulfields going out as we were coming back."

"Yes, we can verify that," Cora said.

"We met up with Ray and Jessi again in the equipment room, and then we all went up to sing carols until my mom called us to lunch."

Chad extended a hand in the direction of his new friends. "Ray?"

"Sure. I was at breakfast and skiing with these two, just as they said. After we all got back, Jessi and I went around the trails again, but this time we did take the longer loop."

"Did you see Viviette and Branson?" Frank asked.

"No, but we can say that we followed fresh ski tracks the whole way. You know, the groomer made the first tracks, but there had been a couple of people skiing in the grooves ahead of us."

"So that suggests Bran is telling the truth. That he and Viviette came back to the house together," I said.

"Of course I'm telling the truth," Branson said in a strangled voice.

"Right," Jessi added. "I can't tell you anything more than Ray just did. Oh, maybe except that there wasn't anywhere that the ski tracks went off-piste into the woods or something. It just looked normal."

"Pissed? We're going to have to account for when we take a leak? This is too ridiculous!" exclaimed Harry.

36

"P-I-S-T-E, off-piste. It means to ski off the maintained trail. It's French." Jessi was trying hard not to sound condescending, but it was obvious she thought Harry was boorish. Her nostrils flared and the nose ring caught the firelight.

"For heaven's sake, shut up, Harry," Belinda ordered. "You sound like you have something to hide. Do you?"

Harry set his mug down on the floor at his feet and wiped his flabby lips with a Santa Claus napkin. Crumbs bounced off his belly and scattered on the carpet. "Of course not. And I can tell you where I was every minute. I never saw that woman after breakfast."

"Please let Ray finish," Chad said

Harry started to open his mouth, but Ray beat him to it and continued. "You've covered the rest of it. We met up with you and Mariah and went to the music room. Paul joined us there at some point. I'm not sure exactly when.

"All right. We'll get to Paul. But now, Harry can tell us where he was, since he's ready."

"By all means, give each person time to get their story straight," Earl sneered.

Chad cracked his knuckles. I knew he was getting exasperated. "Look, Mr. Pyrtle. We can't all talk at the same time. Anyone who is telling the truth doesn't need to put together a 'story.'"

"Except those of us who weren't with anyone. We can tell the truth, but it won't help us," Belinda said. "Oh dear, I should have waited. Well. I'll be patient now."

"Are you folks done discussing this circus, because I think it was my turn," Harry growled.

Every eye turned toward him.

"All right. I was at breakfast. You people saw me. Then Belinda and I came in this room to read. I wanted to finish an article about pheasant hunting in that issue of *Field and Stream* over there." Harry pointed at a basket full of magazines. "You'll have to ask my wife what book she had. Then those two women," he paused and pointed again, at Doreen and Betty, "went into the library and started yakking."

"What time was that?" Chad asked.

"Maybe nine-thirty, quarter to ten. I didn't look. Anyway. Belinda went upstairs, and I went outside to find that young guy, Sam. Walked all around the outbuildings, but he wasn't in sight."

Samson looked perplexed. "What did you want me for?"

"Wanted to ask you if there's an air compressor. My right back tire goes low if it sits too long."

"So you were out by the cars around ten this morning? Did you notice if the gas tanks had been tampered with then?" Sam asked.

"They sure as heck had not. Whoever did that was out later. There were no puddles by the cars," Harry said with finality. "Anyway, so then I came back inside. It was quieter because Betty was gone, and Doreen was alone in the library. I tried to finish reading that article."

Earl casually reached into the basket Harry had been pointing at and pulled out the top magazine. "This one?" he asked, tilting his head.

"Yeah, the cover story," Harry said, sticking out his bottom jaw.

Earl flipped open the magazine and ran a finger down the page. "So, what does this guy recommend as a good time of day to hunt?"

Cora stood up and grabbed the magazine away from Earl. She threw it on the floor. I was shocked. I'd never seen her act rudely toward anyone in the several years I'd known her.

"Just stop it, Mr. Pyrtle," Cora said, her eyes flashing. "We need to at least extend enough courtesy to our fellow guests to allow them to explain themselves without being harassed. There will be plenty of time for an evaluation of the facts as compared with individual accounts afterwards."

"I don't deserve an Alpha Charlie," Earl sneered, but I didn't know what that meant.

"Yes, you do deserve to have your ass chewed," Harry countered. "This isn't fun, but we need to tell what we know without being bullied."

There was complete silence for half a second and then sort of a collective sigh, a collapsing of tensions. Cora sat down.

"Thank you," Chad said.

Jerry smoothed his mustache. I thought he was trying not to chuckle. "It would be good if we could be a bit more respectful, and I think we should be adding a little more information to these recitals," he said.

"Like what?" I asked.

"Well, there's time after lunch we have to account for. Belinda didn't find the body until about three o'clock. Did anyone get the exact time?"

I fiddled with the camera and called up the time stamp info. "The first picture I took was at three-oh-seven."

"So, you think she could have been alive earlier, just avoiding us or something, and killed later?" Betty asked Jerry.

"It's possible. Although rigor mortis was pretty complete. Does anyone remember how long that takes to set in?" Jerry asked, looking around.

"I know it's faster if the body is cold," Jessi said. "Or if the person was exercising right before they were killed. I'll look it up." She pulled out her phone, then shook her head. "No, wait, I can't. No service yet."

Frank said, "Bran says she was alive around eleven. That would be four hours. I don't think she could have been killed after lunch or she wouldn't have been so stiff."

"If Bran is telling the truth," Earl said.

Cora gave him a withering look.

Earl spread out his hands and shook his head. "Can't you people GOFO? That's 'grasp the flaming obvious' for you civvies," he derided.

Branson Owens stood up. "You all are talking about my wife.

And me... us... as if we aren't even here. We were happily married— there's no way I would hurt Viviette. I was with her until about eleven. We'd had a long ski, and she was tired. I assumed she was going upstairs to rest before lunch. But she wasn't there an hour later, after I helped with the shoveling."

"So you admit you were the last one to see her?" Earl insisted.

"There you go again," Cora accused.

But Bran was summoning some backbone. "I couldn't have been the *last* one, Earl, because she was still alive when I saw her."

37

"We need a break," Jerry said, standing and extending his arms over his head.

There was a murmur of agreement and almost everyone rose. Jessi began doing bends and stretches. Several people headed for the ground-floor restrooms.

"Don't be going too far," Earl taunted, "or the mistletoe police will be after you."

Chad stepped across the room to talk with Cora and Jerry. The conversation looked serious in nature. Not one of them was smiling.

"I'll get more cookies," Jimmie whispered to me. "We need comfort food in here."

"I'll help you. Just to follow that 'no one goes alone' rule," I said, half joking. I doubted that more sugar was going to solve anything, but it was good that Jimmie was trying to be helpful.

Soon, almost everyone was re-seated, a few with more cookies, but Chad remained standing. He began, "I apologize to you all. We've been doing this wrong. It doesn't matter where anyone was before the judge was killed, but what we need to do is determine when she was last alive, preferably with at least two witnesses. Branson says he left her about eleven, after they skied. Did anyone else see her then?"

Cora wiggled her fingers in the air and spoke. "I did not see her, but I recognized her skis in the equipment room when Jerry and I got back from our little snowshoe walk. That was shortly after eleven. But, I suppose anyone could have returned them there. And, incidentally, Jerry and I went to our room to freshen up after we came in. We were together."

"Now that's interesting," Ray straightened. "About the skis. Were Bran's red poles there too?"

"I wish I could say for certain, but I can't," Cora admitted. "I only noticed the judge's skis because they were right beside where I hung my snowshoes, and they are distinctive— purple, like so many things she wore."

"So, she either returned them herself, or she was already dead by then, and someone else put the skis there," Ray concluded.

"Yes, that must be true," Cora said.

Chad took a deep breath. "All right, I guess we can't say with certainty that the judge was alive after eleven, but perhaps she was all right until she returned from skiing. Does anyone dispute this conclusion?"

I was afraid an open-ended question like that might start a lot of wild speculation, but no one challenged the statement.

"Great. That's something." Chad said, sounding a little more upbeat. "Let's switch topics. I think it will be more productive to know people's relationships with the judge than these lengthy accounts of where we spent every minute of the day. That way, those of us who barely knew her can probably be discounted as, um... suspects."

"I don't care one way or the other," Belinda said. "But my earlier point is the same. Anyone can lie, and if what they keep hidden is a secret from everyone here, they'll get away with it."

"Let's give it a try," I said. "We can at least ask anyone who has contradictory information to speak up. And I have a suggestion. Those who had never heard of Viviette, or only saw her on television, raise your hand."

Cora, Chad and I were the only three people to lift an arm. So that meant Mariah had met the judge in person, whether she knew about her father's relationship to her or not. If I was correctly recalling the tales I'd heard so far, everyone else present had appeared in her courtroom— either family court or on television— except our hosts. And Frank and Betty had been friends with her since childhood. Well, and Branson, her husband. I really knew nothing at all about how he had met Viviette.

"That didn't reduce the pool by much," Earl scoffed. "But it's no secret how Doreen and I knew her. My darling wife has been telling you our sordid family history since we arrived."

"Let's hear the formal version," Chad said. "We may have heard scraps, but we need to get these things out in the open now."

Earl waved a hand in his wife's direction. "Tell it one more time, dear."

Now that she was in the spotlight, Doreen seemed even more eager to speak. Her makeup wasn't as perfect as it had been earlier— all of us probably looked less than fresh at the end of this traumatic day, but she suddenly struck me as a brilliant and glittering drama queen. Her eye shadow sparkled silver and lavender. Her long purple nails fluttered at the ends of caramel fingers. She wore a silver tunic that flowed in liquid folds over lavender leggings. With her long thin body, she was, in a word, gorgeous. No wonder she'd gone into cosmetology. Most women would pay a lot to have her advise them on how to achieve such stunning looks.

"The judge's rulings hurt us very deeply in the past," she began in an even tone. "As I've told several of you, I was heavily into drugs. Her face crumpled. Oh, please," she gave a little sob, "I'm so sorry I've been talking about this all the time. Having the judge here really rattled me, and I wanted to justify how I felt. Forgive me, Earl?" She turned to her husband and then continued. "The way I've been acting— it's what's making him such a grouch with you all. I know he can be blunt, but he's not always so nasty."

Doreen had been seated beside Earl in one of the library chairs, but now she stood and stepped behind him, placing her hands on his shoulders. Earl sighed and reached up to grasp her fingers. She leaned forward and kissed the top of his head.

"I won't belabor the points," she continued. "It's true that I was a mess. I was doing all kinds of drugs, and the judge was right to put our children in foster care. Earl never gave up hope of my recovery, and he got me into a great program where I broke the addiction. I was angry, for sure, because I thought she should have let Earl continue to watch the kids, but the truth is that he was way too busy supporting me in the recovery process. And, don't forget, Judge Viviette also allowed us to have the children back after I got well again."

Belinda reached over and squeezed Doreen's arm. "And you did a marvelous job as a mother after you got things straightened out."

Apparently Belinda was just being affirming, since I had the impression they hadn't known each other before this party.

Earl added, in a softer tone than we'd ever heard from him, "It was hard, you know, because we lost out on some of the best parts of the kids' lives, but we did put things back together. I do resent those years we missed, but I certainly didn't hate the judge enough to kill her. I've seen enough killing."

There was silence for a few seconds, then Betty started clapping, and some people joined her. "We're so proud of you for what you've become," she said.

Paul jumped to his feet. His Adam's apple was bobbing up and down. "Let me go next. I... this... Branson, my sympathy goes out to you since you seem to really have cared for Viviette, but I'm not sorry at all that she's dead. You might even think I had a good reason to kill her.

38

Dee looked at me and nodded, as if to say, "I knew it." The Dee I knew wasn't really a gossipy person, but she did look smug.

Paul placed the palms of his hands together, stuck them between his knees and bowed his head. It wasn't clear if he was organizing his thoughts or praying. After a few seconds, he straightened and rotated his neck until it cracked. His eyes had that frightened look I'd seen earlier.

"Mariah, come sit with me," he said.

The girl looked baffled. "Sure, Dad. What's the matter?" She crossed to Paul's chair and sat cross-legged on the floor beside him. He reached out and placed a hand on her head, smoothing her hair

"Some of this is going to come as a shock to you, sweetheart," he whispered. "Try to forgive me."

"OK," she said, drawing out the last syllable and looking up at her father, her eyes full of unspoken questions.

Paul began. "The first part of this story was reported long ago by certain sleazy publications, so although I try to keep it under wraps, it's possible some of you may know who my father is."

Dee nodded and spoke, "I know, and I want you to understand that the only person I've told is Ana. We were talking about people with reasons to dislike the judge."

"And I've told no one," I put in.

"Thank you for that," Paul said to me, shifting in his seat. "It's really not as sordid as this buildup probably sounds, it's just that... well, I'd better make it clear what I'm talking about. My biological father is Viviette Velvet's first husband, Carlton Wegner."

We were becoming immune to bombshells. No one gasped. Heads nodded, and Harry even made an impatient "so what" gesture.

"That's the big secret, Dad?" Mariah asked. "I know you've asked me not to spread it around, but I didn't know you felt that strongly. Why would that make you want to kill the judge? It's not like she's actually related to us."

Paul patted her head as if she were a puppy. "Hush, Mariah. This is only the beginning." Seeming to mentally brace himself, he spoke more loudly, "Viviette refused to give Carlton a divorce so he could marry my mother. She made the rest of that man's life a living hell."

"What happened to him?" Doreen asked, flicking her curls absently with a silver nail.

"He died of a massive stroke in ninety-nine. Some people said she killed him with her constant harassment."

Bran leaned forward. "That's not true. He'd had high blood pressure for years, a-fib, earlier TIAs, and high stress levels."

Paul pulled his mouth sideways, "My point, exactly. *I'm* not accusing her of being the source of his stress just pointing out the scuttlebutt. Anyway, she had the same attitude toward his illicit offspring as she had toward Carlton. She went out of her way to cripple my mother economically, and put as many stumbling blocks in my path as possible. I learned to be gun shy of any public opportunities at a very young age. No one had to explain to me that Viviette VondaVay Velvet was not a nice person."

Jessi had tucked one leg beneath her bum, and now she straightened both legs and stretched them. "What could she do to you? You weren't her kid."

"That's true enough, but she had a lot of influence. When I was very small, I remember seeing her at school functions. For example, in first grade I was one of the reindeer at the Christmas play. I had two lines. She coughed loudly during the entire time I spoke my piece."

Branson threw down the pillow he'd been holding in his lap. "Oh, grow up. You can't believe she singled you out with something as innocent as that."

Paul turned haunted eyes toward the judge's widower. "But I do. It continued in various formats throughout my childhood, and culminated with her preventing my acceptance to any college. And that was despite being in the honor society."

"You seriously believe this nonsense?" Bran exploded. He stood and began pacing the room.

"It's true. My mother eventually got one of the colleges to admit as much. Viviette wrote letters accusing me of being a security risk with an unstable emotional makeup and pyromaniac tendencies. I have a copy of one of them."

Bran settled back into his chair and crossed his legs. "I'm not buying it."

"Dad?" Mariah said.

Paul shook his head at her and continued. "We're still in the preliminaries. You can accept it as truth or not, it's merely background. Now we get to the difficult part."

"If that's the easy stuff, I'd say you had as good a motive as anyone to want to get rid of the Velociraptor," Earl chuckled. "This is getting good." He might have mellowed a bit after Doreen's apology, but his comment still had a bite.

"Did she go after Mariah, too?" Dee asked. "That would be pretty awful."

Paul sighed impatiently. "I need to tell the story in order. My mother held up pretty well during this whole time. She managed to make sure I had good male role models in my life, and we treated Viviette's vendetta as a running joke, trying to predict where she would strike next. But blocking my way to college was the last straw. My mother started drinking, and then met a man who made her feel important for a few months. She got pregnant when I was twenty."

Mariah twisted around to face Paul. "I didn't know you had any siblings. That means I have an aunt or uncle that's pretty much my own age."

Paul looked into her eyes and shook his head sadly.

Mariah's face suddenly contorted. "Dad... what happened to that baby and my grandma? I always thought she had a heart attack."

"She died in childbirth, sweetheart."

"But that's what happened to my..."

"I'm sorry you had to find out this way. I'm sorry I ever tried to keep it a secret. You're actually my half sister, although I did adopt you."

"Why, Dad? And what does it have to do with the judge? Oh! but you're not my dad..." Tears sprang to the corners of her eyes.

"Legally, I'm both your brother and your father, Mariah. Viviette was threatening to reveal the secret and give you a hard time, too. I'd kept her at bay for twenty-two years... made her leave you alone.

"How? How did you do it?" Mariah cried.

"I accidentally saw her buying some uncommon pesticide one day, shortly before my father died. In one of those odd coincidences, I'd read an article only the week before about how methyl iodide could bring on a massive stroke. And that was the active ingredient in the product she purchased. It wouldn't have taken much to hasten along someone who was already at high risk. I threatened Viviette with what I knew."

A log crashed in the fireplace. Engrossed in listening, we had hardly noticed the room was becoming chilly. Frank moved the screen, stirred up the coals and placed more wood on the fire.

"That's a little bit of a stretch," Jerry said. "It would have been difficult to prove anything conclusive."

"Probably, but guilty or not, the publicity would have ruined her. She couldn't take the chance, and she was willing to leave Mariah alone. I didn't ask for any money. But two months ago, Viviette started threatening to block Mariah, whom I love as a sister and a daughter, from being hired as a teacher. She said Carlton's death was too far in the past to concern her any longer."

"Why confess this now? Why cause this young lady so much pain?" Cora asked. She had a point. This seemed like unnecessary personal catharsis.

Paul's voice had become faint, but now he spoke with confidence. "If I had killed the judge, it would have been to protect this secret. Now that it's out in the open, it demonstrates I have no motive to need her dead."

He stood, pulled Mariah to her feet and embraced the weeping girl.

39

Branson Owens broke the silence. "I don't know about the rest of you, but I've had enough of this for tonight. For ever, actually, but I suppose we have to tolerate these tales of woe. Gemini have no time for serial complaints."

"Well, somebody sure as heck killed the lady," Harry said irritably. "I'm sorry she was your wife, because you seem like an OK guy, but stop blaming your life on mystical golden circles and weird symbols in the sky. Nothing so far points to her being a nice person, and I think one of her pet projects to ruin somebody finally caught up with her."

"But which one?" Belinda asked. She yawned and picked at her broken nail. "I'm going to bed. Stars aligned or not, Bran is right. This is more than enough for one session." She leveraged her bulk out of the recliner she'd been seated in since dinner and pulled at the lower edge of her sweater where it had hitched up in the back.

Dee did a sort of dance and waved a hand like a school girl. "Oh, please. What I have to say is brief, and we'll be busy making breakfast in the morning. Let me tell you."

Belinda huffed a sigh of defeat, but remained standing.

Looking around, Dee sensed she had our attention and began to speak rapidly. "Our story is a lot like what Earl and Doreen experienced. Well, I wasn't on drugs, but we were quite poor. Jimmie's father had died in a horrible car accident. I re-married and had the girls, but then their father, Wes Ward, left me. I slipped into depression, and he filed for custody. The judge ruled in his favor and sent them to live with their father."

"But here they are," Belinda extended a hand in a hurry-up gesture, her voice cold.

"Yes, things got really bad with me for a while. That's when

Jimmie met Ana, and we got ourselves straightened out. Meanwhile, Wes' new wife ran off, and he took to the bottle. Judge Viviette gave Beth and Lindsey back to me. I hated the woman before then, but I've got no reason to want to hurt her any longer. That's all."

Jerry put his arm around Dee. "Thank you for sharing. You've obviously been a great mother. Cora and I can certainly attest to that." He scanned the room with his eyes. "And I can't imagine anyone thinks the children are involved in any way with this murder. We think of these three as our own grandchildren."

"Oh!" Dee perked up and added brightly. "And, no one will go hungry. We're fixing bacon and eggs for breakfast."

"Not so fast," Bran said. "That boy is as big as Viviette was. He'd be physically capable of overpowering her. I want to hear from him."

"Me?" Jimmie's voice squeaked and he turned red. It seemed unfair to put him on the spot, but although unusually thin, Jimmie was taller than I am. And I knew he was strong. Of course, I understood Jimmie well, and couldn't believe for the life of a snowflake that he'd had anything to do with the judge's murder, but others in the room only knew him as one of the caterers. It was probably good to get the question out in the open.

"Speak up, son. You're nearly grown and you need to account for yourself," Harry said.

Jimmie gulped and said, "I was a little kid when Beth and Lindsey went to live with their dad. I wanted them to come back home, and they did— after my mom got well and we moved into town. I don't understand all the legal stuff. I didn't even recognize the judge until my mom told me who it was. Hey! And I was in the kitchen and dining room after Ana and I came back from outside. You saw me yourself."

He handled the question well, I thought. And he certainly didn't sound or look guilty of anything except being a teenager.

Earl also stood up. "I need a nightcap." He headed for the bar.

Others also rose.

"Not quite so fast," Jerry said.

Doreen groaned and flopped forward to touch her toes, making her mop of hair bounce. "Now what? I've had it. We aren't going to figure out anything this way."

"Maybe not, but we've got a basic chain of custody problem. Who's got the key to the room where the body is being held?"

"I do," Sam said, jingling the ring he carried on his belt.

"Hand it over, and we'll put it right here on the mantle. I assume it's not the only copy," Jerry said.

Frank pulled a single key from his pocket. "I've got the spare. Far as I know, there are just the two."

"And the ballroom key," Jerry said.

Frank pinched the large antique key and the smaller modern key between thumb and finger. "Only one key for the ballroom. Too hard to get duplicates made of these old babies."

Jerry took the three keys and placed them on the mantle in plain sight.

"And now everyone knows where they are," Chad said, looking puzzled.

"That's true, but I think we've got to have someone on watch during the night. There's no other way to secure the building," Jerry said.

"Fine, who's going to take on that thankless job? And why should we trust them?" Paul protested.

"I agree, it's a problem," Jerry answered. "But Cora and I will stay here until two, if Ana and Chad will take over after that. You've previously agreed we have little motive to be killers, and someone has to do it."

"You can't stay on watch with Cora— no couples allowed," Frank quoted the house rules we'd decided upon.

"All right, Ana and I, followed by Chad and Cora," Jerry granted.

"Knock yourself out," Harry said, lifting an imaginary glass. He walked toward the dining room. "But I assume we all get to bed down with our spouses. I doubt you're advocating musical mattresses."

"For sleeping arrangements, we will have to make concessions to the earlier restrictions," Jerry admitted, smiling.

40

Most everyone was hobbling out of the front room as fast as they were able on joints stiff from the long evening of sitting.

Belinda called over the heads in front of her, "Pour me one too, Harry. I need it."

Mariah had left Paul's arms and returned to Chad's side. He hugged her and rubbed her back comfortingly. They were whispering, but I couldn't make out any of the words.

Frank and Betty approached Jerry and Cora, and I hurried to join them.

"You're really willing to do this?" Betty asked. "It seems so officious. Are you sure we need to?"

"Oh, we must," Cora said. "The Sheriff will be highly displeased if we haven't made every effort to keep things as they were. And we've already moved the body. That alone will make him unhappy, even if it seemed necessary."

I pointed out that it might have been moved once before we put it in cold storage.

"Panda Bear and I could help— take a couple of hours to watch," Betty said. She sounded overly eager.

"No, I don't think you should do that, especially not together," Jerry said. "You two have known the judge as a friend for decades. I really think those of us who knew her least have to take on this responsibility."

Chad joined us. "I'm in," he said, with perhaps more enthusiasm than was appropriate for a murder scene, but at least he wasn't grumbling like so many of the guests.

"Good," Jerry clapped him on the shoulder. "I thought you'd help. How about if Ana and I stay up until two and then you and Cora can take over after that?"

I looked at my son and felt a great sense of pride welling up as he nodded solemnly.

"No problem on my end. Ma?"

"Sure, we can do that. Will we need to stay in this room?" I asked.

It was decided that we should keep watch from the dining room. The kitchen doors could be propped open, making one outside door visible, and it would be difficult for anyone to approach the utility room exit without being seen or heard. The main entrance and stairs off the foyer were in sight, as was the front door Betty had shown us earlier in the evening.

Cora verified those were the only exits. It seemed to me as if there must be one at the far end of the sleeping wing for safety, but Betty said there was not. Probably the large windows were adequate for egress in case of fire. We couldn't guard all the windows. There just weren't enough people. We'd all have to give up sleeping, and that would make tomorrow an egregious test of everyone's patience.

If anyone was going to try to make a run for it during the night, we could at least assure that it would be a challenge to get out of the house. If someone bolted, that would also declare their guilt. It seemed much more likely the purpose of a nightly foray would be to doctor certain pieces of evidence. I wondered what might be out there yet to find. Where had the judge been killed?

I was certain that Cora and Jerry's love for local news and heritage would keep them vigilant on their shifts. This was a fulsome new chapter unfolding in the volume of dastardly local crime, perhaps on a scale of the death of Judge Reuben Pierce Oldfield in 1924, memorialized in Cora's museum. The museum Judge Velvet had disparaged.

"Just let me run up and get a warmer sweatshirt while people are still milling around. Don't want to be accused of going somewhere alone," I said.

"I'll wait down here till you get back," Cora said.

I ran up the stairs; running was only possible because almost everyone had already retreated to his or her room.

Jessi was standing in her partially open doorway. "Ana! we

weren't sure we'd see you until tomorrow. Can you come in a minute?"

Since I knew Jerry wasn't alone downstairs, I agreed.

She looked back and forth in the hall and pulled me into her room, shutting the door quietly. "We know some things, but they may not mean anything."

"I told Jessi not to say anything when we were all together." Ray gestured to the desk chair, and I sat down.

"What's up?" I asked.

Jessi pulled the elastic scrunchie from her ponytail, shook out her blond hair and replaced the stretchy fabric as a headband. It made her look very young, like Alice in Wonderland. "We were walking down by the ruined mill," she began.

"Not snooping, but sort of exploring," Ray said. "Frank mentioned it could be dangerous, but he hadn't really told us to stay away."

"Well, we're young and fit. We know how to be careful scrambling around, so we thought we try to figure out where the mill wheel used to be."

Ray took up the story. "That's really only half the truth. We didn't bring any ropes or crampons with us, but Frank talked about steep banks and we thought maybe there could be a place where we might teach an ice climbing class. With his permission, of course."

The tone of his voice alerted me that he had more to tell. "But you found something else, instead?" I asked.

Jessi nodded. "Again, we don't know if it means anything, but if it does, someone might not be happy that we were looking around."

Jerry was waiting for me. I was impatient. "And?"

"There's a long narrow building that's still standing. Mostly, anyway. Some of the roof has caved in. We were going to see what's in it," Jessi said.

"But the door was locked from the inside," Ray added. "There were no other entrances. No windows low enough to get through. We decided it must just have been jammed shut by something that fell against it, but with everything that's happened..." His voice trailed off.

"I doubt that this means much," I said.

"Maybe someone hid something in there," Jessi said, almost hopefully.

"Seems like a poor location to do so. If the roof is gone, it's open to the weather. I really should get back downstairs."

Jessi looked conflicted. "Actually, there's one more thing you should know."

<h1 style="text-align:center">41</h1>

Were these two deliberately trying to waylay me, or did they have genuine guilty knowledge they wanted to get off their chests? Either way, I mentally sighed and settled back to hear the rest. "Tell me," I said, hoping the next bit of knowledge might be more valuable.

"It just that everyone is so focused on Judge Viviette. But someone might believe we wanted to harm Frank and Betty. Perhaps enough to ruin their party," Ray said.

Jessi quickly added, "We didn't kill the judge and have no idea who did, but we sort of have a motive to sabotage the party. Then maybe someone else took advantage of all the bad feelings to kill her when there were a lot of people around who didn't like her. Does that make sense?"

"Maybe," I said tentatively. "Tell me more."

"I'm distantly related to the Janes," Jessi said. "My great-great-grandmother was the youngest sister of Henry, the man who built this house. So I've known about this place since I was a child."

"We were even looking into buying it and fixing it up," Ray explained. "But then the Farnsworth's got interested."

"They have lots more money than we do," Jessi said. "It would have been risky for us, but we thought it would be a great base location for an outfitter— right here in the forest. We were thinking more about leading trips then, less emphasis on selling gear, although that would have been part of the equation."

Ray said, "In fact, we'd already made an offer on the place, but it was low... there was so much work that needed to be done. Then Frank and Betty stepped in and agreed to the asking price."

"They were more like a monied bulldozer," Jessi's voice was bitter. "We never even had a chance."

"So you really don't like our hosts very much?" I wanted confirmation that this was what they were telling me.

"That's true," Ray said. "But when we were invited here— and that doesn't make much sense to us— we accepted because we wanted to see what they've done with the house. I have to admit we never could have restored it so nicely."

"Thank you for trusting me with this information," I said. "But it doesn't seem like anything you've told me is a big enough deal for anyone to accuse you of murder, or even sabotage. I think you should stop worrying and get some rest. I really need to go back down to be with Jerry."

Jessi walked me to the door and whispered as I left. "You should also know that I saw Frank in this hallway when I came up to change for lunch. But he didn't see me."

"He owns the house," I pointed out.

"Yes, but his rooms aren't on this floor. I only thought you should know. If he claims he was somewhere else..." she let the sentence trail off.

On the way downstairs I recalled that Frank had said he'd cleaned snow out of the TV dish. That was probably why he was above the ground floor before lunch. We'd become a suspicious bunch, analyzing each move anyone made.

In the dining room, Jerry and Cora had settled in with steaming mugs.

"We thought you'd gotten mixed up about who was taking first shift," Cora said.

Now I felt guilty for messing up the planned schedule for the night watches. "Sorry, Ray and Jessi thought they had important information, but it was really nothing much," I explained. "Hardly worth bothering with."

Cora leaned forward and showed me what was in her mug. "I've already had one cup of regular coffee, and this is my second. I'll never be able to sleep now. Just leave this shift to us, and you and Chad take the next one."

"I think that's the best idea," Jerry added.

I sighed "Some people will have a fit, say we were deceptive."

"Let them," Jerry said. "Off with you, and leave that to me if anyone even finds out."

I climbed wearily to my room and set the alarm.

At two in the morning, Chad and I descended the stairs as quietly as possible to relieve Cora and Jerry at their post.

"Ah, now I can concede this hand with honor. No nighttime prowlers to report," Jerry said, tossing a fan of cards on the table.

"Quiet has ruled, although I need to tell Betty I heard a few mice in the walls. Dee made us more strong coffee. It's in the carafe over there." Cora nodded toward the buffet table, straightening and shuffling the deck.

"I've been thinking, though," Jerry continued, "about Paul's story."

"What's wrong with it," Chad asked sharply, displaying a keen interest. I suspected that came more from an interest in Mariah than in Paul, directly.

Jerry caught the nuance in Chad's voice and answered cautiously. "I'm not saying this is true, you understand, but it could be that revealing Mariah's relationship to him, after killing the judge for revenge, could provide him with a great psychological alibi. He's now convinced us that he had no motive. But if he were cruel enough to kill, why would he care if Mariah knew she was his sister?"

"Convoluted reasoning, but a valid point, I think," Cora said.

I could see that Chad didn't like this line of thought, but he was tactful enough not to challenge Jerry. Instead, he threw out a topic for discussion. "All right, if it wasn't any of us, or Jimmie's family, or Mariah— I won't believe she did it— who's left? Who makes a valid suspect?"

"Fair enough question," Jerry responded. "I think Branson's a dark horse. The judge's track record with husbands is not good, according to Paul. We have only Bran's word for the acceptable quality of their marriage."

"And only his word for the last time Viviette was alive, as well," I pointed out.

"Samson sneaks around the entire property without being

noticed," Chad said. "I don't like him much."

"He does seem unnecessarily surly," Cora agreed, "but we don't know anything at all about him yet. Perhaps we should ask the Farnsworths how he came to work here."

"If he knew the judge was coming before he was hired, that would be a point to consider," I said.

"Earl, Doreen, and Paul have strong motives relating to vengeance, at least at certain points in the past," Jerry said. "What about Ray and Jessi, Chad? You seem to have become friends with them."

"Yeah, they're angry, that's for sure. But they're young, and the business is bouncing back. Losing a few dollars selling skis is not like having your kids hurt. I don't see them as killers," Chad said.

"Me neither." I kept silent about what the Crocketts had told me. None of it struck me as important, except maybe seeing Frank. "How well do you know Frank and Betty?" I asked Jerry and Cora.

"Only professionally," Jerry answered. "There's lots of room in a lifetime to find reasons to hate someone, and we know the judge seemed to make it a point to torment anyone she could. We need to hear more from them. After all, they invited her here in the first place."

I laughed, recalling Betty's Christmas story. "Little tiny Viviette holding up the mistletoe over her neighbors. Maybe that was the last time she was nice to anyone."

"We'll pass the watch to you," Jerry said, standing. "Wake us if you need help."

"Oh, wait," Cora said. "What about Harry and Belinda?"

"Now there's an odd couple," Chad said.

"Could there be something malignant behind their crediting the judge for bringing them together?"

"They are pretty tight with Frank and Betty," I said. "I've seen them talking. And Belinda was saying something about rare coins or gold, or something. She shut up fast when she saw me."

Cora pulled the hairpins that held her braids in a coil around her head, and they fell loose around her shoulders. "Interesting.

There's more going on there than meets the eye."

"Go get some rest," Chad said. "We're on guard now, and we don't have nearly enough information to really accuse anyone."

"And the guilty party— or pair— knows that," I said.

42

Chad and I settled in to spend the early hours of December twenty-sixth on high alert for something to happen, something we could not predict. We started playing cards, but tired of that long before dawn.

I had brought the camera down with me and began pushing buttons to display on the screen the photographs I'd taken earlier. I assessed my work and decided I'd done a good job of picturing the body from all kinds of angles. Even though I hadn't gotten first reactions when the ballroom was opened, there were shots of each person as they'd stepped forward to look into the room. Belinda looked curious but horrified. Earl's eyes were hooded, making him appear suspicious. Or maybe I'd just caught him in the middle of a blink. Mariah's mouth was opened in an "O," and Chad's eyes angled to the side rather than into the ballroom. He must have been looking at Mariah. I showed him the snapshot, and he admitted it, laughing.

Cora looked annoyed and Jerry had a supercilious smile on his face. Doreen looked angry. The rest just seemed curious or even bored. There wasn't much one was going to be able to deduce from those pictures.

Around three-thirty Chad said, "Ma, can I ask you something?"

"Of course."

"Listening to all these people with broken marriages and sad lives... it makes me scared of thinking about finding a person to spend my life with. You and Dad didn't even last."

"People change. It's impossible to predict some of that," I said.

"Were you happy?"

"With Roger? Your father?"

"Yes."

I sighed deeply. These were memories I hadn't wanted to revive since moving to Forest County. But, this was my man-son, and he deserved answers. "We were wildly in love at first, and then we had you. Life was everything I had hoped for. You were adorable. Smart, too." I reached across and tweaked his cheek.

Chad wrinkled his nose.

"I don't know exactly what happened, but it was mostly after you went to college. Did things seem OK to you in high school?" I asked.

"You two were awesome parents. You were there for me, you didn't nag but checked up to be sure I wasn't prowling around getting in trouble..."

I raised my eyebrows in mock horror.

Chad laughed. "Oh yeah, I knew you operated under the 'trust but verify' principle. But I also knew it meant you cared. I could see that you and Dad weren't very close, but you didn't fight, not really."

"Yes, Roger started working more and more hours. He hit that stage where he felt as if his life wasn't going to amount to much. That really got to him. I think he decided we were in too much of a rut— that he needed to try something wild."

Chad held up a hand to stop me. "I know his choices have hurt you a lot. I've met Brian, and he's nothing special. I guess what I'm getting at is... how can we be sure we won't turn into some kind of horrible person later that seems beyond imagining now?"

"We can't, not really," I said. "But we can make choices today that will result in good consequences for tomorrow. And at every stage of our lives, when things change, we can meet new situations with more good choices. I'm beginning to think there is some divine help available to us as we learn that process."

"Seriously?"

I nodded my head. "And, I have to honestly say I think your dad made some poor choices, ones that destroyed our family."

"How are you dealing with it, Ma?"

How honest should I be? I could deflect the question back on Chad, but that would be evasive. I rubbed my eyes and took a deep breath. "I had a really hard time at first. I ran away up here to figure out if I was as repulsive a person as I felt like after Roger chose Brian. I was angry."

"I was, too," Chad admitted. "How could he do that to us? Just dump the people he'd promised to love for life."

I shook my head. I never had come up with an answer to that question. "I've made a new life here, and I'm very happy. Maybe I'm a country girl and never realized it because I was stuck in the suburbs."

"Would you ever want to get married again?"

"Right now, I don't think so. The independence I've discovered is wonderful. I'm enjoying making all the decisions without checking in with someone else."

"Not even me?" Chad teased.

"Yeah, I'll be sure to ask your permission if I fall in love." I winked

"Me, too," he winked back.

I grinned and pushed the cards across the table. "Your deal."

43

Six-thirty came, and Dee appeared in the kitchen with a sleepy Jimmie. I was awake but in sort of a trance-like stupor, and the banging of frying pans snapped me to attention. When I returned from the bathroom, the aromas of fresh coffee and sizzling bacon drew me to the kitchen.

"Good morning, Ana," Dee said. "Come share the first breakfast shift with us."

Jimmie wanted to know what had happened during the night.

"Not a darned thing," Chad said, finger combing his hair as he entered the kitchen.

I heard the creak of the main staircase and poked my head around the corner in time to see Ray and Jessi coming into the dining room from the foyer. I realized this would be the perfect time for someone to slip away. We'd all assume footsteps and banging doors were ordinary wake-up sounds.

"Jessi and I have decided we should try to ski out for help. Right after breakfast," Ray said. "The wind has died down again. Does anyone know how far we'd need to go to find a house with a land line or a road that will be open and have traffic?"

Frank entered from the utility room. He must have come through the basement passage. "Better than five miles to the highway. It's not that far as the crow flies, but you have to go south and west to Kirtland Road to reach a bridge that crosses the river."

"If it's frozen we can ski across," Jessi said.

Frank headed for the coffee pot. "Better not. The current keeps the ice soft. Trust me. We don't need any more fatalities."

"Five miles isn't that much, though. We've skied farther than that lots of times," Jessi said.

"On groomed trail," Ray admitted. "But I'm sure we can do it."

Chad spoke up. "You'd better not leave unless everyone agrees to it. Surely the plows will be out today."

"Definitely," Frank said.

"What's this? Who's leaving?" Earl's voice barked across the room.

Ray explained his plan.

Earl took in everyone with his response. "Nope. They don't get to walk away that easy. We haven't heard about them and the Vivisectionist yet. How do we know they won't just thumb a ride and keep going."

Jessi rolled her eyes and slammed a piece of bread into the toaster.

Dee and Jimmie had set up the buffet for a mostly help-yourself breakfast, but were cooking the eggs to order.

"Two, over easy," Earl said.

Before nine o'clock, I was dozing in one of the comfortable front room chairs. Everyone had straggled down to breakfast by that time.

"We're going to hear the rest of the stories," I heard Branson snarl. "I don't care how long it takes; I want to know why you each disliked Viviette." Apparently he'd changed his mind about hearing it all. Were Gemini inconsistent? I had no idea.

"So you can decide who to hate most?" Doreen shot back.

Coming awake slowly, I listened to the conversations. Tempers were short, and no one was willing to let any person, or couple, take off on their own. There were threats of physical restraint.

Ray's voice rose above the rest. "O well, I suppose talking it out is better than more board games. Let's get it over with. We'll go next."

Although I was technically awake, my brain wasn't fully engaged. My mind drifted as Ray and Jessi told their story, minus the parts they had told me in private. At the end, they confirmed what Chad had said: the business was recovering, and they emphatically stated they weren't going to risk their futures by committing a murder. If they were still truly angry with anyone it was the competitor who kept playing the recording of the judge's negative comments. I didn't hear any new information.

Chad must have seen me struggling to wake up. He brought me a fresh cup of coffee. The smell alone was heavenly.

Bran was running the show. "Did you know that a huge percentage of serial killers are Cancers? Maybe we should check birthdates."

"Get real, man," Ray said. "That stuff is one step away from alchemy and hocus-pocus."

But Bran commanded, "Belinda, Harry, you're next."

"You go first," Belinda said to her husband. "Your case was before mine."

"By my whopping fifteen minutes of fame," Harry guffawed. "Yeah, I didn't like that woman, even though it's how Belinda and I met." Then his voice sobered. "She didn't have to have Sparky destroyed. Most of you have heard how she found me negligent for the dog bite, and I had to pay for that kid's medical bills. But she could have just ordered me to keep the dog fenced or chained. Other than that, I didn't know her at all."

"And we'll always be so grateful we found each other, all because our cases were heard on the same show." Belinda patted Harry on a wide knee.

He winced. "Careful, lover, that's the sore one."

"Your turn," Branson prompted the simpering woman, not giving anyone a breather.

"Oh, well... such a small thing. It could have gone either way in any court. Judge Viviette didn't single me out. My situation was so ordinary. I had rental properties and this man had done a great deal of damage in his apartment. He moved out and I sealed the door and claimed the things he left behind to compensate for the expenses. The judge ruled that he could have his belongings. Hardly a big deal. Happens every day."

"So you had nothing against her?" Jerry asked

Belinda looked offended. "No, of course not."

Something about that story was off. "Tell us about the gold coins you've been whispering about," I said.

"Oh, just a collection I used to have," Belinda answered

quickly, but her face colored.

The coffee had brought my mind into focus. "No, I don't think it's that simple," I said. "Your gift— those chocolate coins— it looked so innocent, but it upset you. Every other embarrassing present had something to do with Viviette."

Belinda must have wanted to cover her reaction, but it was no good. Her eyes flew to Harry for support, and her shoulders drooped.

44

"What the hey," Harry said, his face full of resignation. "Go ahead and tell 'em. You haven't done anything illegal, and it's not like we're ever going to find the blasted things."

"Oh, Harry, do you really think so? I still have my hopes up. We must be close."

"You're just sounding suspicious, lover. Better tell."

This exchange had caused people to perk up in anticipation of a juicy story no one had yet heard.

"Well, if you say so, but you do it, Harry," Belinda said.

"Nah. The beginning is all yours. You start."

Belinda perched her large behind on the front of the chair. Today she wore a denim kaftan with navy blue beads decorating the bodice. They sparkled as her chest heaved, and she clasped and unclasped her pudgy hands. "All right. See, it began by accident. I owned a boring little four-flat complex, and tenants came and went. I'd always been interested in buried treasure, ever since I read *Treasure Island* when I was nine. Then Casper J. McKay rented a room. The J stands for Janes."

"Oh ho!" Doreen said, "I know where this is going. I read the tabloids, too."

Paul groaned. "I can't tolerate those rags. Is there going to be something of substance here, or just rumors?"

"Hold your horses," Harry cautioned Paul.

"There's more than rumors, I assure you," Belinda continued. "At first, I didn't think anything at all about his name. But then we come to the day the pipes burst. Casper was at work, and I had to unlock his apartment to let the repairmen in. Lying in plain sight on the table was a vast coin collection. I threw an afghan over it so no one else could see, but after the men left I went back and took pictures, just for my own curiosity."

Dee grinned at me and wiggled her eyebrows as if to say, "I knew it!"

Earl sniggered. "Of course, *you've* done nothing wrong."

Belinda gave Earl a dark look and smoothed her skirt. "I'd read the story about the Janes' lost fortune, the one Doreen must have seen, too. It took me a while but I found a copy. This was before everything was on line. The Janes family moved here from Ohio, and the mythical treasure was supposed to be a portion of the tons of gold that was lost in 1758 while it was being transported from Pittsburg to Detroit. The French buried it to keep the British from finding it."

"I know that story," Chad put in. "They buried it along the Tuscarawas Trail, but almost all the Frenchmen were killed, and it was never found. People are still hunting."

"That was Fort Duquesne and Fort Detroit back then," Harry clarified.

"Yes, yes, I can never remember how to say that French name," Belinda fluttered. "Looks like Dookeznee to me. Anyway, there was a list of the coins known to have been part of that treasure. I bought a book with pictures and some of the list matched the pictures I'd taken. Casper wasn't exactly a model renter. He really did all kinds of damage to the woodwork and even cracked the bathroom sink. So, when he moved out and left all his stuff, even though he said he'd be back for it, I had to give it a try. He had no more right to that gold than anyone else. I changed the lock and filed a claim."

"Which Judge Viviette denied, so you lost a lot, not just an everyday security deposit issue," Ray concluded.

"Well, I didn't lose it, since I never had it. It was just a shot in the dark," Belinda huffed.

My wheels were turning. "But someone besides you knew about Casper, unless those chocolate candy coins were from Harry."

"Or maybe the gifts were all from you," Cora waggled a finger in Belinda's direction. "Setting yourself up as a fellow victim is a classic way to divert suspicion onto others."

Belinda looked horrified. "I didn't! Really, I didn't. I don't know who was responsible for those gifts. I brought the popcorn." She covered her mouth as if she'd just revealed some calamitous secret.

Betty sighed. "It doesn't matter who brought which silly gift to exchange. It's obvious the person who provided the unwelcome packages isn't going to 'fess up."

"How did they get here?" Jessi asked.

"They came by UPS on Monday. All boxed with names on them. I just wrapped them in the pretty paper to match the tree," Betty said.

"Oh, I'm so confused. You tell the rest, Harry." Belinda grabbed a tissue and dabbed at her forehead. It seemed a bit over-dramatic to me.

"Yeah, OK... Well, Viviette did find out. We were never sure how. Maybe McKay told her why he needed his belongings returned— that their worth was way more than what he owed Belinda. She threatened to pull Belinda's housing business license if she ever saw her in court again. But we did fall in love; that's not just a cover for a treasure hunt."

"And Frank and Betty also knew about the coins," I said. "I heard the four of you talking about them."

Branson jumped to his feet. "I don't think you're telling the truth. How could Viviette know about that? You're just climbing on the bandwagon with everyone else to give her a bad name."

"Think what you like, Mr. Owens," Harry said, suddenly turning formal. "The rest of the story has nothing to do with your wife, so why would we make that up? Casper McKay was killed in a construction accident the following summer, and the treasure never turned up in his estate. So he must have stashed it somewhere. He was some cousin, umpteen times removed, to Henry Casper Janes, who built this mansion and the mill, and this seems as likely a place as anywhere for him to have hidden it. The house was empty back then. When Frank and Betty bought it, we asked if we could search around the property."

"But we didn't feel as if we needed to tell the world what we might find," Frank added. "And if Ana heard us talking about the coins, anyone might have. So that doesn't eliminate a single person from providing that gift."

My face felt hot, but then it hit me. "Sure it does. Nobody overheard you talking and then went out to buy something. Every one of the 'bad' gifts was in place before we arrived. They had to have come from a person who'd seen the guest list and already knew all these stories. How many people could that possibly be?"

45

"It could be you, Branson... Viviette might have told you about all of us," Betty cried in alarm.

"I agree," Earl said. "Who else would be able to find out all this information?"

Bran put his head in his hands and rocked from side to side. "You've got it all wrong. I had no idea who was coming to this party. Maybe Viviette did, but she certainly didn't share that information with me. I'm no fan of social gatherings, and I wish I'd paid attention to that part of my horoscope. I never should have come. With the betrayal of Mercury, any silly accident can cause serious problems."

Frank said, as if Branson hadn't just made an impassioned speech, "'Silly accident?' That's how you characterize her death? It seems to me this would be a perfect way to cover up getting rid of an inconvenient wife... lots of other people around who didn't like her who would also be under suspicion. A person could actually get away with murder."

"I'm a Gemini, remember?" Earl protested. "We don't kill people, we talk."

Chad asserted himself as the leader again. "Look, accusing each other isn't going to solve anything. Where's Samson? We haven't heard from him yet."

Sam stepped from the shadows of the elevator alcove where he'd been lurking. He wore a greasy brown coverall. It was unsnapped from collar to waist and curly hairs protruded above a stained red v-neck t-shirt . "I'm just the handyman, and I don't know anything about that lady. If I'd known it was a bunch of crazies coming to this party, I'd have quit a week ago."

He would have sounded more convincing if his physique was less menacing. His muscular, blocky body and pinched features gave him a classic gangster look.

"I don't believe Sam had anything to do with this." Betty came to her employee's defense. "We hired him through an ad we ran in the paper last summer. He could hardly have been planning ahead for a crime that would have taken months to set up, at a party he didn't know would be given."

Sam perked up. "Yeah. That's right. And I'm not even from around here. I grew up in New Jersey. Cantcha tell from the way I talk? I moved here last year to live with my cousin."

"So, who's left?" Earl asked. "We haven't heard from our gracious host and hostess yet." The words were polite, but there were teeth in Earl's tone.

Betty was horrified. "You don't think we'd throw a party and kill one of the guests."

"That would be economic suicide for the business," Frank added. "As it is, this disaster isn't exactly going to be something we can use in an ad campaign."

"Well, I'm an Aries," Earl declared. "Not that I believe in Bran's zodiac claptrap, but I've read that we're a suspicious lot. And I am. Better tell us more about how you knew the judge."

Frank lifted his hands in a gesture of surrender. "Fair enough, I guess. But there's nothing very sinister to tell. Our families grew up on the same street, just like we said the other night. Betty, Viviette, and me were in grade school together, although Betty was younger."

"She did pick on me because I was smaller," Betty said, "but she picked on everyone. Our houses were right in a row, and so we ended up spending a lot of time together. Frank beat her up to defend me once, and she didn't bully me after that. We became friends."

"So, you have a history of violence toward Viviette," Bran said quietly.

"Damn it, man, you are getting too pushy," Frank blustered. "We were little kids. I suppose you never got in a sidewalk fight?"

Bran smiled and looked smug, "Like I said, I'm a Gemini."

Chad tried to bring us back to the story and a calmer emotional state. "And you've stayed in contact with her throughout your lives?" he prompted.

Frank responded. "We have. It's not like we were bosom buddies, but Viviette felt as if she could talk to us. She didn't have very many friends."

"Yeah, I can't imagine why," Doreen said dryly.

"Knock it off," Branson ordered through tight lips.

"And sometimes she was there for us, too," Betty said. "It's true that she was prickly, but she wasn't completely without compassion."

"Oh, yes," Belinda put in. "Tell them about your baby."

Betty certainly did not look happy at this suggestion, and since I hadn't heard a word about the Farnsworth's having a child, I guessed it was not a pleasant memory.

"A very sad time in our lives," Frank said, but he was still generalizing, not giving any specifics.

"It's probably time to share, even if it's painful," Cora prodded gently.

"We... we had a little girl, but she died before she was a week old. She had a terrible defect..." Betty faltered and stopped.

"Now you've upset the woman," Frank grumbled. "Viviette was supportive to Betty through that time. We don't like to think about it very much, as you can well imagine. That's all."

"And, I say it's enough talk," Harry said. "As predicted, no one confessed to killing the judge. What a surprise."

Sam came up with the best suggestion. "How about all of you men come grab a shovel? Even if the county gets down our road today, we've got to open up a lane north of their turnaround. Let's do something productive before somebody spazzes out."

"Sounds good to me," Branson said, standing. "I'm tired of this inactivity."

"You girls have to stick together," Ray reminded us. "Nobody goes off alone."

Doreen groaned, "Whatever. Does anyone want to ski?"

"Some exercise sounds great. I'm sick of sitting around," Jessi said. "Let's go."

"Could you tolerate a slower companion?" Cora asked.

Jessi threw an arm around Cora's shoulders and steered her

toward the main door. "Absolutely. Let's get out of here. Too much doom and gloom."

I headed for the kitchen.

46

Dee was opening a canned ham while Beth drained tins of pineapple.

"Look what we found in the pantry," Jimmie said. This will make a great meal without using so much propane because it's already cooked. We only have to heat it up. Ham and pineapple with some hot cheesy biscuits and green beans." He was balancing multiple cans of the vegetables in his arms and managed to set them on the counter without any rolling to the floor.

I heard a faint rumbling sound, and suddenly Lindsey's head popped out of a hole in the wall.

"What the...?" I said.

Jimmie and Beth laughed. "She thinks the dumb waiter is the greatest invention of the century," Beth said.

"Not this century," Jimmie clarified.

"Every time she doesn't have a job to do she gives herself rides," Beth complained "But we're too big to fit."

I suspected Beth wouldn't have been so critical if she'd been able to enjoy the small elevator herself.

"Come look," Lindsey called to me.

As she uncurled and hopped to the floor, I stepped over to look at the dumb waiter. It was larger than I expected, and the reason I hadn't noticed it before was that there was a vertical sliding door that looked like an ordinary cupboard when it was closed.

"See this rope that goes up the side? You just pull on it, hand over hand, and you can make the whole thing go up or down," Lindsey said. "It's easy. Even with something in it. Like me."

"Up? Upstairs?" I asked.

"Yes, I think it goes to that big room that we all went to see last night."

"The ballroom? That makes sense. I'm sure they served food at parties. You've been walking around up there?" I was dismayed. If the girl had been tracking through that room after we'd carefully locked it, we couldn't claim to have protected any evidence.

"No, 'cause I couldn't get out into the room. The door is locked from the other side, or nailed shut or something. I go up till it won't go any farther and then I come down again. Just for fun."

"Good, I'm glad to hear you haven't been in there, Lindsey. We need to have everyone stay out of that room," I said.

"OK. But I can get into the basement. The first time I did it, I ran around and came up the stairs. I sure scared Mom." Lindsey pointed at Dee and giggled.

"Yes, you did," Dee said. "Now it's time to stop fooling around and help us. I need you to see if there are any maraschino cherries in the pantry. Those pretty bright red ones. Do you know the kind I mean?"

"I know," Lindsey said with a flounce, and scampered toward the pantry which was part of the utility room.

I followed the girl. "Lindsey," I said. "Have you seen anyone in the basement who looked like they were doing something they shouldn't have been?"

"Uh, huh." She giggled again and put a finger to her lips. "That man, the fat one. He's been in the basement a lot."

"Mr. Farnsworth, the one who owns the house?"

"Of course not. I know him. The other one."

I was suddenly very concerned for Lindsey's safety. "Mr. Hack, Harry Hack? Lindsey, does he know you were watching him?"

"I guess that's his name. But he never saw me. I just sat curled up in the dumb waiter and watched. What's the big deal?" She located the cherries and started back to the kitchen.

I put a hand on her arm. "Wait. Let's keep this our secret. What did you see Mr. Hack doing? Was he going to the exercise room?"

"Nope. He wasn't ever doing anything interesting. He went up and down the stone hallway a bunch of times, that's all."

"But, he looked like he was doing something secret? That's

what I asked about."

"I don't know. But he did keep looking back, like he didn't want anyone to know he was there. That's part of the reason I kept still. It was a little scary. I'd better take these to Mom," Lindsey said.

She ran back to the kitchen, clutching two jars of the cherries. I stayed where I was and thought about this new information. Maybe it was important to try to find out when the girl had seen Harry. And I certainly needed to keep her from telling anyone else what she'd observed. It wasn't a sure thing that the man was up to no good, but what she had described to me didn't sound completely innocent.

Glancing at the washing machine, I realized the bathrooms and towels hadn't been attended to this morning. I shook my head and decided I wasn't going to worry about it. Maybe I could take care of them after lunch. Maybe not. With everything that had happened, it was hard to care.

I went back to the kitchen and spoke to Dee. "May I borrow Lindsey for a few minutes? I want her to help me with something."

"No problem, Ana. This meal is really simple."

Lindsey skipped across the room and followed me down the stairs to the basement.

"Show me where the dumb waiter comes down," I said.

"Over here."

She led me to the opposite wall and pointed to an open hatch that did not have any kind of door or cover. The control ropes fed through holes on the side, but other than that it simply looked like a deep recessed shelf. I probably could have figured out the location without the girl's help, but I wanted to talk with her alone.

"Lindsey, I want you to promise me something," I said, kneeling down and taking the girl by the shoulders.

"Sure, Ana. Why do you look so serious?"

"You know that a very bad thing happened here yesterday, right?"

"Yes that lady was killed," she said, frowning. "I think that's sad, although everybody talks about her like she wasn't very nice. And mom says she was the judge that sent us to live with my dad for a while, but I don't remember her."

"She hurt a lot of people. Some of that was because of her job, but she seems to have enjoyed being a bully, too."

"Yeah, there's a girl at school like that. I just try to stay out of her way."

"Sometimes that's a really good idea," I said. "I think that's what you should do here. Don't tell anyone you saw Mr. Hack in the basement. Just keep that between you and me."

"OK," she said.

"Lindsey, did you see anything else, anything at all that was strange?"

"I saw someone in the ballroom."

"What? I thought you said you couldn't get in there?"

"I can't," she gave her head an impatient little shake. "But there's a crack beside the door. Yesterday before we served lunch I was riding up and down, and I looked through because I heard a noise."

Trying to keep my voice even so I wouldn't alert the girl that this was potentially a critical piece of news, I asked, "And what did you see?"

"I couldn't see much at all. But there was someone there, walking across the room, real slow, like they were moving something heavy."

"Could you identify who it was?" I held my breath waiting for her answer.

"Nope. The crack is too tiny. All I could tell is that they had on something red."

47

Red? It was Christmas when Viviette was killed. Nearly everyone had been wearing something red. Even I had worn a red sweatshirt with snowmen on the front. Bran's ski jacket, hat and those deadly poles were bright red. Frank had been wearing a red corduroy shirt. Belinda's gaudy sweater was mostly red, and Harry's shirt was red plaid. Mariah had worn a black sweater over red leggings. Betty had been dressed as Mrs. Claus before lunch, a role her looks were perfectly suited for, except when she was caught with an incongruent cigarette dangling from her lips. What had Earl been wearing? For a moment I couldn't remember. Then a mental picture of him swam into focus. He'd had on a gray shirt with a maroon sweater vest. Not bright red, but still red, especially if viewed through a narrow crack. Even Samson had a red t-shirt.

I took Lindsey back upstairs and called Dee into the utility room.

"We're going to tell your mother what you saw in the ballroom, but no one else. Not Beth, not Jimmie, or anyone," I said.

"Gosh, Ana. What's going on?" Dee asked.

I pulled the two of them into the small half bath, shut the door, and pushed the lock button. In that cramped but private space I told Dee what Lindsey had seen upstairs. I wasn't nearly so concerned about Harry's behavior in the basement. That was a public space, and perhaps he just liked the semi-privacy of that passage.

"As her mother, you need to know this, but no one else can hear it until someone official gets here. Do you understand?" I asked. I didn't want frighten Lindsey by openly saying that she was in danger.

But Dee caught my meaning at once. "Lindsey, I want you to

stop playing in that dumb waiter."

"Aw, Mom..."

"I don't think you have to go that far," I said. "In fact, don't do anything that is a change from how you've been acting. But, remember the 'rules' that we all have. No one goes anywhere alone. In fact, I think you shouldn't go anywhere without an adult."

Lindsey was happy to have me take her side about the dumb waiter, but didn't like having it pointed out that she was a child.

"What about Jimmie? Is he grown up enough?"

Dee answered, "Yes, I think it would be all right for you to be with Jimmie. He's strong." She looked at me for confirmation.

I nodded, hoping I was right, but it wouldn't do if the killer became suspicious the girl had knowledge that was a danger to him or her. Technically, one or more of us was supposed to stay with Jimmie's family, but it wasn't turning out to be practical.

"You two are acting weird," Lindsey said, unlocking the bathroom door.

I found Mariah sitting in the front room. No lights had been turned on. The fire had not been kindled this morning, and the room was dim and chilly. She was in one of the easy chairs, with knees pulled up and her arms wrapped around her legs. Her face was partially hidden behind her knees. Betty and Belinda were in the library, chatting quietly.

"How are you doing?" I asked her.

Mariah sighed deeply and looked up at me. "I don't know." She swept her long bangs away from her eyes. "I'd like to go upstairs and have time to think, alone. But we aren't supposed to do that. At least those two aren't right here in the same room." She tossed her head in the direction of the library.

"Want to tell me about it?" I asked.

"It's just that in the course of a few minutes last night my entire perception of my personal reality was altered."

"I'm sure that's troubling." I hoped to encourage her to talk to me.

"For the first time, I think I understand how some of the kids

I work with must feel. Sure, I grew up without a mom, but she had died. It wasn't like she didn't want me and left us. But, now, everything I thought was true isn't."

"Everything?" I asked.

"OK, not everything. Dad, Paul— I don't know what to call him— loves me. He's always taken care of me. But I don't even know who I am any more," she said.

"My guess is, he was feeling pretty emotional about how his mother, and yours, went off the tracks. Then, once he'd made a decision about adopting you as his child, he couldn't change his mind."

"I know he was trying to protect me," Mariah said. "So many of the kids I work with don't have anyone who cares a fig about them, but they come to school and tell me about a new 'uncle' who has moved in, or they find out their cousin is really their brother. They get their chains yanked all the time. That's how I feel. My chain just got yanked." She stared at the unlit Christmas tree, but her face looked blank.

"Do you think you can survive this?"

"Oh, of course." Mariah looked at me, and her eyes were warm and damp. "If eight-year-olds can survive trauma and neglect and come up smiling, I should be able to make it through this shift in identity. I mean, is anyone really going to care if I'm Paul's daughter or sister? I guess I'm both. Once I work through it all, maybe I'll be a better teacher." She straightened her legs, stretched, and smiled at me.

"I'm pretty sure you are going to be a great teacher," I said.

Although an entire room away, we heard a thunderous stamping of feet on the porch and the scraping of metal and plastic blades as shovels were stacked against the outside wall. The men began to come in from the foyer to the dining room. Even Harry had been outside, although I wondered how much actual work he'd done.

"Smells great," Frank said. "Ham?"

"When's lunch," Earl asked simultaneously, unwinding a scarf from his neck.

"As soon as the girls come in from skiing," Dee said, pushing open the pass through. "We just put biscuits in the oven."

I glanced toward the library, but Betty and Belinda were no longer there. They must have left quietly while I was talking with Mariah.

48

Rivulets of sand cascading through the darkness. An hourglass of memories. No shadows now. *Shadows are revealed only in the light. Tenebrae, my friend. Mine.* She drew a bag from beneath the loose earth.

49

The men seemed unexpectedly happy about something, and we didn't have to wait long to learn what that was all about.

"We punched a footpath through to the bridge," Frank announced. "It's not quite as far as we're supposed to clear, but we stuck an orange marker flag at the end, and spray-painted HELP on the snow."

"In really big day-glo letters," Ray clarified.

"Hopefully, if the county comes down the road they'll see the message and cut us some slack. The bridge probably won't hold the county plow, but if they would even come up to the bridge that would be great. We'll try to widen the cut to a car width after we eat," Frank added.

"It is easier to shovel after the first pass," Jerry admitted, "but I'm not sure how much more you'll be able to get out of us older guys." He folded himself into the chair Mariah had vacated, pulled out a handkerchief and blew his nose, which was red from the cold.

Jessi and Doreen, with Cora a few steps behind, came through from the kitchen. Cora joined Jerry and me in the front room.

We chatted, killing time until lunch. "I don't understand why there's no passage from the utility room to the foyer," Cora grumbled. "Dee wasn't exactly happy that we tracked through the kitchen, and I can't say as I blame her."

"Maybe there used to be," I said. "It's all closets on the walls that must be back to back. Betty probably wanted more space for guest's coats."

Cora continued to fuss. "One door width wouldn't have taken much space. The foyer is large enough. I suppose it would have offended Betty's superb sense of architectural unity."

This comment set my mind in motion, comparing houses. I'd

178

rescued a house just slightly younger than this one, although far less handsome. But my focus had been on functionality. Cora and Jerry's place in Cherry Hill was a lovely Victorian home, however it was much smaller than this rambling mansion. I knew Cora could be content either with the luxury Jerry could afford, or with much less. I recalled the warm atmosphere of the vintage cabin where she'd formerly lived. Betty, however, seemed to be all about the decor; she'd been so determined to explain each of the themed bedrooms to us. She and Frank were in the process of transforming this palatial home into a genuine showcase of Victorian grandeur. The fantastic modernization of the utility systems might have been Frank's doing, rather than Betty's, but the whole project made me discount them as serious suspects in Viviette's murder. It seemed unlikely they would jeopardize this expensive undertaking that wasn't yet completed. Of course, murderers seldom thought they would be caught. Then, too, the Farnsworth's were the judge's friends. Where was their motive? Motive. Who most wanted Viviette gone? I still had no idea.

Jimmie called from the dining room, "Lunch is served."

Those of us who were in the sitting room rose to head for the buffet just as the nearby roar of a snowmobile assaulted our ears. I ran to a front window and pulled back the drapes.

"It's Sam. He's taking off."

"Drat that boy," Frank exploded.

"He must have found some gas." Cora pointed out the obvious.

"Or he lied to us before," Branson said. "He's a shifty sort of fellow. I wouldn't doubt if he's the culprit. He'll be gone to New Jersey or anywhere he wants before we ever get away from this wretched place. He must be a Pices."

Betty lost her temper. Her normally cute and doll-like features turned dark, and her eyes narrowed to slits. "Wretched!" she screamed. "Wretched? You watch your tongue. We throw the best party of the season, and some fool ruins everything by committing the most dastardly act possible against a friend of ours, and you have the nerve to call us wretched?"

"Oh, for Pete's sake," Bran countered. "Not you or your precious house. Just the circumstances. Forget it; let's eat." He grabbed a plate and forked a slice of meat onto it with considerable violence.

From watching body language I could tell that everyone was thoroughly tired of the animosity. People openly avoided Branson as they silently filed to the table to help themselves to ham and pineapple and the delicious fresh biscuits. No one joined him at the table where he sat hunched with his back to the room.

I was closest to the widower and from the corner of my eye saw a tear drip from his cheek and splash on the tabletop. He muttered, "Venus sextile Jupiter. This was supposed to be a great month for parties and making love. What went wrong? What?"

Leaning across to Jerry and Cora, who were sitting with me, I whispered. "Do you think Sam is guilty?"

"I doubt it," Jerry said, also *sotto voce*. He's probably gone for help. I don't think he liked to be ordered around very much, and being forced to work with us wasn't his style."

"Yes, I got that feeling, too," I said. "He wasn't happy that I was doing housekeeping. Not that I've done any today." I lifted an eyebrow and grinned.

"The bathrooms are fine," Cora soothed. "No one here is a pig."

Feeling as if we couldn't continue in this atmosphere of ceaseless tension much longer, I asked my friends, "Look, I've found out that Harry was prowling around in the basement— in that dismal stone passage for the staff. Should I challenge him on it? Maybe we can break something loose."

"Good idea," Jerry said.

Cora craned her head around, perhaps to locate Harry. "Where's Belinda?" she asked. "Actually, I don't see Betty either."

"That might be good. Call him out when he doesn't have Belinda to run interference," Jerry put in.

"How did you learn he's been spending time in the cellar?" Cora asked.

"Lindsey saw him. More than once," I whispered.

"Oh, dear," Cora said, reaching up to twiddle her fingers nervously in the gray braids wrapped around her head.

"Exactly," I replied.

"Let me try it," Jerry suggested. "I'm farther removed from the source of the information."

I nodded.

Jerry pushed back his chair and cleared his throat. "In light of the fact that Sam has disappeared— perhaps to summon help, or possibly for purposes of his own— we need to work even harder to be more transparent with each other. This constant suspicion could lead to another unfortunate incident, and no one wants that to happen. I will begin by adding a little more to my own story."

"Nobody thinks you killed Viviette," Chad said.

"Nevertheless, I think a frank and open attitude is called for," Jerry went on. "I mentioned that I knew the judge in college, and that she started some gossip about me. What she said got me in a lot of hot water back then. I confess that I was not happy at all to discover she and I would need to share the same house for a few days at this party. You need to recall that we were at university in the sixties. She accused me of using marijuana, a common but serious offense at that time. I had difficulty shaking that rumor, and it prevented me from being hired at the *Chicago Trib*."

"But you had the *Herald*," Earl said.

"Yes, but that wasn't my first choice. It was due to Viviette that I ended up coming home and working on my family paper. In the long run, I've never regretted it, but for many years I harbored a great deal of ill will toward Ms. Velvet as she climbed the career ladder that was her first choice."

"I'm so glad you stayed local," Cora murmured.

"Now, I'd like to hear from Harry Hack," Jerry continued, turning to face the man. "It's been reported that you were seen prowling around in the staff passage of the basement. I suspect most of us didn't even know of the existence of that hallway. So maybe you'd share what you were doing there."

<h1 style="text-align:center">50</h1>

Harry lumbered to his feet awkwardly, favoring his sore knee and yelling, "What are you implying?"

"The rest of us had to explain our every move, so get on with it, Hack." Earl raised a level hand to his forehead. "And I salute the officers of our own little kangaroo court-martial."

"Better can the indignant posture, Harry. It's a legitimate question," Frank said. "And, of course, I knew you were down there. It's no big deal, in light of what you told us last night."

Harry's eyes darted around the room. If he was hunting for Belinda, he was out of luck. She and Betty had still not appeared for lunch. His face fell as he realized he'd either have to explain himself or at least come up with a believable lie. He'd probably need to communicate that to Belinda quickly. I was certain that whatever they were up to, they were in it together.

"You're OK with me showing them?" Harry asked Frank, mysteriously.

"You said last night that you didn't find anything," Frank replied.

"All right, who wants to come see the original basement of this house?" Harry asked, wadding up his paper napkin and throwing it on the table. It bounced and fell to the floor.

I certainly wanted to follow Harry downstairs, but not everyone was as enthusiastic.

"We already know the ballroom is the place one should avoid being associated with," Branson said without even turning to look at us. "I, for one, don't care what Harry was doing in the basement."

In the end, only Frank, Cora, Jerry, Chad, Mariah, and I followed Harry.

As we passed through the kitchen, Jimmie decided to tag

along, too. Not wanting to miss anything, we all tried to crowd close to Harry as we descended.

"Back off," he ordered, with a certain amount of menace. "There's nothing to see yet."

Turning into the stone corridor, Harry pushed the button that flooded the dark rocks with blinding light. We continued behind our guide, squinting against the glare.

We reached the end of the hallway where the back stairs rose to the first floor. On our left was the small alcove where I'd caught Sam smoking. Harry stepped into this space. He ran his hands over the stones, but with his back to us, we couldn't really tell what he was doing. Suddenly, the entire back wall of the alcove slid quietly away from Harry. There was only the slight sound of wheels rolling in a track. The stones had been carefully fitted so the corners appeared normal, but in actuality the movable section was not mortared to the rest of the wall.

"Watch your step," Harry said, " sidling around the displaced stones and snapping on a small flashlight.

"Wow!" Jimmie whispered in my ear. "Just like a pirate movie."

Harry must have heard the comment. He turned around to face us, and backed up enough to make room for all of us. Then he began speaking as if we were simply on a tour of some historic structure, which, in a sense, we were.

"Yes, this might seem a bit like a pirate movie, but more accurately, a movie about a mill. This really isn't all that surprising, given the climate here. The Janes family simply wanted an easy way to get from the house to the mill, year round. It's probable the tunnel wasn't much of a secret when they lived here. But as the generations passed, people forgot. This first hallway is underneath the servant's quarters."

"This is fantastic!" Cora cooed. "How can it be possible I've never heard of the tunnel? Right here in Forest County."

"I doubt that anyone alive remembered it. Frank found the latch for the stone panel by accident and with a little Liquid Wrench and some grease got the mechanism working smoothly again. Well, anyway, we thought Casper Janes McKay might have known about it. Maybe heard the story from his grandfather or another relative."

"So you've been hunting in the tunnel for those coins, thinking he might have hidden them here?" Chad asked.

Harry spread his hands and nodded. "That's all there is to it. But we didn't find anything."

"How far does this go?" Jimmie asked. Even in the dim light, his eyes were sparkling with adventure.

"Supposedly all the way to the mill, although the passage is blocked by a cave-in farther ahead," Harry explained.

"Can we see? Didn't you dig it out? Maybe the treasure is on the other side." Jimmie's questions tumbled out eagerly.

Harry was starting to get fidgety. "No point to it. If we can't get through, Casper couldn't either. We're not searching for something Henry Janes hid. We don't even know if Casper was ever here. Let's go back."

But Cora was not so easily put off. "We've come down here to see the tunnel, and I think we should follow it all the way to the end. No disrespect meant, but we want to verify anything that's been said, when possible."

"Lady, you sure can be pushy, but all right," Harry conceded. "Anyone else got a flashlight? Once we get around the first bend, none of the light from this doorway will help a bit."

No one was even carrying a smart phone— and thus a light— since without service the phones were little more than paperweights. Chad ran upstairs to find a couple more flashlights, and Harry turned his off to save the batteries. There was enough spill from the main hallway that we weren't left in complete darkness.

We stood there quietly, surrounded by the chilly stones, waiting for Chad to return. I reached out to touch the oppressive walls. The rock was rough but dry, perhaps covered with mold or lichen. How many rocks had it taken to build this, I wondered, and how many men and horses to move them all into position nearly one-hundred-fifty years ago. Looking upward, in the faint light, I could make out wide beams that looked like railroad ties spanning the rock walls to form a roof. Why hadn't these rotted?

The faint odor of creosote answered my question.

We continued to wait. Mariah coughed; a few feet shuffled on the concrete floor.

At the far end, where we hadn't yet been, a faint light began to move and bob along the faces of the blackened rocks. A monstrous shadow bulged into view.

<h1 style="text-align:center">51</h1>

Mariah clutched at me, gasping, and Jerry moved protectively in front of Cora. Even Harry seemed surprised.

The shadow advanced until the flesh-and-blood body of Belinda revealed itself, attached to the dark menace. Betty walked behind, holding the flashlight. Belinda carried something, a satchel of some sort with a strap, but it seemed heavier than a purse. She was carefully watching her footing. The women were unaware they were being observed by an entire group of people.

Harry flicked on his flashlight.

Startled, Belinda looked up. She pivoted and pushed past Betty to return the way she had come. We heard her footsteps echoing down the passage.

Betty turned her head away, raising an arm to cover her face. "Who is that? Get your light out of my eyes."

"Sorry," Harry called, lowering his flashlight. "It's just me. Frank said I might as well show people the tunnel, since there's really nothing down here worth seeing. Where'd my wife go?"

It was Betty's turn to use her light to advantage. She played the beam slowly over each of our faces. "She'll be right back. She forgot something," Betty said as she walked slowly toward us. She was still keeping her light in our eyes. That had to be deliberate.

She reached Harry and physically turned him around, as if he were a child she were directing. Then she gave him a little push.

"What's up?" Harry asked.

"I understand what's happening here," Cora said with a voice as cold as the stones. "You've found something interesting. Belinda had some kind of bag. Did you actually find the coins?"

Mariah said, "Where did she run off to? She acted afraid of us."

"Perhaps she's afraid we'll steal the treasure from her," Cora suggested.

"That doesn't make sense," Jerry said thoughtfully. "I think I recall that the laws concerning old treasure recovery on land favor the person who discovered it, with some rights for the person on whose property it was found. Stealing it after we've all heard the story would be a non-starter."

"And with the road still closed there's no way to escape fast enough to disappear with the treasure, anyway," I added.

"Maybe she's known the coins were down here all along, but couldn't let on. Here she comes." Mariah pointed to the returning Belinda. "Let's ask her."

"What did you forget, Belinda?" Cora asked pointedly.

"Forget? Oh! I thought I dropped something, but I must have been mistaken. It's getting chilly down here. Denim isn't really warm enough. I'm going upstairs." She rubbed her arms and tried to elbow her way past us.

"Not so fast." Jerry grabbed her arm. "I suspect the French coins have been located, but this attempt to be coy strikes a false note with me. You could almost certainly establish a claim even if there were still living relatives of Henry Janes. In legal terms, Casper abandoned the treasure if he buried it here on property his family no longer owns. So there's something more going on."

Something stirred in my brain. Something I'd been told.

Frank raised his light again and played it over Belinda's face. "I think Jerry's right," he said. "How about this? Belinda and Harry had to get rid of Judge Viviette because she was threatening to throw some kind of monkey wrench in the works."

"What could she possibly do?" Belinda challenged. "Jerry just said we've got a good case." She twisted out of Jerry's grasp.

"I'm not sure," Frank said, "but there's something fishy here."

"You think I'm acting fishy? I smell rotten crappie all over you, and we're not even in Denmark," Belinda tossed back, mixing her idioms with ease.

Betty defended her husband. "What are you talking about? Frank's not the one who's trying to cover something up."

"Oh, I know things," Belinda said mysteriously. "Things like the results of your DNA tests."

"You can't possibly," Betty gasped. She nearly cowered under the force of her friend's words.

Belinda now had some kind of psychological advantage, although the rest of us were completely clueless as to what was happening. "You shouldn't leave papers lying around on your desk," she chided.

Betty's eyes narrowed and her apple-cheeked face contorted to look more like an apple-head doll that has started to go bad, "Lying around? I don't think so, you sneak thief. I thought you were my friend."

Frank stared at Belinda and then gave his wife a look that must have communicated something. Suddenly, Betty whirled around and began running down the hall, toward the mill. We had no time to recall that the end was supposedly blocked, because simultaneously Frank charged us and headed toward the house. He was large enough to knock Mariah and Jimmie off their feet, and they crashed into me. I stumbled into Jerry whose back banged against the stones as I fell against his chest.

"Oof," The air rushed from his lungs, and he slumped to the floor, the wind knocked out of him.

Cora reached to stop Frank, but she was too small to be effective. Harry was hard on Frank's heels. We heard them start up the stairs and then the sound of two bodies colliding, followed by a thump and a metallic patter as several objects hit the concrete and rolled.

"Hey," Chad yelled. "What's going on?"

Then there were more footsteps moving quickly away. Chad limped in to the midst of our disabled group. Jerry was just beginning to get his breath back, trying to suck in air, but unable to make a sound. He stumbled to his feet.

"Quick, after them," Cora pointed in the direction of the house. "Betty's trapped anyway."

Chad turned and ran back through the camouflaged opening in the stones and along the hallway toward the stairs. We followed with Jerry hobbling at the rear, still struggling to breathe.

<h1 style="text-align:center">52</h1>

As I reached the top of the steps, Chad was coming inside through the back door. "I checked to see if they ran outside this way, but there's no tracks in the snow," he yelled.

The kitchen was empty. Dee and the girls must have finished cleaning up. I ran through to the dining room where Ray, Doreen, and Jessi were playing a game.

"Where's Frank?" I demanded.

"Not here. We haven't seen him since you went downstairs." Doreen said in a languorous tone. "What's all the fuss?"

"What about Harry?"

"Nope, not him either," Paul said.

There was no time to explain that Frank, Betty, and Harry had bolted. I turned around and practically crashed into the others who had rushed up from the basement. "They must have hidden in the utility room and gone back downstairs," I said.

"I'll bet they lied about the tunnel being blocked," Chad yelled over his shoulder as he clattered down the steps. We followed hard on his heels.

The LEDs blazed in the public section of the stone passage. We were about halfway to the alcove when a hand snaked around the corner ahead of us, and the light suddenly went out. Our eyes were unable to adjust to the inky dark and we piled into Chad who had stopped abruptly. In the quiet darkness, we heard the faint sound of the metal wheels rolling the stone door into place. Then there was utter silence. But only for a moment.

"Come on," Jimmie yelled, taking the lead, but moving slower, with one hand on the wall as a guide.

We reached the stone wall in the alcove that was also a door if one knew how to open it. We didn't.

"It can't be that hard," Jimmie said. "Frank was pushing

something along here."

He and Chad began to run their hands over the bulging stones and into the mortared joints between them.

The light in the hall flared on again, making us all blink and squint. Cora came up behind us. "I turned on the light and picked up the flashlights Chad dropped," she said. "Two of them still work."

"That'll be great if we can get this open," Chad said.

Jimmie grunted and something clicked. "Got it."

The stones rolled away from the opening once again, and we charged through. We could see well enough without the flashlights until we reached the bend where we'd first seen Betty and Belinda appear. Then I realized Belinda was no longer with us.

"Where's Belinda?" I asked.

"She stayed upstairs," Jerry answered.

"What if she and Harry are actually working with Frank and Betty?" Mariah said, somewhat breathlessly.

"I'll go find her," Cora offered. "You'll be faster than I am down here, and someone upstairs will help me if she's trying to get away with Harry."

Jimmie and Chad took the flashlights and led the way, while Jerry, Mariah and I followed. Neither beam was very bright, but together they were enough to keep us moving steadily forward through the unfamiliar passageway.

It ran straight for perhaps a hundred feet— the part that was still beneath the house. Distance was really difficult to judge in the dim light while trying to hurry, but then Chad halted and called over his shoulder, "There's steps."

He reached out and touched the wall to steady himself then carefully descended.

"They're really uneven. Be careful," Jimmie added.

"Wait till I'm down and I'll shine the light on them," Chad said.

Soon we were all on a different level. We'd gone deeper into the earth by the height of ten rough stone steps.

"Listen for a minute," Jerry said.

We stood still, but at first all that could be heard was the sound of our own breathing. Then a tiny waterfall of sand slithered, hissing and pattering, down the wall and came to rest atop a cone of dirt at the base of the stones.

"There could be more than one passageway," I whispered. I wasn't sure why I kept my voice low, but it felt right. "You guys with the lights need to check the walls for openings as we go."

We proceeded slowly as the tunnel zig-zagged onward, presumably toward the river and the mill. Every so often there would be another descent of three or four steps. I knew Betty was ahead of us— mixed with the damp and earthy scents of the walls were floral perfume and the stench of stale cigarettes. Echoes of dripping water joined the hissing of sand rivulets, creating eerie background music for our journey. We were chilly but not too cold.

"It stays about a constant fifty-five degrees underground," Jimmie said. "We learned that in science class. The snow must melt from the bottom and drip through the roof."

We found no intersections, but eventually the passage came to a pile of rubble with a broken beam from the ceiling sticking out at a crazy angle. A pencil of light drew a tiny white oval on its dark surface. Jimmie aimed his flashlight upward. Only one beam had broken and fallen from the ceiling, and the space was much too narrow for anyone, even Jimmie, to squeeze through to the outside. From above, this might look like a depression in the snow, but from where we stood we only saw the underside of a snowbank, gray and slightly translucent, with a small hole where the sunlight entered.

"They didn't get out here," Mariah said. "Can we get past this?"

Jimmie ran the light across the pile of fallen rocks and dirt "Yup, we can climb over where there's a space at the top. Look! There are marks where someone already tried it," he said.

One at a time we scooched across the top of the mound in the narrow space that hadn't filled in between the dirt and the ceiling. Jerry had the most trouble since he was tall and the space wasn't wide, but eventually we were all beyond the cave-in.

"They're probably way ahead of us now," Jimmie said in despair, wiping dirt from his lips and tongue and making raspberry noises. "They know where they're going, and we don't."

"We'll find them. Even if they get to the mill, we can follow in the snow," Chad reassured us. "Let's keep moving."

Instead of having more steps, the tunnel soon narrowed and began to angle gradually downwards.

"How much farther?" Mariah asked, but no one answered.

Jimmie's flashlight died. "Darn," he said, slapping it against his leg and thumbing the switch back and forth with no results. We were now reduced to one light.

Behind me there was a thump. "Ouch."

Chad turned the light on Jerry, who was rubbing the top of his head.

"The ceiling is getting lower. Watch yourself."

I asked, "Are you all right?"

"Just a bump. No problem," Jerry said, motioning us to continue.

We kept moving slowly and steadily downhill. Jerry had to shuffle with his knees bent, and occasionally Chad's hair would brush the beams. We could also tell the last flashlight was almost out of power. Only a watery yellow circle illuminated the way ahead.

I'd been running one hand lightly along the wall to orient myself in the uncertain passage, but suddenly there was nothing beneath my fingers.

At the same time, Chad flung out an arm and cried in alarm. "Stop!" His voice came from open space, not the echoed confines of a tunnel. The temperature was colder here, too, and none of us had on clothing that would be warm enough outdoors.

"What's the matter?" Mariah asked, her voice tense.

"Just don't push," Chad said. "It's pure luck we're not all wet. I stopped on a landing, just in time. This must be part of the mill. Maybe there are steps under water that go down to the floor, but now it's like a swimming pool."

Thin points of ice jutted into the water from the brick walls, and the surface was greasy with oil slicks and clotted with brown frozen leaves and broken branches. A couple of dead saplings reached for the far door, victims of either the deep water or an unsuccessful quest for light.

"Where did Frank and Betty go?" I wanted to know.

With the final bit of power from its batteries, Chad's flashlight revealed a narrow catwalk that followed the left wall around to the opposite side of the room, at the same level as we'd entered. It was dry. Pearly daylight gleamed from somewhere ahead of us.

"They must have gone around to that other door," Jimmie said. "Nobody would go in the water on purpose at this time of year. Let's go."

"Not all at once," Mariah cautioned. "That doesn't look too sturdy."

One at a time, we worked our way to the next room. I was feeling that we'd never catch up with Frank and Betty. Their head start, combined with knowledge of the route, would defeat our likely better fitness levels. It was a race in slow motion.

Once we reached the far door, the floor was once again on a level with the catwalk. Broken pieces of machinery lay scattered around, and we had to avoid slick patches of ice, but we were able to move quickly through this room, which led us to yet another section of the old mill. However, here the roof had partially caved in. This must be the place Ray and Jessi had seen. We had full daylight, and it didn't matter that the flashlights were dead, but we had to pick our way carefully through the broken trusses, deceptively hidden by piles of fallen leaves— blown here, trapped, and then covered with snow.

A wooden door barred us from exiting. There was a sliding deadbolt on our side, but it was open. Of course, Frank and Betty had not been able to lock it after they went through. But maybe they had a way to lock the door from the outside.

Thankfully, this was not the case, although it was slightly jammed from hanging crooked. Jimmie wrenched the door open. Then we were outside, no longer enclosed by walls of any kind. Chad slipped and sat down hard, but bounced quickly to his feet.

I pointed to my right. "Look, out on the ice."

Frank was nowhere to be seen, but Betty was attempting to cross the river on the remains of some low structure that didn't really look like a bridge, although there was a single line of pilings connected by planks showing above the frozen surface. What pieces remained were tilted and curled, sagging at the middle. Betty was kicking the freshly fallen snow from the boards as she minced her way forward. With no railing and working at snow removal, the woman was making slow progress, However, she was more than halfway. Slung across her chest, and also impeding her progress, was the heavy bag Belinda had been carrying earlier.

"Stop," Jimmie yelled.

Betty carefully twisted her body, looked shocked to find us in pursuit, and then continued inching her way along the narrow boards which led to the far bank.

"We have to follow," Chad said. "At least some of us. If we can catch her we'll restrain her while the rest of you go for help. Come on, Jimmie. Time to be a man."

With that, Chad began working his way out on the makeshift boardwalk.

"Only one of you at a time on each plank," Jerry yelled as Jimmie began to follow Chad.

Jimmie turned to Jerry wearing a stunned expression, "Gosh, you're right. I didn't think about that. Thanks." He waited a few seconds till Chad had passed the first junction, then followed.

The better balance of the two young men allowed them to close in on the dumpy middle-aged woman, but there were still several lengths of board separating her from them.

"Stay away," Betty shouted. She tried to wave her arms to gesture us off but thought better of it as the large motions began to make the board beneath her feet rock.

"You need to come back here," Chad returned. "Even if you make it across, where are you going to go on foot? You don't even have a coat."

"Neither do you," she yelled back.

She stepped to the next board, which bowed badly under her weight as she approached the middle of the span. Splintering and groaning with the torque, the board broke. Betty fell to the ice and clawed at the shattered wood. She pulled herself toward the nearest piling and tried to stand.

Forgetting his own safety and running nimbly to reach the woman, Chad reached down and called, "Give me your hand."

With a tremendous cracking and sucking sound, the ice beneath Betty gave way and she slipped into the river.

<h1 style="text-align:center">54</h1>

Swirling water tore the woman from the board she was attempting to grasp and swept her downstream a dozen yards until she caught against a raft of broken branches and a tree trunk cemented together with a shelf of thicker ice.

"Grab that tree and hold on. We'll get you," Chad shouted. Then he turned to Jimmie and said something we couldn't hear.

Chad eased himself carefully off the plank, lowering his body until he was stretched on his belly on the ice, crawling toward Betty.

Jimmie hurried back to us as quickly as he was able. "We need to find a long branch or another board, or something like that," he said. "Then I have to try to get close enough. Hopefully, the ice will hold."

"Inside that building," Mariah pointed back the way we'd come. "Maybe we can pry off one of those roof pieces."

We all started in that direction, but there was another loud crack and I looked over my shoulder just in time to see Chad go in the icy water.

"Fifteen minutes. That's how long we've got to get them out and warmed up," I yelled, pushing Mariah ahead of me. With Betty in the water I was concerned. With my only child in the water I could feel tendrils of panic creeping toward my heart. I was cold just standing in the winter air. I knew the water was pulling heat from Chad's body faster than I could tolerate the thought of it.

Jerry and Mariah were already wrenching a long two-by-six away from the fallen trusses when I stepped through the doorway. With an agonizing squeal the nails pulled from the wood, and Jerry landed on his back as the board came loose. He got up slowly, rubbing his spine, but said, "Never mind me. I'm fine. Go help those two. Hurry."

Mariah and I dragged the heavy and unwieldy board to the river's edge. Jimmie was already trying to work his way carefully toward Chad and Betty who were now both clinging to the tangle of branches.

"Let it go," Chad was shouting.

Betty was shaking her head and pulling ineffectively at the strap of the pouch that still hung around her neck. It seemed to be caught on one of the branches. Her motions were sluggish.

"She's slipping into hypothermia," I told Mariah.

"This way, Ana," Jimmie yelled. "The ice is stronger here."

"Get down flat. Spread out your weight," Chad commanded Jimmie.

Jimmie carefully lay down on the ice. Mariah and I inched toward Jimmie and pushed the board ahead of us until he could reach it. He began playing it out toward Chad.

Meanwhile, Chad had worked his way over to Betty who was clearly losing control of her muscles. She could barely hold on. Chad tried to free the strap of the heavy bag but couldn't manage it against the pull of the current.

He must have said something to Betty because I saw her shake her head violently and struggle. She actually tried to push her rescuer away.

Chad tugged on the leather strap and must have managed to undo a buckle because the brown belt suddenly whipped over Betty's shoulder and was swept out of sight under the ice.

"Nooooo," Betty wailed, just as Chad grabbed her with one arm, and began hauling the woman toward Jimmie, walking his other hand along the fallen tree trunk.

"This is the dangerous part," Chad called. I could hear his voice shake. "I have to let go of this tree and switch to your board. Do you have a really good hold on it?"

I had now crawled to Jimmie's side and grabbed the two-by-six as well. "We've got you," I told him with all the protective instincts a mother can bring to bear on a situation like this.

We jockeyed the end of the board into a position where Chad shouldn't have to let go of the branches for more than a second.

I prayed the current wouldn't be strong enough to pull my son and this greedy woman under the ice.

I saw Betty's form bob as Chad tried to tighten his grip around her chubby body. She seemed to be unconscious. Maybe that was better. She'd be dead weight, but she wouldn't fight.

A look of extreme resolution crossed Chad's face.

"We're ready," Jimmie said, his voice quavering. "There's a nail in the end you can brace against, but don't stab yourself."

Chad let go of the tree trunk and was momentarily at the mercy of the river. I didn't want to watch, but couldn't turn my eyes away. Then he grabbed the end of the two-by-six. The extra force threatened to yank it out of our hands. My arms ached, and the board see-sawed against the edge of the ice. Chad's head disappeared and then surfaced. He was still holding the board. And Betty.

Slowly, Jimmie and I inched our way toward shore. At first the ice kept cracking and breaking away where Chad and Betty's weight dragged against it, but finally a section held and we pulled them onto its surface.

"Stay down, keep pulling," Chad commanded through chattering teeth.

I felt someone behind me, drawing us all to safety. Jerry had recovered from his fall and was lending his strength to the rescue. In another few seconds we were all on shore. But Betty was unconscious and Chad was barely functioning.

"Let me lie here a minute," he said, rolling on his side.

"No. No, you can't," Jerry prudently insisted, putting a toe in Chad's ribs, which made him sit up and howl.

Jerry already had his arms under Betty's armpits and was dragging her toward the ruined mill. "Back through the tunnel. It's a little warmer than out in the air. We've got to wake this woman up." He slapped her face, somewhat gently at first, but with increasing fervor.

Mariah peeled off the sweatshirt she was wearing and began helping Chad put it on. She supported him as he got to his feet and led him in the direction of the building. But she was now wearing only a t-shirt. I could see her breath, and goose bumps rose on her arms.

Betty groaned.

"Get up," I said. I was probably more gruff than I needed to be, but I didn't care. "Stand up, or you're going to die."

Jerry and I half hauled, half guided Betty, following Chad and Mariah.

"I'll try to make a clearer path," Jimmie hollered, running ahead of us.

By the time the remaining five of us made it to the room with the fallen roof, Jimmie had managed to drag some of the lumber out of the way so Chad and Betty didn't have to step quite so high to get over the obstructions.

"Hurry, hurry," he coaxed.

When we reached the room with the catwalk, Betty collapsed. "I can't," she sighed.

"You can, and you will," Jerry said through clenched teeth. This brave young man didn't save your life in order for you to give up at this little difficulty."

She couldn't manage it without help, so we had to trust the planking would hold two of us at once. It did, but the traverse took precious time. Chad and Betty were out of the frigid water, but their clothes were wet and their body temperature had to still be dropping. It would have been good to give the hypothermic duo our coats, but we didn't have any to offer.

In fact, the rest of us were now marbled with wet streaks from helping them, and we'd also been outside without adequate clothing for many minutes.

We no longer had any light for the return trip, but we knew there were no side tunnels where we could get lost. We only had to keep going. Personally, I didn't feel cold. I was numb, knowing that my only child could die from saving this miserable woman's life.

We hustled the two who had been in the water through the passage, more or less stuffing Betty through the opening where the way was partly blocked. Jerry and I pushed from behind and we heard her roll down the other side, where Jimmie and Mariah got her back on her feet.

Jimmie was acting as our life-and-death cheerleader. "Keep it up, Chad. We're going to make it. Don't fall asleep, lady,"

Betty could barely stay on her feet, but Jerry was strong enough to keep her upright.

"Watch out, there are steps soon," Jimmie said. "I'll find 'em." He ran ahead and returned in a moment. "Twenty-one paces ahead, then we'll be at the first ones. Count. That way we won't trip."

We chanted in unison. "Twenty-one, twenty, nineteen... four, three, two, one."

"Here we are," Jimmie said. "I'll go find the next set. He scampered ahead into the darkness.

The counting did help. It made me feel as if we were actually getting somewhere, and in this fashion we arrived at the turn where some light was visible around a bend to the right.

"The stone door is just down the next hallway, and it's still open. We're almost there. You can do it." Jimmie cheered us on.

55

Minutes later, we were standing in the dining room, no longer dripping, but more than damp, and looking as if we'd been rolled in dirt, which was exactly what had happened. The Pyrtles, Crocketts, Paul and Branson looked up and stared at us, uncomprehending. Then Ray realized that something was terribly wrong. Something beyond being filthy. He jumped to his feet.

"Chad and Betty are hypothermic," Jerry said. "They've been in the river. The rest of us are just cold."

"Go start running two baths," Ray ordered. "Not super hot, but we've got to warm these people up. And someone fix some hot tea."

"Don't leave Betty alone. She's guilty of something. We don't know what just yet," Jerry added.

Jessi grabbed Doreen's hand. "Come on. I know what to do." She yanked Doreen to her feet and they dashed out of the room. Jerry supported Chad. The adrenaline was wearing off and he was starting to falter. At least that's what I assumed, because that's certainly how I felt. Ray and Bran stood. They picked Betty up by lifting her under her arms and unceremoniously followed, carrying the exhausted woman like a sodden sack of grain.

"I'll put on water for the tea," Paul said, heading for the kitchen.

"Where's Frank?" I demanded. "We didn't find him."

Earl seemed confused. "Who cares?" he asked, raising a hand and taking a sip from a can of beer.

I was getting annoyed now that my fear for Chad was subsiding. "Frank Farnsworth, you know, our wonderful host. We think he and Betty killed the judge. We don't know why. We don't

202

even know for sure, but they bolted when Belinda asked them something about a genetic test."

"I saw him getting a coat out of the foyer closet about a half hour ago. Then he went down the hall," Earl said. "That did seem odd. There's no outside door down that way."

There wasn't time to think about how Frank had gotten from the utility room to the foyer without being seen earlier.

My stress level was rising again. "How about Cora and Belinda? Have you seen them?"

"Yup. They came through a while ago. Cora seemed quite determined about something, but she didn't say what. I think I heard them go upstairs." Earl said, again without much feeling.

Finally, some useful information. Harry was still unaccounted for, but I'd worry about him later. Pounding up the stairs, I knocked on Cora's door. It was closest.

"Just a minute," I heard her call.

That instantly made me feel better. She sounded fine.

She opened the door a crack and her eyes widened. "What happened to you?"

"It's a long dirty story." I said, trying to joke, since I knew I looked like I'd just been unearthed from an archaeological dig. "Have you seen Frank? Supposedly he came this way, although I don't know how."

"I haven't heard or seen anyone," Cora said quietly, shaking her head. "Lots of noise from the third floor, though. I've got Belinda in here. I don't know what's going on, but I think we want to keep track of where she is. How about Harry?"

"No idea," I said. "Keep Belinda calm. That was good thinking. The treasure is at the bottom of the river. But don't tell her yet."

Cora's eyes widened. She nodded sagely and shut the door. I heard a key turn in the lock.

The master key was still in my pocket. I unlocked the stairway door and climbed to the attic. If one of the missing men had gone up, it probably wasn't Harry alone. He wouldn't have had a key. I hoped the Wards were in the lounge and had seen someone, but that semi-public space was empty. I knocked on Dee's door and she answered, with Beth and Lindsey giggling from the depths of the room. They were running back and forth, ending each pass by sliding across the wood floor in their sock feet. That must be what Cora had been hearing.

"Hi Dee," I said calmly, not wanting to alarm the girls. "Have you seen Frank, or possibly Harry?"

"I don't think so," she said, looking at me in astonishment. "Someone came through the hall a while ago, and I assumed it was Jimmie. When he didn't find us after a bit, I looked out, but no one was here. Are you all right?"

"Yes, everyone is fine, just dirty. Jimmie's been with me. Keep your eyes and ears open. We think Frank or Betty killed the judge. Maybe you should lock your door. And we have no idea where Harry is, either."

Dee thanked me and shut the door to her suite. Where could Frank have gone? I wandered to the third floor window at this end of the house. Resting my hands on the sash I peered out. Footprints in the snow leading toward the bridge caught my eye. Of course! The fire escape, right under my hands. I twisted the lock and pulled up the window to see how easily it opened. The track was clean and the sash cords in good repair because the window slid up soundlessly. Frank could easily have gone out this way and over the ballroom roof to exit the house out of sight of anyone. Or were those Harry's prints in the snow?

Leaning out, I tried to determine where the escape ladder went down the outside wall. There were depressions along the ridgeline, leading to the TV dish. Frank probably had cleared that, as he said. Small avalanches had cleared valleys from the ridge to the eaves. Someone could have slid down any of those without leaving tracks. However, I thought the ladder was near the elevator shaft, and that's where the footprints on the ground seemed to start. It would be easy to walk away from the house without being seen from that point. Only someone in one of the tower rooms could have observed the fugitive, and since all those windows were heavily curtained, it was unlikely anyone was looking out at the right moment.

I retraced my steps to head downstairs. Would there be any point in going after Frank, or was it Harry, now that one or both of them had such a big head start? Maybe. Ray or Jessi on skis could easily catch up to someone postholing through deep snow.

Leaving the attic door unlocked— seriously— who cared at this point, I entered the second floor hallway and heard sounds coming from the suite I shared with Chad. His door was open, and I stuck my head in.

Jerry was standing in the entrance to the bathroom with his back to me. I could hear Chad talking. That was a good sign.

"How's my boy?" I asked.

"Ana, come in," Jerry said. "He's doing great. Ray's in there keeping him talking. I think it's Betty we might need to be worried about. She was much colder, and we sure can't get medical help here."

"Where did they take her?"

"To Doreen's room, just down the hall," Jerry pointed in that general direction.

I knocked, and Jessi opened the door. "How is she," I blurted, with no preliminaries.

"It's touch and go," Jessi said. "Her core temperature was really low. A bath isn't ideal under those conditions because it can warm the extremities faster than the body, but it's the best we can do here. She's conscious and drinking hot tea. That's really good, because it will help heat the core. We're raising the water temperature gradually."

"Then why the concern?" I asked.

"Shock or heart attack is the danger now. Sometimes the arms and legs warm up so fast they put more demand on the organs than what they can handle in a cold state. Doreen's watching her closely." Jessi tipped her head toward the bathroom.

"Wow, you know a lot about this."

"Wilderness medicine. It's necessary in our business," Jessi said nonchalantly.

56

Where and who was the missing man? I could only account for one person walking away. It was possible the second one had carefully stepped exactly in the footprints of the leader, but that would have defeated the goal of getting away quickly. It didn't seem likely. And Earl had only mentioned seeing Frank.

My questions were partially answered the minute I returned to the dining room. Harry was seated at a table holding an icepack to the side of his head. Paul was hovering behind him and rubbing his shoulders, and Jimmie came through the kitchen door carrying a mug with a dangling teabag tag.

"Here you go, Mr. Hack," he said. Handing the drink to Harry.

Jimmie did not seem to be suffering any ill effects of his experience on the ice. Oh, to have the stamina of the young!

"Ana, you need some hot tea, too," he said. "We've all been drinking it to warm up our cores. Ray said that's important. I'll fix you some."

I nodded my acceptance and sat down, suddenly drained again. So, it was Frank who had escaped, but we couldn't do much about it now.

"He slugged me," Harry said, his eyes practically striking sparks, but without being completely clear as to who had hit him.

"Frank did that?" I asked.

Harry pulled the ice pack away from his head and revealed a huge goose egg just above the temple. "Yup, and not with a fist. Had to be something hard. I never knew what hit me." He replaced the ice, and a deep moan escaped his lips as he touched the large bump.

"Do you know what's going on here," I asked him.

"Not really," Harry said. "Some friend, eh? We only know one thing. Belinda's a snoop... not her best feature, but I knew it when I married her. It's how she learned about those coins in the first place."

I didn't think it was wise to tell Harry the treasure was gone, either.

"She read some report from one of those ancestry places where you send a bottle of spit. Meant something to her. I don't know what."

"But where were you?" I asked, remembering that no one had seen Frank or Harry after we'd chased them up the basement stairs.

"You won't believe it," Harry said.

Jimmie had returned with tea for me. "I'll show you," he said. "Come on."

I took the mug and sipped as we walked, following him through the kitchen to the utility room. He opened the doors to storage cupboards on the inside wall and pushed aside racks where tablecloths were hung to keep them from retaining the multiple creases caused by folding.

"Look at this! Another secret door."

At the back of the cupboard was a pocket door which connected to the foyer closet. Now I understood. Frank only had to slip through, and when Earl had seen him getting a coat, he'd actually come from inside the closet.

It was looking less and less as if Harry and Belinda were guilty of anything except greed for the French treasure. If Frank was willing to bean his good friend— hard enough to leave him unconscious for nearly an hour— and hide him from sight, then Frank was capable of almost anything. And desperate.

I ran back upstairs to check in with Jessi and Doreen.

"Watch Betty extra closely," I whispered. "We found Harry, and I'm pretty sure it's the Farnsworths who are up to no good. She might pretend to be in worse shape than she is, and then run off. Frank already managed to get away. And he conked Harry on the head and stuffed him in a closet."

"Wow! That's good to know." Jessi whispered back. "We'll keep any dry clothes away from her, and I'll lock the door. She'll have to get the key away from me, and I'd like to see her try that."

Jessi flipped her ponytail and grinned. She looked as if she would gladly anticipate an actual wrestling match with our overweight hostess.

Doreen stepped quickly to the bathroom door and turned a cold eye on Betty. I could just see the woman's flabby arm resting on the edge of the tub.

"Keep us posted, please." Doreen requested.

I filled in Ray, Jerry and Chad on the current situation and headed back down the main staircase to the first floor.

At the bottom of the stairs stood Detective Dennis Milford, my least favorite county official; Harvard Brown, one of his deputies whom I liked very much; and between them in handcuffs was Frank Farnsworth. Our renegade snowmobiler, Sam, was on the far side of the foyer, hanging coats in the closet, and grinning widely enough to split his face.

57

"Well, well, well," Milford drawled. "If it isn't the intrepid Anastasia Raven. Death certainly seems to follow you around."

I rolled my eyes. "You must be kidding. I had nothing to do with what's happened here."

"You never do," the detective said dryly. "Fetch everyone down here. We'll just make ourselves comfortable."

Fetch? So now I was assigned to be Milford's pet servant? The man had a way of making my blood boil every time I ran into him. He had on a black overcoat, but beneath it I detected one of those gray suits he always wore.

"You're welcome that we've been working hard to preserve any evidence." Sarcasm was my best defense against the burly and aggressive detective. "It will take a while to roust everyone. We've got two people upstairs soaking in hot baths after being dunked in the river. But they're going to be all right, we think. One of them is this man's wife. Her name's Betty. We're watching her pretty closely because she ran away," I explained. "But we don't know exactly what's going on."

"Good. I'll send Harvey up with you to get her," Milford said. He took Frank by the elbow and steered him toward the front of the house. It was then I realized Frank was also wearing leg irons. What had he done to provoke the detective to restrain him so carefully?

Harvey said, "Lead the way," and extended a hand toward the stairs.

I craned my neck to make eye contact with the handyman around Harvey's confident frame. "Thanks, Sam. We weren't sure if you were a good guy or the bad guy."

"Yeah, I figured there would be lotsa talk, but I found a can of gas that was missed when they got dumped and thought I should just go for it," he explained.

"Thank you!" I said sincerely.

"Looks like all you-know-what broke loose while I was gone," Sam grinned. His close-set features would never give his face a truly open look, but when he smiled he almost seemed jolly.

I laughed. "Pretty much."

"Come on," Harvey urged. "We'll need to go over it all once we account for everyone, so let's collect people"

We went to Doreen's room first. It seemed like a good idea to place Betty in the deputy's care right away. I knocked and told Jessi what was happening, and that I had a male officer with me.

"We'll get Betty out of the tub and dressed. She's in pretty good shape now. Jimmie even brought hot soup up to her. He's such a dear boy," Doreen said. "Just let me shut the bathroom door, and you can come in."

I left Harvey with them and hustled to "fetch" the men in Chad's room and the Wards from the attic.

We assembled in the front room of the house. Frank was still in cuffs and leg irons. He was fuming, but quietly. Whatever had happened, he apparently thought his best option at this point was to be silent.

Betty was not restrained, but she was seated in a straight chair brought in from the dining room, and Officer Brown stood nearby and facing her, vigilant. She wore fleece pajamas and clutched a blanket that had been wrapped around her shoulders. She looked warm, but she also looked frightened.

Chad appeared, wearing a hooded sweatshirt and jeans, and he also had a blanket wrapped around him. Mariah was cozied up to his side. He grinned at me.

Cora entered with Belinda in tow. A piece of me wished we could also restrain the treasure hunter. She seemed unpredictable, and her role in the story behind the story was unclear to me.

Everyone else arranged themselves around the room.

Milford cleared his throat and began. "Mr. Lyghtner here," he nodded toward Sam, "notified us that the possible murder of celebrity Judge Viviette Velvet had occurred at this house. He accompanied us to investigate. On the way here, just as we reached the end of where the road commission has managed to plow, we met Mr. Farnsworth, who was on foot. He had a conversation with Mr. Lyghtner and Deputy Brown then suddenly assaulted Mr. Lyghtner.

"He popped me a good one too," Harry said, pointing to the still visible lump on the side of his head. "Keep those cuffs on him, if you will."

Frank glared at Harry.

"I don't think there's any doubt about the murder," Earl said. "We've got a body in cold storage with a ski pole through her middle. I've seen a lot of death— Desert Storm— and people rarely jump down elevator shafts with half a ski pole to commit suicide. Besides, I'm pretty sure she was dead already, before she took that tumble."

Uncharitably, I thought this sounded more like Earl was taking the opportunity to point out that he was a veteran, rather than to provide vital information.

"What makes you think that. Mr....?" the detective asked.

"Earl Pyrtle. I write under the name Pratt. No blood around the wound. You check, but I'm pretty sure she'd been strangled or suffocated first."

"I think you can count on us to investigate all the options," Milford said. "Now, we need to hear what's happened since Sam left you earlier. It appears you've had an active day. Ordinarily, we'd speak with you individually. And we will do that, but perhaps someone can give us an overview first."

Several people started talking at once, but then there was general agreement that Jerry should tell the story, which he proceeded to do.

The only hitch was that Jerry hadn't gotten the word that Harry and Belinda didn't yet know the gold coins were at the bottom of the river. But as it turned out, that piece of information was the key to revealing the motive for murder.

58

Those who hadn't gone on the tunnel adventure listened with rapt anticipation as each step of our way was revealed. Jerry had just gotten to the part where the strap of the leather bag slithered across Betty's shoulder and disappeared beneath the surface of the water. Jerry poetically described it as a snake coiling around her neck threatening destruction.

Belinda heaved herself out of her chair, looking wild-eyed. She pointed a finger at Betty.

Deputy Brown took a step forward.

"Don't you fuss," she said to him, but still staring at Betty. "I'm not gonna do anything rash, but that... that woman! We trusted you to help us find those coins, and agreed to give you half their value, but you tried to make off with the whole thing."

This was also news to Harry.

"What a couple of dirty rats," he spat. "We don't owe you anything now. Tell 'em what you know, lover."

"I can prove that Casper Janes McKay was my third cousin," Betty snarled. "I've got more right to that money than you."

Cora had known Betty was related to the Janes. That was the detail I'd been trying to recall.

Frank stood and tried to aggressively shuffle toward Harry. But Branson, who had been seated beside him, reached out and grabbed the link joining the handcuffs that held Frank's hands together behind his back. Frank was yanked backwards and fell awkwardly into his chair.

"Enough of that," Milford said. "We can cuff you to that railing if you can't behave." He pointed toward the spiral staircase.

Frank hunkered down in the seat and shook his head.

Belinda sat down and responded to Harry's instruction. "I certainly will tell. We began to suspect something when I read

212

the results of the DNA tests the Farnsworth's took, but it didn't make sense until they told that "innocent" story about how little Viviette held up the mistletoe at a Christmas party fifty-some years ago."

"You've been reading papers on my desk." Frank accused.

"Maybe, but I'm no killer," Belinda retorted.

"So, the Velvet Velociraptor began slashing lives at an early age," Paul chuckled.

"What are we talking about? I don't get it," Mariah said. "What's up with this mysterious DNA test we keep hearing about? Did they find out they're related to the judge somehow?"

Doreen pondered, "Why would that make them want to kill her?"

"I had suspicions, but it was none of my business," Belinda said self-righteously. She added, almost offhandedly, "they're brother and sister."

Detective Milford held up a hand like a traffic cop. "One at a time, or we'll separate you all right now."

"Oh, cripes," Frank bellowed. "If you're going to tell it, get it right."

"Perhaps you'd do just that," Milford commented. "Would you like to make a statement."

Frank hung his head. "Sure, why not? We've been caught out, now."

"Speak for yourself," Betty said, sitting up and trying to look prim and innocent.

"It all started when we had Zoe. That was our little girl." A look of genuine misery came over Frank's face. "She was... she had... a terrible deformity. And she died when she was only a few days old. But the doctors said it was genetic, that it was usually seen as a result of incest. They were pretty rough on Betty— an interrogation almost. But there was no question in our minds that I was Zoe's father."

"So we did one of those tests," Betty explained.

Frank continued. "And it turned out we are half-siblings. Apparently after my father kissed Betty's mother under Viviette's mistletoe, a bit more than kissing ensued. We grew up as neighbors and friends, but we were much more than that. We never knew."

"My mother died before we were dating, or maybe she would have stopped us," Betty said as a tear ran down her cheek. She didn't even try to wipe it away.

"But why take it out on Viviette?" Branson asked. "Surely one childish joke wasn't the cause of such grief."

Frank's lip curled into a sneer and with his square head he looked obstinate and menacing. I'd read that the adorable Giant Pandas could be dangerous and aggressive when cornered. Perhaps Betty's odd nickname for Frank was appropriate.

"Why not make her pay?" he demanded. "She's been no great boon to society. I'll admit we collected a bunch of you people who had every reason to hate the judge. We let natural selection take its course. Someone cashed in. This party is only a cross-section of the people she's hurt. Except maybe you. You can have her."

"But, I can't," Bran said quietly. "You've killed her."

"Not me," Frank needled. "Must have been Betty."

This was enough to make Betty throw off the blanket and leap to her feet. In the pink fleece pajamas decorated with scattered flamingos she hardly looked dangerous, but Harvey stepped toward her. "It wasn't me," she shouted, pointing at Frank. "He did it."

"Prove it," Frank said sullenly.

Grinding and scraping noises drowned out the responses to Frank's challenge, and since I was seated near a window I pulled back the curtain. A county truck fitted with a wedge plow, with two Sheriff's cars behind, and an ambulance behind that, came to a stop in the front yard.

Within minutes, Frank and Betty were taken into custody, crime scene techs were being shown where Viviette's body had been put for safekeeping, and more techs were given the key to the ballroom.

Detective Milford had, of course, radioed for reinforcements before walking to the house with Harvey, Frank, and Sam.

We each were fingerprinted and told we'd be contacted within the next couple of days to make our statements. Jerry and Cora offered to make sure the house was closed up properly, but Detective Milford gruffly pointed out that everything was now in the hands of law enforcement.

It was nearly suppertime. Dee offered to fix food, but the deputies wanted us off the premises as quickly as possible after persons, rooms, and cars were searched. They didn't let us take our luggage.

"You'll get it all back as soon as we're done with it," Milford grudgingly admitted, as if it was a personal affront that he had to return our belongings at all.

"But we can't leave," Ray pointed out. "All our gas tanks are damaged."

Milford fumed and muttered, but there was nothing else to be done. He had to walk back to his vehicle and radio for more transportation.

We weren't allowed to shower or change, so those of us who were covered in sand stepped outside and used a broom to clean each other off as much as possible. It was totally unsatisfactory.

Jerry, Cora, and I were finally ready to leave. A county car was waiting to return us to Cherry Hill, but we were unable to locate Chad. We checked upstairs, but he wasn't there. As we came down the main stairs and entered the dining room we were just in time to see Chad and Mariah entwined in a long kiss beneath the Dead Mule Swamp mistletoe.

59

My friend Adele, whom I mentioned at the beginning, was seriously peeved that she'd had no part at all in this adventure. But while we were gone she did hear that Charlie Dixon was perhaps getting remarried, and she also showed me a picture of Roy Sendak's firstborn son that he'd sent her from Poland. She was especially thrilled that he'd written to her rather than me.

Anyway, of course I had to tell Adele the entire story, which is why I was able to present it here in so much detail.

Frank and Betty quickly lawyered up, but not with the same lawyer. Frank continued to insist he was innocent— that Betty must have killed Viviette, and Betty said the same of Frank. They readily admitted engineering all the unpleasant gifts except, of course, the mistletoe ball. They had planned a different present for themselves, but when I appeared with the fake mistletoe it was perfect. The trinket provided a prompt so they could tell the story of young Viviette at the neighborhood Christmas party so long ago. This put the judge on notice that they knew their parents' kiss held a hidden meaning. Perhaps they later confronted Viviette with the rest of the story. There were too many ways the situation could have turned ugly.

The last I heard, both of them were out on bond and the county was trying to decide if they could be prosecuted together for conspiracy, despite each of them insisting on personal innocence. It was rumored there wasn't enough solid evidence to convict either one of the Farnsworths, or anyone.

Frank confessed to getting rid of the gasoline, and he had to pay for all the repairs to the damaged cars. He admitted that the dramatic tension of being isolated gave him a rush. Frank and Betty jointly claimed they had only hoped to assemble some of the judge's victims and make them angry enough to frighten her into changing her ways.

Well, anything is possible, at least so I've been told.

So far, Frank and Betty retain ownership of the Janes' mansion. Rumors are flying that they will have to sell if one or both of them is convicted of murder. However, at present, I hear that reservations for the summer are coming in at a good pace. Everyone wants to see the no-longer-secret tunnel to the mill. Chad mischievously concluded the house did turn out to be a dragon with a secret in its belly. Of course, he carried that one step too far and likened the tunnel to the dragon's guts. It had pooped everything that was giving it indigestion into the river.

I also know that if the house does go on sale, Ray and Jessi might still be interested in purchasing it and moving their business to the heart of Thousand Lakes State Forest.

We haven't received much news about Earl and Doreen. He's still the sportswriter for the *Ledger,* and I suppose Doreen is making over the female population of Emily City. I simply have no need for make-up or hair styling, and never will. Adele says the Pyrtles are eagerly awaiting the arrival of their first grandchild.

The satchel of French gold remains at the bottom of the Petite Sauble River, waiting for the next treasure hunter. Perhaps the river of time has teased the coins from the bag and buried them in a tantalizing swirl as they are carried downstream into the sands of their future. Perhaps Harry Hack and Belinda Kramer are planning a summer treasure hunt of their own.

As soon as the story of the Christmas party at the Janes Mill Bed and Breakfast hit the news, Cherry Blossom Cuisine received so many requests for business that they began selecting only the best venues. Jimmie had the historic section of damaged sign mounted and protected with resin. It's going to be incorporated into an optimistic billboard he's designing that reads: "Cherry Blossom Restaurant – reopening soon!"

Cora is digging into the history of the Janes family and plans a temporary display at the museum in the near future. And Jerry? He plods along, keeping the *Cherry Hill Herald* in the spotlight with journalism awards as an outstanding weekly paper. And he keeps me on my toes as its one-and-only crime reporter. That said, I'm back to writing about petty thefts and domestic mishaps. In January, Marj Brinker stole forty dollars from the cash register at Aho's Service Station when John wasn't looking. But he didn't prosecute. Instead, he gave her the money and bought the family enough food (at Volger's Grocery, of course) for a special meal. She had only wanted to buy her twins birthday gifts. Life in a small town is good.

Paul and Mariah, in their new relational roles are doing great. Paul has experienced a great release from the guilt he felt though all the years of pretending to be Mariah's father. You might think I have no way to know this for certain, but my information comes straight from Mariah. Let's just say that she and Chad stay in touch on a regular basis. And, much to my delight, Mariah telephones me fairly often, telling me that she feels like I'm the mother she never had. Heady stuff.

The most intriguing follow-up story might be Branson Owens' actions. Even before our personal belongings were released to us by the Sheriff's Department, he hopped on a plane and moved to Togo. Yes, Togo in Africa, where he has established permanent residency. I had to look it up to find out exactly where the small republic is. Interestingly enough, it's one of the few countries in the world that does not have an extradition treaty with the United States.

Just for kicks, I looked up the horoscope for Gemini in December. In addition to all the love and harmony mumbo-jumbo, I found this: "Gemini will have enough resources to face any problem head-on and get out of the situation as the clear winner."

But who believes in astrology?

Challenges and Acknowledgements

I first decided to write a Christmas mystery in the Anastasia Raven series after reading *Tied Up in Tinsel* by Ngaio Marsh. Marsh is one of my favorite British authors, who has an exceptional talent for throwing a large group of characters together and making their interactions both intriguing and more-or-less possible to keep organized. I began roughly formulating the setting in my head...rambling Victorian bed & breakfast, snowbound guests, etc. Then I read *English Country House Murders,* edited by Thomas Godfrey. This overview sampler volume of the style was, for me, a research book, and it includes excerpts from twenty-two mysteries of the sub-genre. I like to call them the closed-suspect-pool mystery. Godfrey gives a fourteen-plus-two point definition, all of which I have carefully followed (mostly by accident, but someone has to be telling lies) except points one and fourteen. More on this in a moment.

The mystery genre, and the seeds of the English Country House setting, were introduced by Wilkie Collins in The Moonstone, 1868. A century-and-a-half later, this story is a rather boring read. But there are those who say 2001: A Space Odyssey is a boring movie, and yet it introduced many of the visual sci-fi techniques that became standard. Never despise your roots. Early twentieth-century writers like Agatha Christie and Sir Arthur Conan Doyle perfected the English Country House story, and more recently P.D. James has written more-than-satisfactory additions to the collection. Oddly enough, I dated the construction of the Janes Mill to 1868. You are welcome to make something of that, or not.

Godfrey also includes eleven rules that make an "English Country House." These I have also followed... entirely by chance, as I didn't re-read the list until *Dead Mule Swamp Mistletoe* was finished. Nevertheless, they are all incorporated into the setting. Apparently a lifetime of reading this sub-genre built the requirements into my psyche.

One oft-occurring ending of this type of book is that the country house is destroyed... fire, earthquake, violent storm, rogue ocean wave, pick one, invent another. I chose not to allow such devastation within my Forest County series setting. But for those readers who thought that would have been an appropriate closing, my nod to the destruction of dreams and fortunes is the loss of the French coins to the river. The source of the original treasure is an actual historical event.

The gauntlet was thrown down on my keyboard when Godfrey said in point one: "Americans... may study the form and give it a go, but invariably give themselves away as pretenders to the tradition." Sure, he's writing this all tongue-in-cheek, but one should never tell me I can't do something. Point fourteen states that "the crime must take place in a proper English Country House." I say, the only thing lacking for the Janes Mill Bed and Breakfast to make the grade is for it to be located in the British Isles. You can decide for yourself if the setting and the story work. My DNA test proved my British ancestry. I'll have to say "close enough."

Point fourteen-two? Also inadvertently, I followed this rule: "No one named Lefty has ever appeared in an English Country House Mystery." If I'd re-read this precedent before typing my last word, I'd probably have thrown in someone called Lefty just to be obstreperous. It's one of my best qualities.

In addition to acknowledging *Tied Up in Tinsel* as the direct seed for the germination of this story, the broken-down portions of the house were inspired by descriptions in *Fen Hall*, by Ruth Rendell. Although that setting was pen-ultimately Brit, I tried to create a similar feeling with appropriate American flavor.

The basic outline of Janes Mill Bed and Breakfast is loosely based on the Inn at Ludington B&B, in Ludington, Michigan, a typical Victorian home of the lumber baron era.

A small hike around the remains of the American Wood Rim Company in Onaway, Michigan provided the visual images of the ruined mill rooms. There, in the early 1900s, rock maple (fine-grained sugar maple) was fashioned into bicycle rims and steering wheels. The facility burned in 1926, but many of the foundations have been incorporated into a park to memorialize the city's history. The mill rooms in my book would not have been as interesting had I not taken that little walk.

I need to give a nod to Jody Hartley, retired Undersheriff of Mason County, Michigan. I asked him where, in Chapter 56, Deputy Harvard Brown would have placed himself to keep an eye on Betty Farnsworth. He graciously answered that question, but also said the typical "group reveal" of this kind of book would never happen. Subjects would be separated immediately and interviewed individually. So, don't blame Jody that I've fudged reality a bit and allowed some general parts of the tale to be given to Detective Milford in a group setting.

Also, I've fudged the safety conditions surrounding the unfinished elevator. In this era of heavy regulations, those openings would have been more secure.

And, if you think a child could not give herself rides in a dumb waiter, I can only tell you that I delighted myself over and over when I was small, doing just this very thing. I've never looked up the workings of the mechanism— counterweights and brakes and rope diagrams would destroy the magic.

Finally, several advance readers have made this a stronger book. Barry Matthews, of Ludington Writers, helped me determine that the pace of the story was appropriate and not too boring. Pam Blais contributed to my confidence as well, as I stepped into a slightly different formula from the previous books in the series. Two other authors: J.L. O'Rourke, author of the mystery *Deep in the Shallows*, and Donald Levin, author of the Martin Preuss mysteries, also read the manuscript and offered valuable suggestions. Margie Hayward actually volunteered to proofread during the week before Christmas. She deserves a huge thank-you.

As always, any remaining mistakes are my own.

Joan H. Young, December 21, 2018

Both Anastasia Raven and Adele Volger find their peaceful worlds interrupted in *Dead Mule Swamp Singer*.

Dead Mule Swamp Singer

1

"We can pull this off. When someone wants to believe it's true, they trust you."

2

Chester Alan Arthur Schoellkopf was assuredly a hunk, if you liked aging hunks. Hunks who were a little too sure they represented a gift of the gods to the human race. But he was Adele's old friend. A "dear friend," she had confided, when she told me he was coming to visit, so I kept my opinions to myself.

Adele and I, and more than half the population of Cherry Hill, were at the Spring Strawberry Shortcake and Sundae Social– advertised as the 5S Sunday– being held on the lawn of the Lutheran church. It was a warm Memorial Day Sunday, May 29th that year, and despite stomachs being full of barbecued chicken and potato salad, the ice cream and strawberries were disappearing quickly. I was doing my part to prevent the unnecessary melting of any frozen dairy products. Chocolate syrup drizzled over the real whipped cream topping was the pinnacle of perfection.

Caught with a spoonful halfway to my mouth, Adele and Chester approached the folding chair where I was perched.

"Ana, meet Chester," Adele crooned. "I've been telling him all about you!"

I had to choose whether to delay the carefully balanced treat or go for it. Of course, I filled my pie hole. Or in this case, my ice-cream hole.

Chester smiled unctuously and held out a tanned but hairy paw. I replaced the spoon in my styrofoam bowl, set the remaining sundae on the grass beneath my chair and stood up so that we were meeting more as equals than as vassal to lord.

"Call me Chet," he said as we shook hands, and I quickly forced the cold ice cream down my throat.

"My pleasure," I choked out, hoping I wouldn't get brain freeze.

Chet was above average height, but not too tall. His tightly-curled blond hair was going gray, but the effect was of a silver-gold mixture that sparkled in the sunshine. Hair was his signature feature. Not only were his knuckles hairy, but he sported a full mustache in the middle of a long face. Two buttons of a creamy silk shirt were undone, and curly hairs rioted everywhere in the exposed triangle, leading me to believe the curl was natural. It would be a little too weird if he permed that. I wondered if the chunky gold chain he wore around his neck tangled enough to be painful. A square gold signet ring with a central diamond glittered on his right hand. His clothes were not synthetic, his shoes not imitation leather. Everything about Chet screamed money. Well, money and hair.

Adele beamed and offered some new information. "Chet has rented the apartment above the drugstore for at least a month. That's a nice place for our little downtown, with its own enclosed stairway. And it's furnished, too. I'm so happy to have him nearby. We have a lot of catching up to do."

She slipped her arm through Chet's, and he smiled down at Adele. They were an incongruous couple if that's what was happening here. Adele is at least matronly, if not downright heavy. She looks exactly like what she is, a middle-aged businesswoman who doesn't have time to worry about fashion or makeup. Her one nod to beauty is a trip to the hairdresser every couple of months for a wave and to catch up on the gossip she might have missed. Not that she misses much.

Out of the corner of my eye, I saw my young friend, Jimmie Mosher, walking toward us. He wore a black apron embroidered with a cluster of pink flowers and the words Cherry Blossom Cuisine. Clipped to the strap of his apron was a set of car keys. Jimmie was justifiably proud of his new driver's license, even though it would be provisional for a few more months.

"Hi Ana," he called. Then, realizing he might be interrupting, he stopped and waited for further encouragement.

I waved him in. "Come meet Mr. Schoellkopf, Jimmie."

Then, to Chet I said, "This is my buddy. Adele's too."

Adele had long been a friend to Jimmie, so they were on a first name basis. In the year when Jimmie was picking up and selling scrap metal from roadsides to feed himself, he would often leave her store, Volger's Grocery, with a bit more food than his pocket change technically covered. But Adele was wise enough to refrain from giving him items for free. She would claim the label on a can was ripped, or the produce was old. I'd actually seen her smush a loaf of bread on the sly so she could sell it to Jimmie as damaged. Adele may be a busy-body, but her heart is pure gold.

Jimmie and Chester shook hands.

"So, young man, you work for the caterer who made these shortcakes? Excellent baking, and the strawberries are the rosy perfection of sunshine."

"Thank you, Mr. Schoellkopf," Jimmie said as a sly smile spread across his face. "Actually, the business is mine, although it has to be registered in my mom's name until I'm eighteen. We all pitch in. Sometimes my little sisters help too, but dishing up ice cream is simple. They get today off."

"Wonderful. Amazing," Chet gushed. "What drew you to the food services, young man?"

"My dad used to own the Cherry Blossom Restaurant out on the highway. Do you know it?"

Chet shook his head in the negative.

"Well, it's a wreck now. Dad was killed in a car accident when

I was a baby, and the building was lost in a tax sale. But Mom and I are hoping we can buy it back. I want to re-open it. The Pine Tree Diner is great for a sandwich, but there's no place in the whole county to dine out in style any more."

"I'll have to check it out. The Pine Tree is all right, but not quite what I'm used to. I'll be in town for a month. I don't suppose you'll be up and running by then."

Jimmie grinned at the obvious teasing. "No sir. It's not likely."

Everyone chuckled. My ice cream was melting.

Jimmie turned to me. "Ana, do you think maybe you can help us take some of the equipment back to our house when this is over? The portable freezers take up a lot of space. We can't get it all in one trip, even with the van, and Lindsey has a piano lesson at four."

"Sure, Jimmie," I replied.

"Great, thanks!" He headed back toward the serving tables.

I glanced sideways at my sundae, sat down and rescued it. Definitely softer now, but still edible.

"Chet and I hope you'll join us for some outings," Adele said.

"I'd like that," I said, digging my spoon into the deflating mound of dessert and hoping they would get the message that this conversation was over.

"Looking forward to it," Chet agreed, running slim fingers across his mustache, then patting Adele's arm, still linked in his.

As Adele steered Chet in the direction of someone else she wanted to introduce, I had to wonder what was going on. Adele usually stuck tight to her store, watched television in the evenings, kept tabs on everyone, and ran the Family Friends Committee at Cornerstone Fellowship where we attended church. Her husband, Henry, had died long before I moved to Cherry Hill, and I'd never seen her show any interest in another man. I like Adele, and Chester seemed oily. I felt a tinge of concern.

3

The annual Strawberry Social was a big deal in Cherry Hill, and I wouldn't have missed it for anything, but it was people-intense for my tastes. Funny how I'd changed. I used to live in a suburb of Chicago. I had a busy life teaching literature at a community college and thought my marriage to an upper level manager of a chain store was solid, if not exactly great. I was always involved in social gatherings. But Roger had informed me he was in love with someone named Brian. In shock, I'd bought the last house on a dead-end road several miles outside of a very small town, miles and miles north of the Windy City. I wasn't sure it would work out, but I had to make some big changes to be able to move forward. In retrospect, the decision was just perfect. Now, I valued the privacy and enjoyed a few close friendships. Roger got his freedom, and I got enough money to create my new life.

That evening, I was relaxing in my upstairs screened porch that overlooks Dead Mule Swamp. I'd taken the winter shutters off only the week before. Spring in the Northwoods is fickle before Memorial Day. I was more than ready for warm evenings simmered in slanting light and the cheerful chorusing of peepers and vesper sparrows.

The sky to the west was turning pink, and the light spread across the swamp, causing every puddle of open water to glow with the pink satin of early roses. The trees were barely leafing out, so the reflections shimmered and winked as small gusts of the light breeze stirred the nascent greenery. Beyond the swamp ran the Petite Sauble River. But that was too far for me to ever see from the house. I could trace its course on chilly mornings by the line of mist that rose beyond the trees.

I'd discovered the foundations of an old cabin near the shore of the river on my property. Last summer, my son, Chad, who was now looking for his first post-college job, had rebuilt the small structure. Just one room, but it was a wonderful place to camp when the mosquitoes weren't too obnoxious. We'd added a fire ring and benches. My kayak was stored inside, and I hoped to build some bunks this summer. Although this section of the river was not generally popular with paddlers, I could work my way through the braided backwaters whenever I wanted to. I'd enjoyed some birdwatching forays in the little-visited area.

The breeze was dying down, and the peaceful quiet seeped into my bones. This, this was why a fixer-upper house on the back side of nowhere was right for me.

"Deep river, ... home ...over Jordan." Snatches of an old spiritual drifted from the direction of the river. The voice was male and deep, but not bass. More like a rich baritone.

Must be someone trying to paddle down from the Turtle Lake Dam to Cherry Hill, I thought. Spring, when the water was high, was about the only time of year anyone had a very good chance of making it through. Most of the time, there were shallow spots netted with sandbars. Snags and deadfalls meant that anyone trying to paddle this section had to watch carefully and do a lot of extemporaneous portaging. In some places it was almost impossible to tell where the main channel was, and as a result, people sometimes got lost back in the swamp. But not usually ones who calmly sang spirituals. And not usually at sunset. The swamp could be dangerous after dark. Soft sand, unexpectedly deep pools, broken winter trees hung up and waiting to fall if disturbed all threatened anyone who went astray.

I hoped the man was just passing by and knew what he was doing.

"Oh, don't you want to go-o to that Gospel feast..." The voice was now coming from upstream of its previous location. That was definitely odd. Hardly anyone paddled upstream. Even more remarkable was that the voice was now accompanied by some stringed instrument. A guitar? It didn't sound quite right. An autoharp? I barely knew what that was, but I didn't think it was capable of the complex notes I was hearing that blew to me in snatches of sound.

"To that promised land where all is peace. Deep river..." These words were followed by an instrumental interlude. Then it came to me. No one can paddle and play something that requires two hands at the same time. A radio? More than one person? The paddler had stopped somewhere?

In fact, the music was definitely coming from the general direction of my cabin. Should I have concerns about some mystery singer? Who could it be?

Chester Alan Arthur Schoellkopf– Adele had made sure I knew his whole name– was the only stranger in town that I knew of. Was he a closet crooner? More likely, I was hearing holiday weekend vacationers oblivious to the dangers of the river after dark.

This is ridiculous, I said to myself, swinging my legs off the ottoman on which they had been resting. It took me a couple of minutes to find and put on my sneakers. Then I grabbed a light jacket and ran down the stairs. It was dark enough by this time to want a flashlight, but finally I was working my way down the compacted pathway that led to the cabin.

"Who's there?" I called as I entered the clearing, swinging the light in arcs across the opening and throwing shadows everywhere.

No one was there. I saw no drag marks on the bank where a canoe or kayak might have pulled up. There were no obvious footprints. I checked the lock on the cabin door, shrugged and headed back to the house.

PUBLISHED WORKS BY JOAN H. YOUNG

Non-Fiction:
>North Country Cache: Adventures on a National Scenic Trail (2005 Independent Publishers, third place Regional Non-fiction)
>North Country Quest: Completing my National Scenic Trail Adventure
>Would You Dare?
>Devotions for Hikers
>Get Off the Couch with Joan
>Fall Off the Couch Laughing

Fiction:
Anastasia Raven Mysteries
>News from Dead Mule Swamp
>The Hollow Tree at Dead Mule Swamp
>Paddy Plays in Dead Mule Swamp
>Bury the Hatchet in Dead Mule Swamp
>Dead Mule Swamp Druggist
>Dead Mule Swamp Mistletoe
>Dead Mule Swamp Singer

Dubois Files Mysteries for Children
>The Secret Cellar
>The Hitchhiker
>The ABZ Affair
>The Bigg Boss
>The Lonely Donkey

Other
>Accidentally Yours- a chaotic collection of short works

ABOUT THE AUTHOR

Joan H. Young has enjoyed the out-of-doors her entire life. Highlights of her outdoor adventures include Girl Scouting, which provided yearly training in camp skills, the opportunity to engage in a ten-day canoe trip, and numerous short backpacking excursions. She was selected to attend the 1965 Senior Scout Roundup in Coeur d'Alene, Idaho, an international event to which 10,000 girls were invited. She rode a bicycle from the Pacific to the Atlantic Ocean in 1986, and on August 3, 2010 became the first woman to complete the North Country National Scenic Trail on foot. Her mileage totaled 4395 miles. She often writes and gives media programs about her outdoor experiences.

In 2010 she began writing more fiction, including several award-winning short stories. *Dead Mule Swamp Mistletoe* is the sixth story in the Anastasia Raven mystery series.

Visit booksleavingfootprints.com for more information.